MEDIAEVAL AND MODERN WELSH SERIES

General editors: P. Mac Cana, T. Arwyn Watkins

IX

A WELSH BESTIARY OF LOVE

MEDIAEVAL AND MODERN WELSH SERIES

Published

I. Pwyll Pendeuic Dyuet, ed. R. L. Thomson

II. Branwen Uerch Lyr, ed. Derick S. Thomson

III. The Poems of Taliesin, ed. Sir Ifor Williams and J. E. Caerwyn Williams

IV. Owein, ed. R. L. Thomson

V. Brut y Brenhinedd, ed. Brynley F. Roberts

VI. Armes Prydein, ed. Sir Ifor Williams and R. Bromwich

VII. Cyfranc Lludd a Llefelys, ed. Brynley F. Roberts

VIII. Poems of the Cywyddwyr, ed. E. I. Rowlands

IX. A Welsh Bestiary of Love, ed. G. C. G. Thomas

A Grammar of Middle Welsh, ed. D. Simon Evans (Supplementary Volume)

MEDIAEVAL AND MODERN WELSH SERIES
Volume IX

A WELSH BESTIARY OF LOVE

being
a translation into Welsh
of Richart de Fornival's
Bestiaire d'Amour

EDITED BY
GRAHAM C. G. THOMAS

DUBLIN INSTITUTE FOR ADVANCED STUDIES
1988

ISBN 0 901282 90 1

Printed in Great Britain
at the University Printing House, Oxford
by David Stanford
Printer to the University

PREFACE

THE Welsh translation of Richart de Fornival's *Bestiaire d'amour* is found in two 'versions', one Middle Welsh (texts AB) and the other Early Modern Welsh (texts CD(J)). For this reason, the work provides important evidence for the development of Welsh during the fifteenth and sixteenth centuries. The texts of B, C, and the A fragment are printed here in that order. Where D(J) varies from C, the variant forms are listed as footnotes to the C text. The corresponding text as it appears in Cesare Segre, ed., *Li Bestiaires d'amours di Maistre Richart de Fornival e li response du bestiaire* (Riccardo Ricciardi, Milano, Napoli, 1957), is appended, and I gratefully acknowledge the ready permission given by the author and publisher to print the relevant extracts.

My thanks for assistance go to Professor T. Arwyn Watkins, University College, Dublin, for his comments and general advice, and for his thoroughness and patience in supervising the preparation of the typescript for publication. Professor Emeritus J. E. Caerwyn Williams and Professor Proinsias Mac Cana read the typescript and made many useful suggestions. Dr Ceridwen Lloyd-Morgan helped with translating the French text into English, Professor Edmund Fryde provided information concerning Fornival's library, and Mr Gareth Bevan and the staff of *Geiriadur Prifysgol Cymru* gave willing assistance when required. Finally, I should add that I myself am responsible for any and all deficiencies.

GRAHAM C. G. THOMAS

May 1988

CONTENTS

SELECT BIBLIOGRAPHY

BBCS *Bulletin of the Board of Celtic Studies* (1921–).

Catalogue of Additions to the Manuscripts in the British Museum 1841–5 (London, 1850).

DWB *Dictionary of Welsh Biography* (London, 1959).

EC *Études Celtiques* (1936–).

EGC Stephen J. Williams, *Elfennau Gramadeg Cymraeg* (Caerdydd, 1959).

D. Simon Evans, ed., *Buched Dewi* (Caerdydd, 1959).

GMW D. Simon Evans, *A Grammar of Middle Welsh* (Dublin, 1976).

Handlist of Manuscripts in the National Library of Wales (Aberystwyth, 1943–).

J Dafydd Jones (Trefriw), *Cydymaith Diddan* (Caer Lleon [Chester], 1766).

Anne Elizabeth Jones, 'Gwilym Tew: Astudiaeth destunol a chymharol o'i Lawysgrif, Peniarth 51, ynghyd ag Ymdriniaeth â'i Farddoniaeth' (unpublished Ph.D. thesis (Wales), 1981).

LlC *Llên Cymru* (1950–).

Florence McCulloch, *Mediaeval Latin and French Bestiaries* (University of North Carolina studies in the Romance languages and literatures 33, Chapel Hill, 1960).

NLWJ *National Library of Wales Journal* (1939–).

T. O. Phillips, 'Bywyd a Gwaith Meurig Dafydd (Llanisien) a Llywelyn Siôn (Llangewydd)' (unpublished MA thesis (Wales), 1937).

PKM Ifor Williams, ed., *Pedeir Keinc y Mabinogi* (Caerdydd, 1930).

RB *Red Book of Hergest* (Jesus College, Oxford, MS CXI).

RC *Revue Celtique* (1870–1934).

RMWL J. Gwenogvryn Evans, *Report on Manuscripts in the Welsh Language* (Historical Manuscripts Commission) (London, 1899–1905).

Charles Roth, 'Du bestiaire divin au bestiaire d'amour', *Études de lettres, Lausanne*, ser. 3, ii (1969), 197–216.

S Cesare Segre, ed., *Li bestiaires d'amours di Maistre Richart de Fornival e li response du bestiaire* (Milano, Napoli, 1957).

SC *Studia Celtica* (1966–).

WB *White Book of Rhydderch* (NLW, Peniarth MS 4).

WG J. Morris-Jones, *A Welsh Grammar* (Oxford, 1913).

G. J. Williams, *Traddodiad Llenyddol Morgannwg* (Caerdydd, 1948).

ABBREVIATIONS

(*a*) Grammatical

The following grammatical abbreviations are exceptions and additions to those used in *GMW*.

accus.	accusative	nas.	nasal
adv.	adverb	neg.	negative
aff.	affixed	num.	numeral
affirm.	affirmative	obj.	object
asp.	aspiration	ord.	ordinal
aux.	auxiliary	part.	particle
conjunct.	conjunctive	pos.	positive
cons.	consonant	pref.	prefixed
def. art.	definite article	pronom.	pronominal
dep.	dependent	redup.	reduplicated
f.	feminine	sg.	singular
gen.	genitive	subj.	subject
indep.	independent	subjunct.	subjunctive
inf.	infixed	superl.	superlative
len.	lenition	vb	verb
m.	masculine	vn.	verbal noun

(*b*) Languages

MW	Middle Welsh
ModW	Modern Welsh

(*c*) Manuscript Collections

BL	British Library, London
BN	Bibliothèque Nationale, Paris
NLW	National Library of Wales, Aberystwyth

INTRODUCTION

THE late Professor G. J. Williams maintained that there was a 'school' of professional scribes and translators in Glamorgan from the fifteenth century to the beginning of the seventeenth century, transcribing texts, and translating Latin, French, and English works into Welsh on behalf of a group of landowners who patronized their work.[1] Although his use of the term 'school' to describe these scribes and translators is open to question, there was a long tradition of copying prose texts in Glamorgan. At the end of the fourteenth century or beginning of the fifteenth century the scribes of the 'Red Book of Hergest' (*RB*) and associated manuscripts were copying texts for patrons such as Hopcyn ap Tomas of Ynysdawy.[2] Copying of prose texts continued through the fifteenth century with manuscripts such as Peniarth MS 51, written by Gwilym Tew, *c.*1460, to the sixteenth century and early seventeenth century with manuscripts such as NLW MS 13075 in the hand of Llywelyn Siôn and Llanstephan MS 171 in the hand of Ieuan ab Ieuan ap Madog. Welsh translations were also made of English texts in print such as the *Gesta Romanorum* in NLW MS 13076, 'The Travels of Sir John Mandeville' in BL MS 14921, and 'The Voyage of the Wandering Knight (Y Marchog Crwydrad)' in Llanstephan MS 178, NLW MS 13163, and NLW MS 15533.

[1] G. J. Williams, *Traddodiad Llenyddol Morgannwg* (Caerdydd, 1948), 173–81, and see further J. E. Caerwyn Williams, 'Medieval Welsh Religious Prose' in *Proceedings of the Second International Congress of Celtic Studies 1963* (Cardiff, 1966), 65–97, in particular 72–3.

[2] See below, p. xvii.

Richart de Fornival's *Bestiaire d'amour*

One text which was copied by the Glamorgan scribes, but which up to now has received no attention by Welsh scholars, though it first appeared in print in 1766,[1] is a Welsh translation of part of the *Bestiaire d'amour*, a work written in French by the thirteenth-century Picard poet and cleric, Richart de Fornival.[2]

Richart de Fornival (1201–*c.*1260), the son of Rogier de Fornival and half-brother of Arnoul, bishop of Amiens from 1236 to 1246, is recorded as a canon of the Cathedral Church of Notre Dame at Amiens in 1240 in the cartulary of that cathedral. He was chancellor of the same chapter in 1246. In the same year, Pope Innocent IV granted him permission to practise surgery. He was also a canon of Rouen and chaplain to Cardinal Robert de Sommercote. He died on 1 March in a year not later than 1260, when a mass was celebrated in his memory. His works include a treatise

[1] Printed by Dafydd Jones (Trefriw) in *Cydymaith Diddan* (Caer Lleon, 1766), 22–9.

[2] The definitive edition of de Fornival's bestiary, based on the seventeen known surviving manuscripts, and the lady's response to it, based on the four surviving manuscripts, is Cesare Segre, ed., *Li Bestiaires d'amours di Maistre Richart de Fornival e li response du bestiaire* (Milano, Napoli, 1957). A 13th-c. verse version also exists, see Arvid Thordstein, ed., *Le Bestiaire d'amour rimé, poème inédit du xiii*[e] *siècle* in *Études Romanes du Lund*, ii (Lund, 1941). A 360-line fragment of another rhymed version occurs in Paris, BN fonds français 25544 (anc. fonds Notre-Dame 274 *bis*), written after 1317. This has been edited by Arthur Långfors, *Le Bestiaire d'amour en vers par Richard de Fournival* in *Mémoires de la Société Néo-philologique de Helsingfors*, vii (1924), 291–317. De Fornival's work was translated into other languages, e.g. a version in Middle Low Franconian, see J. Holmberg, ed., *Eine mittelnieder-fränkische Übertragung des Bestiaires d'amour* in *Uppsala Universitets Årsskrift*, 1925, and a version in the Pisa dialect of Italian, see Roberto Crespo, ed., *Una versione pisana inedita del 'Bestiaire d'amours'* in *Collána romanistica Leidense*, xviii (Leiden, 1972).

in Latin on alchemy and didactic works in French on love.[1] He is also remembered as a collector of manuscripts. Our knowledge of his collection is derived from his own catalogue known as the *Biblionomia*, which exists in a fifteenth-century manuscript: Paris, Bibliothèque de l'Université MS 637.[2] It contained about three hundred manuscripts, covering the trivium and quadrivium, philosophy, metaphysics, medicine, civil and canon law, the scriptures and commentaries on the scriptures, the works of the Fathers of the Church, and classical literature. The manuscripts, apart from the medical ones, came into the possession of the anti-Mendicant and Regent Master in Theology at Paris, Gerard de Abbeville, and comprised a large proportion of the manuscripts bequeathed by him in 1272 to the Sorbonne Library, Paris.[3]

De Fornival's *Bestiaire d'amour* is a prose work in the form of a letter from a lover to his beloved in which he analyses his love for her and his relationship with her, and makes observations on the relationship between man and woman with reference to the nature of animals. There is also *Li Response du bestiaire* in which the woman replies to the man's supplications. To understand the *Bestiaire d'amour*, it is necessary to place it within its tradition. Medieval pseudo-science concerning the nature of animals derives, in the main, from the *Physiologus*, a work written originally in Greek, probably in Egypt, and possibly in Alexandria, sometime between the end of the second century and the end of the fourth century AD, and known

[1] See C. Segre, op. cit. xxix.

[2] Printed by Léopald Delisle, *Le Cabinet des manuscrits de la bibliothèque*, ii (Paris, 1874), 518–35.

[3] For research on de Fornival's library, see Richard H. Rouse, 'The Early Library of the Sorbonne', *Scriptorium*, xxi (1967), 42–71, 227–51, and idem, 'Manuscripts Belonging to Richard de Fournival', *Revue d'histoire des textes*, iii (1973), 253–69.

in Western Europe through various Latin translations. The work consists of forty-eight sections and, although it deals mainly with the nature of animals, both real and fictional, it also contains material on the nature of stones and plants. The material is drawn from ancient authors, popular traditions, legends, and the Bible, and is subjected to a moralizing interpretation. In France, it reached a much wider audience when it became the basis of the so-called 'divine' bestiaries, written in the French vernacular by Philippe de Thaun, Gervaise, Guillaume le Clerc, and Pierre de Beauvais, in the period 1121–1217.[1] In these works the number of animals was increased, the 'scientific' part was inflated by additions drawn from the *Etymologies* of Isidore of Seville, and the moralizing interpretation was extended.

The nature of animals described in de Fornival's work is drawn from the *Physiologus* and the traditional French bestiaries, in particular that of Pierre de Beauvais.[2] Where de Fornival departs from these works is in the application of the imagery drawn from the animal kingdom to the domain of love rather than to Christian moralizing. However, de Fornival was not the first to use the *Physiologus* in this way. Charles Roth has shown that the *Physiologus*, which had long provided poets with symbolism for religious poems, was first applied to the domain of love by the

[1] The principal editions of these bestiaries are E. Walberg, ed., *Le Bestiaire de Philippe de Thaün* (Lund, Paris, 1900); Paul Meyer, 'Le Bestiaire de Gervaise', *Romania*, i (1872), 420–43; R. Reinsch, ed., *Le Bestiaire: das Thierbuch des normannischen Dichters Guillaume le Clerc* (Leipzig, 1892); C. Cahier, ed., *Le Bestiaire de Pierre le Picard* in *Mélanges d'archéologie, d'histoire et de littérature*, ii–iv (Paris, 1851–6).

[2] Of those portions of the *Bestiaire d'amour* translated into Welsh, the animals whose natures de Fornival drew from de Beauvais's bestiary include the ass (III), nightingale (V), viper (VII), raven (IX), lion (X), siren/mermaid (XII), tigress (XIII), and crane (XV).

troubadours.[1] He cites in particular the work of Rigaut de Barbezieux (*fl.* 1170–1210), who, although not the first or the only troubadour to have used images drawn from the animal kingdom, was probably the first to have been inspired by the *Physiologus* and to have made constant use of its imagery. De Barbezieux's innovation had a great influence on subsequent poets, and the *Physiologus* became well established as a source for providing them with imagery for their lyrical poetry. As Roth has shown, this profane utilization of the *Physiologus* was most apparent in Italy and Sicily, at first among the poets of the Sicilian School, the most ancient poetic school in Vulgar Italian, and then among the Florentine precursors of Dante. The influence of the troubadours, and in particular that of de Barbezieux, can be discerned in their work. The *Bestiaire d'amour* is to be seen as the apogee in the history of this profane utilization of the *Physiologus*.

The *Bestiaire d'amour* does not seem to have had any direct influence on Welsh literature. I have found no examples of *Bestiaire*-inspired imagery in the *cywyddau* of Dafydd ap Gwilym, who otherwise drew a great deal of imagery from the animal kingdom, or even in the works of Gwilym Tew, the copyist of the B-text of the Welsh translation. It should be noted, however, that the 'divine' bestiary tradition is represented in Welsh literature, e.g. the pelican in 'Cywydd i Dduw' by Siôn Brwynog,[2] and the unicorn in 'Troedigaeth Pawl Ebostol'.[3] Besides the Welsh translation of the *Bestiaire d'amour*, a short bestiary in Welsh is found in Cardiff MS 2. 615, pp. 13–14, copied by one Edward

[1] Charles Roth, 'Du bestiaire divin au bestiaire d'amour', *Études de lettres, Lausanne*, ser. 3, ii (1969), 197–216.

[2] R. M. Kerr, 'Cywyddau Siôn Brwynog' (unpublished MA thesis (Wales), 1960), 138.

[3] Ed. by Thomas Jones in *BBCS* xxiii (1968–70), 35 from Cardiff Public Library, Havod MS 22, 464.

Jones in 1748–9 from a lost manuscript written by John Jones, Gellilyfdy.

Manuscripts of the Welsh Translation of the Bestiary

The Welsh translation of the *Bestiaire d'amour* is to be found in various states of preservation in four manuscripts.

A Aberystwyth, National Library of Wales, Llanstephan MS 4, fos. 526^{v}–527^{v} (fo. 526^{r} also carried the text but it is now almost completely obliterated). The manuscript is incomplete, with gatherings missing at the beginning, in the middle, and at the end. It now consists of only 53 folios. J. Gwenogvryn Evans (*RMWL* ii. 424) dates it *c.*1400. It once belonged to the antiquaries Edward Lhuyd (1660–1709) and Moses Williams (1685–1742). It is one of an important group of manuscripts written at the end of the fourteenth century or the beginning of the fifteenth century by 'the Red Book of Hergest Scribes' (to use Gifford Charles-Edwards's convenient term).[1] The manuscripts were written by one or more of the three main scribes of *RB*. The anonymous scribe of Llanstephan MS 4 also wrote *RB* columns 1–29, 31–376, 381–502, 605–26, 1311, Peniarth MSS 19 and 190, and part of Peniarth MS 32. The main scribe of *RB* identifies himself as 'Howel Vychan uab Howel Goch o Uuellt' in a colophon in MS 8680, fo. 68^{r-v}, of the Public Library Company of Philadelphia, Pennsylvania. He also wrote Jesus College MS LVII in the Bodleian Library, Oxford, Peniarth MS 11, Peniarth MS 12, fos. 39–58^{v}, and an addition in Peniarth MS 4 (*WB*), columns 467–8, Llanstephan MS 27 ('Red Book of Talgarth') (with the exception of fos. 58–59^{v} which are in another contemporary hand), all in NLW, and Havod MS 16, pp. 101–12 (the detached continuation of Llanstephan MS 27) in Cardiff Public Library. The third scribe of *RB* also wrote the 'Llyfr Teg' portion of Peniarth MS 32, namely fos. 1–112.

The colophon in the Philadelphia manuscript, in which Hywel Fychan identifies himself, also mentions that it was written at the request and command of his master 'Hopkyn

[1] G. Charles-Edwards, 'The Scribes of the Red Book of Hergest', *NLWJ* xxi (1979–80), 246–56, 427–8.

uab Thomas uab Einiawn'. Hopcyn ap Tomas is the central figure in the production of the manuscripts written by the *RB* scribes. The poet Dafydd y Coed (*RB* col. 1375) refers to his 'galchlys ger Tawy', and he is generally referred to as Hopcyn ap Tomas of Ynysdawy, although he belonged to the family of Ynysforgan.[1] Before Brynley Roberts[2] drew attention to the Philadelphia colophon, thus proving conclusively Hopcyn ap Tomas's connection with the *RB* scribes, G. J. Williams[3] had brought together indirect evidence to suggest that *RB* and certain of the other related manuscripts were written at his request or belonged to him. *RB* itself contains five poems addressed to him and one to his son, Tomas ap Hopcyn, and a work entitled 'Casbethau Gwilym Hir, saer Hopkyn ap Tomas'. There are references in the work of fourteenth-century poets to some of the books he possessed. Dafydd y Coed in *RB* col. 1376 seemingly refers to copies of the 'Elucidarium', the 'Greal', and the 'Ynyales' as being 'in his court'. It is significant that the earliest copy of 'Y Seint Greal' in Welsh is in Peniarth MS 11, and a copy of the 'Elucidarium' in Welsh is in Llanstephan MS 27, both written by Hywel Fychan. Another copy of the 'Elucidarium' is found in Peniarth MS 190, written by the same anonymous scribe as Llanstephan MS 4. G. J. Williams[4] maintained that the 'Ynyales' was a Latin 'Annales' which he tried to identify with the Latin chronicle in BL, Cotton MSS, Titus D XXII, but it is more likely to have been Peniarth MS 32, which contains on fos. 112^{v}–114^{v} a short history of Wales in Latin in the form of a chronicle. Llanstephan MS 27, fo. 152^{r-v} contains a spell which mentions 'Rys uab Thomas uab Einyavn', who was probably Hopcyn's brother.[5] In Llanstephan MS 2, which has not been identified as a manuscript of the *RB* scribes, the tale 'Ffordd y Brawd Odrig'[6] is said to have been translated by a certain Syr Dafydd Fychan of Glamorgan on the orders and desires of his master, Rhys ap

[1] Prys Morgan, 'Glamorgan and the Red Book', *Morgannwg*, xxii (1978), 47.

[2] Brynley Roberts, 'Un o Lawysgrifau Hopcyn ap Tomas o Ynys Dawy', *BBCS* xxii (1966–8), 223–8.

[3] G. J. Williams, op. cit. 9–14.

[4] Ibid. 13, 190.

[5] Printed by Brynley Roberts, op. cit. 224.

[6] S. J. Williams, ed., *Ffordd y Brawd Odrig* (Caerdydd, 1929).

Tomas ab Einion. The total weight of this evidence suggests that both Hopcyn ap Tomas and his brother Rhys were patrons of the arts, were collectors of manuscripts, and, more important, commissioned scribes to copy manuscripts for them, and to translate texts from Latin and French into Welsh. It is possible that Llanstephan MS 4 was also one of Hopcyn ap Tomas's manuscripts, and that the Welsh translation of the *Bestiaire d'amour*, if not translated for him, was copied for him.

B Aberystwyth, National Library of Wales, Peniarth MS 51, pp. 194–209.[1] The manuscript consists of 210 pages, written by the poet Gwilym Tew (*fl. c.*1460–80). See *RMWL* i. 399. Watermark: an ox's head, probably a variant of Piccard VII, 375–7 of the measurements recorded between 1455 and 1463.[2] It suffers from torn corners and amateurish repair work. The text has faded in parts. Gwilym Tew probably lived at Llangynwyd in the lordship of Tir Iarll, Glamorgan.[3] G. J. Williams[4] describes him as one of the two most important poets in Tir Iarll during the second half of the fifteenth century, the other being Rhys Brydydd. His pedigree is given by Gruffudd Hiraethog in Peniarth MS 178, p. 42, where he is described as 'Gwilym tew prydydd a phenkerdd ap Ieuan'. However, Gruffudd Hiraethog has added 'Rys brydydd' before 'ap Ieuan', which creates some ambiguity concerning his parentage.[5]

Peniarth MS 51 is the only surviving manuscript which we know to have been written by Gwilym Tew, although there is evidence that he wrote others, e.g. on a single leaf of paper (NLW, Poyston Document 12) the poet Dafydd Benwyn (*fl.*

[1] For a detailed study of this manuscript, see A. E. Jones, 'Gwilym Tew: astudiaeth destunol a chymharol o'i lawysgrif, Peniarth 51, ynghyd ag ymdriniaeth â'i farddoniaeth' (unpublished Ph.D. thesis (Wales), 1981).

[2] Gerhard Piccard, *Die Ochsenkopf-Wasserzeichen* (Stuttgart, 1966).

[3] For details of his life and work, see *DWB* 327; G. J. Williams, op. cit., in particular 43–8; C. W. Lewis, 'The Literary Tradition of Morgannwg down to the Middle of the Sixteenth Century', chapter x in T. B. Pugh, ed., *Glamorgan County History*, iii, *The Middle Ages* (Cardiff, 1971), 505–9.

[4] G. J. Williams, op. cit. 39.

[5] For the problem of Gwilym Tew's parentage, see ibid. 43–4.

second half of the sixteenth century) has copied a pedigree of the descendants of William ap Dafydd ap Gwilym 'or llyfr dv y Wilym tew brydydd'. Other pedigrees copied from his manuscripts occur in BL, Harleian MS 2414, fo. 6^{v}, in the hand of Llywelyn Siôn, and also in Peniarth MS 447, p. 21 (eighteenth century). The 'Book of Aneirin' (Cardiff MS 2. 81) was at one time in his possession and he has included words from it in the vocabulary in Peniarth MS 51, p. 119. Peniarth MS 51, like the 'Book of Aneirin', seems to have migrated to Denbighshire by the second half of the sixteenth century. It was in the possession of the poet Gruffudd Hiraethog (died 1564), who inked over some of the faded passages of the bestiary. He probably acquired the manuscript from the poet Lewys Morgannwg (*fl. c.*1520–65), who was his bardic teacher and in whose hand his licence as a *pencerdd* is written. Lewys Morgannwg's pedigree is given by Gruffudd Hiraethog in Peniarth MS 178, p. 41, where he is said to be the son of 'Rissiart Morganwg prydydd a phenkerdd ap Rys brydydd penkerdd o gelvyddyd kerdd davawd ap Ieuan'. Gwilym Tew was probably his uncle. A pedigree in NLW, Castell Gorfod MS 8, p. 92 (eighteenth century) again gives Gwilym Tew as the uncle of Lewys Morgannwg.

The inscription 'per me Roger Kyffin de Gatheryr [*sic*]' appears on p. 171 of Peniarth MS 51 in a late sixteenth- or early seventeenth-century hand. This is probably the signature of Roger Kyffin the poet (*fl. c.*1587–1609). *DWB* 89 says that it is not known whether he was related to Morus or Edward Kyffin. However, Roger Kyffin's pedigree occurs in *NLW*, Cwrtmawr MS 21, p. 332, and shows that he was not related to them, at least not closely. He was a member of the Kyffin family of Gartheryr, Llanrhaeadr-ym-Mochnant, Denbighshire, being the son of Jeffrey Kyffin, and grandson of Lewys Kyffin of Gartheryr. His two sons are given as Godfrey and Sansam (= Samson) Kyffin.

C Aberystwyth, National Library of Wales, Additional MS 13075 (Llanover MS B 17), fos. 98^{v}–104, see *Handlist of Manuscripts in the National Library of Wales*, ii. 360–1. The manuscript is incomplete with folios missing at the beginning and end. It now consists of 124 folios. It was written towards the end of the sixteenth century or the beginning of the seventeenth century by the Glamorgan poet and professional scribe Llywelyn Siôn (1540–?1615).[1] He was born at Llangewydd in the parish of Laleston near Bridgend in the lordship of Tir Iarll. He is probably the Llywelyn Siôn ab Ieuan whose name appears in a rental or taxation list for Llangynwyd, 1584, in the hand of Ieuan ab Ieuan ap Madog (NLW, Lloyd-Verney MS 20). His name also appears in an estreat of fines and amercements, including heriots, in the Lord's Court for Tir Iarll, Michaelmas 1589–Michaelmas 1590: 'Richardus Ienkin quia non procequitur versus llewelin sion in placito transgressionis—iij^{d}; Idem llewelin quia non procequitur versus eundem Richard—iij^{d} (NWL, Foyer, White, and Prescott Deed no. 49). There is some evidence that he was, for some time, a crier in the legal courts. He says in one of his *cywyddau* that Tomas Llywelyn of Rigos was his bardic teacher. About fourteen of his *cywyddau* and *awdlau* survive, but they are of little literary merit. He is more important as a copyist. He was one of a group of professional copyists working in Glamorgan in the second half of the sixteenth century and the beginning of the seventeenth century, copying Welsh poetry and prose texts, including translations of English, Latin, and French works, on behalf of gentry who paid them for their services.

NLW MS 13075 contains an important collection of prose texts in Welsh. Apart from modernized versions of 'Iarlles y Ffynhawn', the present work, and 'Ystori Taliesin', the texts are mainly of a religious, moralistic, and didactic nature. Only a few of the texts have been edited: 'Ystori'r Llong Foel' by Brynley Roberts (*BBCS* xviii (1958–60), 355–7), 'Ystori Saith Doethon Rhufain' by Henry Lewis (*RC* xlvi (1929), 54–83), 'Ystori Alexander a Lodwig' by Thomas Jones and J. E. Caerwyn Williams (*SC* x/xi (1975/6), 261–304), 'Ystori Taliesin' by Patrick Ford (*EC* xiv (1974–5), 451–60), and 'Ystori y Gŵr Moel o Sythia' by Telfryn Pritchard (*SC* xviii/xix (1983/4), 216–33).

D London, British Library, Additional MS 15038 (Caer Rhun MS XXVII), fos. 38^{v}–44, see *Catalogue of Additions to the*

[1] See *DWB* 602.

Manuscripts in the British Museum 1841–5, 76. The manuscript is imperfect with folios missing at the beginning and in the middle. It now consists of 154 folios. The date of its writing, 1575, occurs on fos. 1^{v}, 2^{v}, 11^{v}, 30^{v}. The scribe does not identify himself, but the hand is the same as that of Mostyn MS 159 (NLW MS 3055), which was written in 1586–7 by 'D[a]uid ap Jenkin amhredydd o Vachynnlleth' for 'Huw lewis Syr Morgan or Hafodwen', see *RMWL* i. 222. The following signatures occur: 'Ieuan lloud ap Iohn' (late sixteenth century or early seventeenth century), fo. 41; 'Elliceus Humphreys ar'', fo. 86; 'Dyma lyfr gryffudd ap Rusiart' in red fere-textura, fo. 87^{v}; 'John Powel his hand 1761', fo. 104. On fo. 85^{v} is an additional passage in 'llaw Morgan ap Henri o blwyf llangevelach' (late sixteenth or early seventeenth century). Dafydd Jones of Trefriw, Denbighshire, owned the manuscript during the second half of the eighteenth century, from which he published the text of the bestiary in *Cydymaith Diddan* (1766), cf. 'David Jones is the true owner of this Book', fo. 91^{v}; 'Dafydd ap Sion a Biau hwn 1768', fo. 154^{v}. This text is denoted by 'J' henceforth.

Both Mostyn MS 159 and BL Addl MS 15038 contain prose texts in Welsh. The former contains such texts as 'Dares Phrygius', fo. 1; 'Brut y Brenhinedd', fo. 27; and 'Brut y Tywysogion', fo. 144. Among the prose texts in the latter are 'Mynachlog yr Ysbryd Glân', fo. 1^{v}; 'Pymtheg Arwydd cyn Dydd Brawd', fo. 11; 'Efengyl Nicodemus', fo. 13; 'Statud Gruffudd ap Cynan', fo. 94; 'Ystori Teitys vab Ysbysianys', fo. 105^{v}; 'Ystori Sylfestyr', fo. 124, another copy of which is in Mostyn MS 159, fo. 235. It is significant that it contains at least two texts, the Welsh translation of the bestiary and 'Chwedleu Seith Doethon Rufein' (both Early ModW adaptations of MW texts) which are also found in sixteenth-century manuscripts written in Glamorgan. Such adaptations have been regarded as the work of an anonymous, talented littérateur in Glamorgan in the second half of the fifteenth century or first half of the sixteenth century, who modernized and adapted the language of traditional Welsh prose texts.[1] It would seem that David ap Jenkin of

[1] For a discussion of the work of this adapter, see T. O. Phillips, 'Bywyd a Gwaith Meurig Dafydd (Llanisien) a Llywelyn Sîon (Llangewydd)'

Machynlleth had access to texts which were circulating in manuscripts in Glamorgan.

Relationship between the Welsh Texts

A comparison of ABCD shows that they are copies of a single translation of de Fornival's *Bestiaire d'amour*. Although A is a fragment, it contains accounts of three creatures not found in BCD, namely, the partridge, the hoopoe, and the stork. As there are folios missing in Llanstephan MS 4 immediately before and after these accounts, it is likely that the original Welsh translation contained accounts of more animals than those that now survive, and that A is closer to this translation than the other texts. Unfortunately, only a small portion of the surviving A-text corresponds to the text preserved in BCD, namely, V, and portions of IV and VI, so that the true relationship between A and BCD is difficult to establish. However, there are two textual features which suggest that BCD cannot descend directly from A itself but rather from the same ancestor (*α*) as A, namely,

Am hynny i nakeisst di vyvi 50 B, *ag am hynny i nakaist dithav vinnav* (*nakesti vi* D) 53 CD, which translates the French **m'aveis vous eschivé** (S 11. 10[1]), 'you have shunned me', is omitted in A,

and

i wddf 69 B, *i vwnwgl* (*vwnwc* D) *ef* 69 CD, correctly translates the French **le col** (s 15. 6), 'his neck', whereas A has *t6f y gorff* 19.

It would also seem that BCD descend from (*α*) through an

(unpublished MA thesis (Wales), 1937), 136–209, in particular 159–77.

[1] 'S' is my siglum for C. Segre's edition of the *Bestiaire d'amour*. References to this edition are given in such a form as 'S 11. 10' where the first number refers to the page and the second to the line.

intermediary text (β), in which the number of animals described was reduced to fifteen.

A comparison between BCD and the French original suggests that B is closer to the French than CD. Compare the following:

kail 72 B, *koed ne le dyrys* 72 CD; **une berkerie** (S 15. 8–16. 1), 'a fold'.
ar haflwydd 111 B, omitted CD; **par sa malaventure** (S 20. 1), 'by its misfortune'.
a gwybydd di i gennyf i 130 B, omitted CD; **et sachiez** FG (S 22. 2), 'and know you'.
ac ni ddaliai gariad byth oni bai drwy edrychiad 143 B, omitted CD; **ne ja Amors ne le prisist, s'i n'i eüst esgardé** (S 23. 8), 'for Love would not capture him had he not looked thereon'.
kans nad oes mewn angav chwaith gobaith bywyd. Velly, nid oes obaith lle ni bo trugaredd am gariad 170 B, omitted CD; **Car ausi com en mort n'a point de recoivrir, ausi n'a il point d'esperance de joie d'amour la ou on n'atent merci** (S 29. 5–6), 'For just as in death there is no recovery at all, so too is there no hope of joy of love at all there where one expects no mercy'.
A phan ddarffo iddo ev lladd 245 B, omitted CJ; **Et quant il les a ochis** (S 56. 2), 'And when he has killed them'.
i ysstlys 247 B, *i ddwyfron* 236 CJ; **sen costé** (S 56. 3), 'his side'.

A comparison between B and CD shows that sometimes C is in agreement with B against D and sometimes D is in agreement with B against C. This suggests that neither C nor D can be a copy of the other but that they are probably independent copies of a common ancestor (γ).

C in agreement with B:

kans pob rryw yssgr[iv]enn (ryw ysgryven C) 10 B, 8 C, *kans pob ysgrifen* 8 D.
brevv byth 33 B, vrefy byth 33 C, *brefy* 33 D.
gwedy adeiliad (adailiad C) 44 B, 47 C, *gwedi tyfy* 47 D.
na wneuthvm (wnaethym C) y llythr (llythyr C) hwnn 52 B, 55 C, *na wneythym y llyfr hwn* 55 D.

o damweinia i wryssgenn 73 B, o damchwaina i wrysgen 73 C, *o disgin i wrysgen* 73 D.

y gwna y ssarff 90 B, i gna y sarff 92 C, *i gwnaeth gwnaeth* [*sic*] *y bwystvil* 92 D.

pan welo ddyn noeth, hi a ffy 91 B, pan welo ddyn noeth, ef a ffy oddi wrtho 93 C, omitted D.

Natur y gigvran 126 B, Kans natur y gigfran yw 124 C, omitted D.

y (−y C) ffordd honno 157 B, 155 C, omitted D.

bwriaisst (bwraist C) di vi 167 B, 165 C, *byest vi* 165 D.

D in agreement with B:

hyd hynn (hyn D) 19 B, 19 D, *o'r blaen* 19 C.

nid amgen noc i'r assen (asen D) 32 B, 32 D, *a hwnnw yw'r asen* 32 C.

Kans y mae llawer etto o natturiav (mae llawer o natyrie D) ar y blaidd 68 B, 68 D, omitted C.

y gwr a gatwo kariad 119 B, y neb a gatwo i gariad yn gefrinach 118 D, *yr vn a vo heb wisg kariad* 118 C.

y gwelaf jnnav y ffordd 120 B, i gwelaf i y ffordd 119 D, omitted C.

ac am na bv gallter gennyf (by gallder genyf D) 227 B, 220 D, *ag am na bvm j synwyrys* 220 C.

It is unlikely that the writer of (γ) used B as his exemplar because a number of misreadings and errors in B appear correctly in CD:

kans pan gano, i natur yw yn nes i'r dydd noc haner nos 20 B, with the omission of *kanv* between *yw* and *yn*; *am vod i naturiaeth ef ganv ynes i'r dydd nag i hanner nos* 20 C, *Kans i natyr ef yw kany ynes i'r dydd nac i haner nos* 20 D; **car li cos, de tant com il cante par nuit plus pres de la vespree ou de la jornee** (S 8. 10–9. 1), 'for the cock, in so far as he crows at night nearer to dusk or to day'.

ni wyr Dduw nac y'w mam nac y'w tad ddw[c] [ ] na diod vddunt 128 B, *ny ddwg hi ddim trwydded yddynt* 126 C, *ni ddwgant hwy na bwyd na dim ymborth yddynt* 126 D; **ja ne les regardera ne ne pastera** (−**ne ne pastera** FG) (S 22. 1–2), 'it will never take notice of them nor feed them (−nor feed them FG)'.

There is at least one example where CD preserve a better translation than B:

ac velly y daeth hi i'r exampl hwnn yssydd yn kadarnhav ky[ff]lypu dyn noeth i'r hwnn ni char dim ar ddyn arall dilladoc 115 B, *Ag velly, y sampl honn* (*yr axiampal hwn* D) *a ellir i gefflybv i ddyn noeth a vo heb garv dim, a'r dyn dillatog a gefflybir* (*a ellir i gyfflyby* D) *i vn a vo yn karv* 115 CD; **Cis exemples conferme bien c'on doit comparer l'omme nu a celi ki n'aime mie, et le vestu a celui ki aime** (S 20. 5–6), 'This example confirms well that the naked man should be compared to the one who is not in love, and the clothed man to the one who is in love'.

It is therefore likely that (γ) descends directly from (β) rather than from B. I offer the following stemma:

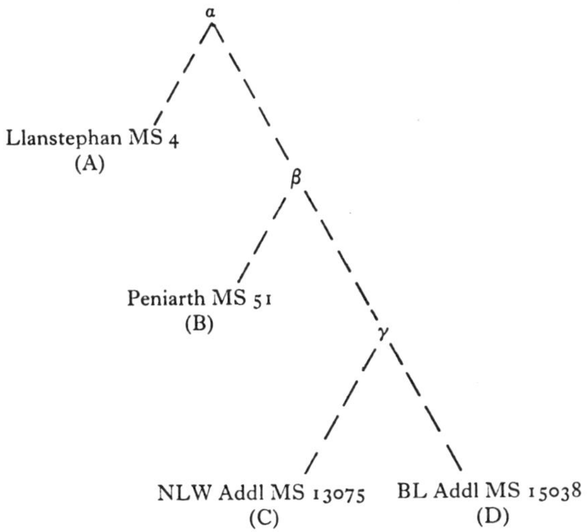

The Welsh Translation and the Main French Recensions

C. Segre's edition of the *Bestiaire d'amour* is based upon the seventeen known surviving manuscripts. He shows that they form two main recensions; ten manuscripts derive from a common prototype *y*, while the other seven derive from a common prototype *x*. Although none of these could have been the Welsh translator's exemplar, the closest to the Welsh are twin manuscripts, belonging to the second recension: Paris, BN fonds français 24406, fos. 141–8 (F), and fonds français 15213, fos. 57–96 (G), both written in the fourteenth century. The following correspondences may be noted.

Readings which only FG have in common with the Welsh:

	FG	*Other manuscripts*	*Welsh translation*
S 12. 5	rossignoil	crisnon	yr eos 54 B, 57 CD, 5 A
S 22. 2	et sachiez quil ne	ains ne	a gwybydd di 130 B, omitted CD
S 22. 3	pere et mere	leur (le) pere	ev mam a'i tad 132 B, 130 CD
S 29. 3	desesperance	desconfort	anobaith 158 B, 156 CD
S 30. 5	l'ocient en dormant	l'ocist	ac i lladd yn i gwssc 184 B, ag a'i lladd ef (−ef J) yn y gwsg 179 CJ
S 30. 6	l'ocist en dormant et en traïson	l'ocist en traïson	i ladd ef (Dyn J) yn y gwsg yn dwyllodrys 180 CJ, missing B
S 43. 9	l'ocient (occist G) en dormant	l'ochient	a'i daliant yn i gwssc 213 B, omitted CD
S 46. 3	touz ces perilz	cest peril	pob perigl 220 B, omitted CD
S 46. 6	de paor	por chu	rrac ofn 224 B, 216 CD

There are also two examples where the Welsh text translates readings which FG share, in each case, with only two other texts, in the first with Brussels, Bibliothèque Royale de Belgique MS 10394–414, fos. 227–238v (K), fifteenth century, and New York, Pierpont Morgan MS 459, fos. 2–30v (M), beginning of the fourteenth century, and in the second with Paris, BN fonds français 1444, fos. 257–265v (E), end of the thirteenth century, and BL, Harley MS 273, fos. 70–81 (L), end of the fourteenth century.

	FGKM	*Other manuscripts*	*Welsh translation*
S 11. 4	Ce est escrit es (ou K, en M) liures dautorite (liure de autorite KM)	omitted	Ef a gyfflypir (a hwnn a gyfflybir CD) yn llyfr (+yr D) awduriaid 43 B, 46 CD
	FGEL		
S 46. 7	entre ses piés	en ses piés	rrwng i ddwy goes 224 B, 216 D, rwng i dwy troed 216 C

Readings omitted in FG and which are not translated into Welsh:

S 9. 7	del monde
S 10. 2	plus s'esforce de braire et ke
S 10. 5	en nule maniere
S 16. 10	par sa bouce
S 18. 3	com il convient, ausi
S 21. 8	pour chu k'il ne sont noir
S 22. 1	ne ne pastera
S 54. 1	bele tredouce amie, ke jou croi
S 55. 1	vostre

However, neither F nor G could have been the Welsh translator's exemplar because a number of readings found in the other French texts (but omitted in FG) are translated into Welsh.

S 12. 5	dont je me sui molt pris garde	yr h6nn y kefeis exemplar ohona6 5 A, yr hwnn y kymerais (+j CD) exampl (sampl C, axawmpl D) ohonno (ohano C, ohono D) 54 B, 57 CD
S 20. 3	en arbre	y (i'r C) prenn 113 B, 114 CD
S 23. 1	en amour	mewn kariad 137 B, 136 CD
S 24. 2	de tant com il est fais a l'ymage et a le samblance le Siengneur des siengneurs	oblegyt i wnevthur o gyffylybrwydd i wyneb Duw e hvn 147 B, am (o achos D) i Dduw i wnaethur ef (−ef D) ar gyfflybrwydd i wyneb i hvn 145 CD
S 43. 5	s'agenoille devant lui et	y daw ef i ddaresstwng iddi, ac 208 B, ef a ddaw eti, ag 204 C, ac i daw ynte, ac 204 D
S 54. 2	medicine	meddiginiaeth 230 B, meddiginaeth 221 C, meneginiaeth 221 D
S 58. 2	de sa nature	o natur 262 B, omitted CJ

Also XIX seems to be a summary of the passage *Ne por chu . . . ma vraie mere* (S 84. 9–85. 5), which is omitted in FG.

Segre argues that FG descend from the prototype *x* through a manuscript *x″*, which had undergone contamination by a manuscript belonging to the first recension, close to Dijon, Bibliothèque Municipale MS 526 (H), thirteenth century, and that FG underwent further contamination by a manuscript belonging to the first recension, close to Oxford, Bodleian Library, Douce MS 308 (O). He has tabulated the readings in FG which he considers the result of the two series of contaminations. However, the examples of contamination by H occurring in those parts of the text translated into Welsh are of no significance in seeking to discover at what point in the stemma from the prototype *x* through *x″* to FG the Welsh translator's exemplar stood. But the fact that the Welsh translates passages omitted in FG suggests that this exemplar was closer to *x* than FG. Of the examples of contamination by O, the only one of significance is the phrase *dont je me sui molt pris garde* (S 12. 5) quoted above. This is omitted not only in FG but also in O and in Paris, BN fonds français 412 (B), written in 1285. As the phrase is translated into Welsh as *yr hwnn y kymerais* (*kefeis* A) *exampl* (*exemplar* A, *sampl* C, *axawmpl* D) *ohonno* 54 B, 4 A, 57 CD, it would seem that the Welsh translator's exemplar had not undergone contamination by O.

Content of the Welsh Translation

De Fornival's *Bestiaire d'amour* describes the natures of forty-six animals (one text, BL, Harley MS 273, adds the scorpion), together with accounts of the five senses, the four elements, and the classical story of Argus and Mercurius. Of these, only fifteen animals are described in the Welsh translation as preserved in BC. D, which is imperfect owing to the loss of two leaves, contained descriptions of all fifteen animals when Dafydd Jones of Trefriw printed it in his *Cydymaith Diddan*. The fifteen animals are: II *keilioc* 'cock'; III *assen* 'onager or wild ass'; IV, VI *blaidd* 'wolf'; V *eos* 'nightingale'; VII *ssarff* 'serpent'; VIII *ab* 'ape'; IX *kigvran* 'raven'; X, XVI *llew* 'lion'; XI *kolendr*/*kalendr* 'heron'; XII *morvorwyn* 'mermaid or siren'; XIII *dygerdav*/*digerfa*/*teiger* 'tigress'; XIV *vnigkorn* 'unicorn'; XV *garanod* 'cranes'; XVII *pelikan* 'pelican'; XVIII *kasstrin* 'beaver'.[1]

The A fragment is written on a conjoint pair of leaves, being all that survives of a possible gathering of six or eight conjoints. The recto side of fo. 526 is so badly rubbed that it

[1] For a discussion of the bestiary tradition concerning these animals, see F. McCulloch, *Mediaeval Latin and French Bestiaries* (Chapel Hill, 1960).

is now illegible, even under ultraviolet and infra-red lights. It seems to have carried the end of the account of the ass (III) and the beginning of the account of the wolf (IV). The legible text begins on the verso side of the same folio and contains the remainder of the account of the wolf (IV), the account of the nightingale (V), and the beginning of the account of the wolf (VI). Folio 527 carries accounts of three creatures not found in the other three texts: the end of the account of the partridge (the name of this bird is not given in the surviving fragment) (XIX); *chuinng* 'stork' (XX); *adar yr up neu'r epopus* 'hoopoe' (XXI).

The fact that A contains accounts of three animals not found in BCD, and that there are folios missing in Llanstephan MS 4 immediately before and after these accounts, suggests that the original Welsh translation was longer than the text as it now survives. However, it was probably never a complete translation, as accounts of *li chingne* 'the swan' and *li chien* 'the dog' (S 13. 2–14. 4) are omitted between the accounts of the nightingale (V) and the wolf (VI) in A as well as in BCD, and the account of *l'estrice* 'the ostrich' (S 85. 10–86. 6) is omitted between the accounts of the partridge (XIX) and the stork (XX) in A.

The Welsh translation as it now survives corresponds to the following pages and lines in Segre's edition: S 3. 1–13. 2; 14. 4–25. 3; 28. 1–31. 4; 40. 9–44. 5; 45. 4–47. 10; 54. 1–58. 8; 84. 9–85. 9; 86. 9–89. 2.

As argued above,[1] AB preserve the text of the original Welsh translation more faithfully than CD. The latter are probably independent copies of an adapted text, in which the language was modernized. It should be stressed that the adapter was adapting an existing Welsh translation, and that he had no access to the original French exemplar.

[1] See above, pp. xxii–xxiii.

Indeed, he was probably unaware that the text was a translation of a French work. Apart from rewriting the work in the language of his own day, he felt free sometimes to omit and sometimes to change the meaning of certain passages. Therefore, any critical appraisal of the work of the original translator must be based on the comparison between AB and the French text. A comparison between the Welsh translation and the French is dealt with in some detail in the Notes, and it suffices here merely to draw attention to certain features.

The translator's aim does not seem to have been to produce a full translation of the original. Passages not translated are sometimes long, as in the case of the account of the asp, blackbird, and the five senses (S 31. 5–40. 8) omitted between XII and XIII, but sometimes only involve single sentences, phrases, or words. As a result of these omissions, the logical argument of de Fornival's work is often destroyed. However, the translator sometimes employs a bridge or link passage to restore the logical argument of the original after he has omitted a passage, e.g. after translating the account of the lion (X), he omits the account of the weasel (S 25. 3–28. 1) and continues with that of the heron (XI). In the original French, the weasel's nature of carrying its young for fear of losing them is compared to the great despair of love. In order to introduce this concept of despair, the translator prefixes the account of the heron with the following sentence, which is not found in the French:

Ac yn enwedic y ffordd honno y kolleis bedwar ssynnwyr a'm gobaith, ac ydd euthvm mewn anobaith am nad ydwyt ti yn mynnv edrych arnaf megys y mae natur yr ederyn a elwir kolendr 157 B.

The standard of the translation varies between two extremes. On the one hand, the translator adheres closely to the French and seeks to provide a literal translation and, on the other hand, he chooses to summarize the original rather than to translate it verbatim. Sometimes this summarizing is so drastic that the original meaning is obscured, e.g.

[*Wrth*] *exampl yr heliwr am yr ab y gwelaf jnnav y ffordd y deliaisst dithav vyvi* 120 B; **Et par cest example est confirmés cil de la wivre, et par ces .ij. voies voi jou bien le raison par quoi m'aveis fait pior samblant puis ke vous seüstes ke je vous amoie, ke devant: et pour chu ke li cinges n'est pris devant la k'il est cauchiés, et par chu ke li wivre cort l'omme seure quant elle le voit vestu** (S 20. 9–21. 4), 'And by this example is confirmed that of the viper, and by these two ways I see well the reason why you have been outwardly less kind to me since you got to know that I loved you than before, both because the ape is not caught before it is shod and because the viper runs up to the man when it sees him clothed'.

The omission of a word or phrase can result in a shift of meaning, e.g.

ti a'm kyrchaisst yn gyn aruthred ac y bu aruthur gennyd vi 95 B: **si me fuistes si fierre com vous volsistes, et me corustes auques sus de paroles** (S 18. 5–6), 'then you were as fierce as you liked to me, and ran at me a little with words'; here **de paroles** 'with words' is not translated.

Sometimes the Welsh differs greatly from the equivalent passage in the French, e.g.

Ac [ ]*bvosst vy mod i'th orvod y buosst kyn valched a* [*chyn*] *drahaussed ac i kyrchaisst vi y'm lladd* 88 B; **Car volentiers voet savor d'autrui chu k'ele ne veut mie c'on sache de lui, et d'omme k'elle quide k'il l'aint se set elle tres fermement garder** (S 17. 2–4), 'For she would gladly know about another person what she does not wish to be known about herself, and she knows how to guard very securely against a man whom she thinks loves her'.

Sometimes the translator has added words, phrases, or passages for which there are no equivalents in the French, e.g. *val y gallwyf torri vy newyn . . . pes medressid* 36 B; *A mi a goll6n heuyt vy neges* 16 A; *kyd gallo hi adel bod genthi* 77 B; *llety* 79 B; *glux*, the name given to the serpent 90 B; *o'i vynwes nev j dan i wregys* 108 B; *ar y ffordd, nev ar y maes* 140 B.

Grammar

(a) *Orthography and Phonology*

Vowels

A /a, e, i, o/ are denoted by *a, e, i, o*. Both /ɨ/ and /ə/ are denoted by *y*. The prep. 'to' is denoted by *y*. The 3 gen. pron. (generally denoted by *y* sg. and *eu* pl.) is denoted by *e* in the reflexive *e hun* 6, and after *a* 'and': *a'e dia6t* (3 sg.) 7, *a* 'with': *a'e gyluineu* (3 pl.) 38, and *o* 'of, from': *o'e naturyeu* (3 sg.) 18. Original /ʉ/ is denoted by *u*, but also by *v* in *vn* 18, 24, 40, and /u/ by both *w* and *6* in free variation. The epenthetic vowel between consonant clusters is denoted by *y* in *ffuryf* 3, *hebyrgofi* 7, *sathyr* 37, *k6byl* 38. /j/ is denoted by *j* or *i* in initial position: *jeueingk* 35, 40, *ieueingk* 43, and by *y* medially: *anyan* 4, *kywydolyon* 9, *caryat* 21, *garyat* 51. /w/ is denoted by *w* and *6*: *gwir* 47, *ch6ant* 7, *ch6itheu* 13, *g6aethaf* 10.

B /a, e, o/ are denoted by *a, e, o*, and /i/ mainly by *i* but sometimes by *j* in initial position, e.g. *jnnav* 60, besides *innav* 58. Both /ɨ/ and /ə/ are denoted by *y*; *i* generally denotes the prep. 'to', the 3 sg. gen. pron. (*e hun* is the exception), and the 3 pl. gen. after *a* 'and': *a'i tad* 132, *a* 'with': *a'i llygait* 242, and *o* 'of, from': *o'i haissiav hwythav* 202. Four examples occur of /ə/ denoted by *v*: *vr* (= *yr*) 90, 96, and *vn* (= *yn*) 7, 72. Original /ʉ/ is denoted by *u* and *v* in free variation, and /u/ by *w*. The epenthetic vowel appears as *u* in *aruthur* 96, otherwise it is not denoted. /j/ is denoted by *j* in initial position and by *i* medially, except for two examples of *y*: *delyaisst* 103, besides *deliaisst* 121, *helywr* 104, besides *heliwr* 106. /w/ is denoted by *w*. It is lost in *atochi* 2.

C /a, e, o/ are denoted by *a, e, o*. Initial /e/ is lost in *wyllys* 244. /i/ is denoted mainly by *i*, including examples where /ʉ/ > /ɨ/ > /i/ before /g/, e.g. *drigarog* 3, *drigaredd* 26, and by *j* in the aux. pronouns *jnnav* and *j*; *i* denotes the preverbal and rel. particles. Both /ɨ/ and /ə/ are denoted by *y*; *i* generally denotes the prep. 'to', and the 3 sg. and pl. gen. pron. Original /ʉ/ is denoted by *u* and *v* in free variation, but also by *y* in a few examples, e.g. *vym* 3, *byost* 91, *vy* (= *vu*) 99, *ty* (= *tu*) 11, *ffyrf* 56, *ffynyd* 92, *plyf* 125, *dwyllodrys* 181, *gariadys* 228, *dolyr* 240, *rythyr* 148, *gysgy* 216, besides *gysgv* 217, and by *i* in *kysgi* 214. /u/ is denoted by *w*. /j/ is denoted by *j* in initial position and by *i* medially, but is lost in *kailog* 20, *anobaithol* 30, *bailchon* 121, *haibo* 143, *gaiso* 193, *gwilad* 215. /w/ is denoted by *w*.

D /a, e, i, o/ are denoted by *a, e, i, o*. Both /ɨ/ and /ə/ are denoted by *y*; *i* generally denotes the prep. 'to' and the 3 sg. and pl. gen. pron. Original /ʉ/ is denoted mainly by *y*, except for a few examples of *v*/*u*: *vn* 13, 68, etc., *hvn* 58, 76, etc., *vnbenes* 67, 130, *dwyllodrus* 181, *ganv* 60, and *garv* 81, 163. /u/ is denoted by *w*. The epenthetic vowel appears as *w* in *gwbwl* 78, and as *y* in *kalendyr* 158, and *wybyr* 35. /j/ is denoted by *j* initially and by *i* medially; /w/ is denoted by *w*, but is lost in *atochi* 2, *arnochi* 3, *vyochi* 3, *genychi* 67, and *chi* 138.

Diphthongs

A /ɑɨ, ɑu/ are generally denoted by *ae*, *a6* respectively. /ɑɨ/ is reduced to /e/ before /l/ in unstressed final syllables: *allel* 22, *gaffel* 51, *vyng gadel* 46. When /ɑu/ is followed by a vowel, it is denoted by *aw*: (*l*)*lawer* 18, 24. /ei, eɨ, eʉ, eu/ are denoted by *ei, ey, eu, e6* respectively; /oɨ/ by *oe*; /ʉu/ by *y6*: *y6ch* 14; /uɨ/ by *6y* and *wy* in free variation; /əu/ by *yw*, and /ɨu/ by *y6*: *y6* 18, 30, 46, 52.

B /ɑɨ, ɑu/ are generally denoted by *ae*, *aw* respectively. /ɑɨ/ is reduced to /e/ before /l/ in unstressed final syllables in *adel* 77 and *kaffel* 112. Original /ei/ is generally denoted by *ai* in monosyllables, but *ei* occurs, e.g. *chweith* 25, *gwreic* 44, besides *wraic* 45, 48. In pre-final syllables, it is generally denoted by *ei*, but *ai* occurs in *haissiav* 202. In unstressed final syllables, it is denoted by *ai* and *ei* in free variation, e.g. *anifeil* 31, besides *anivail* 207, *ereill* 83, besides *eraill* 255, *diveeisst* 190, besides *diveaisst* 191. /eʉ/ is denoted by *eu* or *ev* in pre-final syllables. Finally and in monosyllables original /eʉ/ is generally denoted by *av*, but *ev* occurs, e.g. *chwithev* 63, *parablev* 82, *ddev* 5, besides *ddav* 14. Reduction to /e/ is denoted in *gore* 216, 254, and *gigle* 255. /eu/ is denoted by *ew*;

/iu/ by *iw*; /oi, oɨ/ by *oi*, *oe* respectively; /ʉu/ by *uw* or *vw*; /uɨ/ by *wy*. /ɨu, əu/ are both denoted by *yw*.

C /ɑɨ, ɑu/ are denoted by *ae*, *aw* respectively. Original /ei, eʉ/ are generally denoted by *ai*, *au*. A curious characteristic of C is that original pre-final /ei/ and /eʉ/ are usually denoted by *ai*, *au* respectively, e.g. *adailiad* 47, *damchwaina* 73, *santaiddrwydd* 145, etc.; *ddauthym* 96, *dechrauad* 141, etc. In *wnaethym* 56, *gwnaethur* 106, *ae* represents original /eʉ/. /eu/ is denoted by *ew*; /iu/ by *iw*; /oi, oɨ/ by *oi*, *oe* respectively; /ʉu/ by *uw*; /uɨ/ by *wy*. /ɨu, əu/ are both denoted by *yw*. Aphaeresis occurs in pre-penultimate syllables in *ddwedvd* 37, 185, 239, *ddwedaf* 42, *ddwedais* 164, *gwilyddia* 148.

D /ɑɨ, ɑu/ are generally denoted by *ae*, *aw* respectively; /ɑɨ/ by *ai* in *ddaiar* 35. Reduction to /e/ before /l/ is denoted in *ysgafel* 71, and to /a/ in *imgydnabodath* 96. Original /ei/ is generally denoted by *ai* in monosyllables (*eithr* 42, *lleill* 214, are the exceptions) and unstressed final syllables, and by *ei* in pre-final syllables. Reduction to /e/ is seen in *elles i* 52, *nakesti* 54, *byest* 165, *ymeth* 110, *byse* 162, and to /i/ in *gimint* 59, 231. Original /eʉ/ is denoted finally and in monosyllables by *av*. In pre-final syllables, it is denoted by *ey*, e.g. *wneythyr* 40, 106, 134, etc., *dechreyad* 141, *greylon* 225, and by *ay* in *imgyrhayddyd* 25, *ymgyrhayddyd* 38. /eu/ is denoted by *ew*; /iu/ by *iw*; /oi, oɨ/ by *oi*, *oe* respectively; /ʉu/ by *yw*. /uɨ/ is generally denoted by *wy*, but by *wi* in *mwia* 87. It is reduced to /u/ in *ir wf i* 1, and *rwstro* 219. /əu/ is generally denoted by *yw*, but by *ow* in *kowir* 8, *kowrain* 105, *kowraint* 107, *kowion* 133, *bowyd* 226. As in C, aphaeresis occurs in *ddwedyd* 37, *ddwedaf* 42, *ddwedais* 164, *gwilyddia* 148. /ɨu/ is denoted by *yw*.

Consonants

A /p, t, k/ are denoted by *p*, *t*(*t*), *k*/*c*. Initially, /k/ is denoted by *c* and *k*, with *c* occurring before consonants and sometimes *a*, and *k* before vowels, and medially by *k*. No examples of /k/ occur in final position. Examples of *tt* occur only medially between vowels: *etto* 18, *clyttaf* 37, *attat* 46, *ytti* 50. /b, d, g/ are denoted initially and medially by *b*, *d*, *g*. Finally, /d/ and /g/ are denoted by *t* and *c*. /χ, θ, f/ are denoted by *ch*, *th*, *ff*; /v/ by *v*-, -*u*-, -*f*-, -*f*. One example occurs of *u*-: *uelly* 41, besides *velly* 34. Medially, -*u*- is in free variation with -*f*-, e.g. *kefeis* 5, *gefeis* 4, *hebyrgofi* 7, *ouer* 15, *llauur* 15. Medially after a consonant, it is denoted by *-u-*: *gyluineu* 38, *eistedua* 55. /ð/ is denoted by *d*. There is one example of *x*: *exemplar* 5. /l/ and /λ/ are denoted by *l* and *ll* respectively; both /r̥/ and /r/ by *r*; /s/ by *s*, doubled between vowels; and /m/ and /n/ by *m* and *n* respectively. /n/ and /nn/ are distinguished medially between penultimate and final syllables and finally in monosyllables, e.g. *heneint* 36, *keneis* 9; *gynnal* 40, *wannet* 54; *gan* 6, *hun* 6; *hỽnn* 5, *honn* 4. The symbols *m* and *n* are sometimes replaced by a short suprascript line, e.g. *dī* 32, *nā* 24, *hỽn̄* 3, *gyn̄ull* 41, *hyn̄y* 53.

Initial lenition, except that of /d/ and /r̥/, is regularly shown. Aspiration of initial /t/ and /k/ is shown as *th* and *ch* respectively. No examples occur of aspiration of /p/. Nasalization of initial consonants is shown as follows: /k/: *vȳghlỽyf inneu* 12; /b/: *vy mryt* 24; /g/: *vȳggadel* 46.

B /p, t, k/ are denoted by *p*, *t*(*t*), *k*. Examples of *tt* occur medially between vowels only, e.g. *nattur* 40, 67, besides *natur* 20, 43; *natturiav* 68, besides *naturiav* 75. /b, d, g/ are denoted mainly by *b*, *d*, *g*, but examples occur of /d/ denoted medially and finally by *t*, e.g. *lletrata* 195, *bechot* 187, and finally, /g/ is always denoted by *c*. /χ, θ, f/ are denoted by *ch*, *th*, *ff*, and /v/ initially by *v*, finally by *f*, and medially mostly by *v*. Four examples occur of *-f-*: *anifeil* 31, *klwyfvs* 161, *ofn* 149, *trachefn* 231. Final /v/ is lost in *kynta* 154, *hwya* 262. /ð/ is denoted by *dd*. *x* occurs in *exampl* 55, 115, and *glux* 90. /l/ and /λ/ are denoted by *l* and *ll* respectively. /r/ is denoted by *r* and /rr/ by *rr* in *torri* 36 and *ssarrvc* 123. The distinction between /r̥/ and /r/ is shown, the former is denoted by *rr* and the latter by *r*. An exception is *ruth*[*r*]*o* 123. /s/ is denoted by *s* and is always doubled initially and medially. (*sain* 182 and *gwsc* 183 are the result of the inking over of faded passages of the text by a later hand.) Single *s* occurs only in final position. /m/ and /n/ are denoted by *m* and *n*. /n/ and /nn/ are distinguished medially between pre-final and final syllables and finally in monosyllables, e.g. *vynych* 22, *vyned* 82; *hanner* 26, *hynny* 4; *kan* 21, *dyn* 30; *hwnn* 8, *hynn* 19. However, some examples occur of *n* where *nn* might be expected: *anerch* 2, *genyd* 2, *haner* 22, *hono* 106, *hyny* 17, 47, *amenydd* 156.

Initial lenition is regularly shown. Aspiration of initial /p/, /t/, /k/ is shown as *ph*, *th*, and *ch* respectively. Nasalization of initial consonants is shown as follows: /p/: *vy mhvm ssynnwyr* 201; /k/: *vyn ngeredikaf* 1, *vy nghlwyf innav* 62, *ynghnywillyn* 206; /b/: *vy mod* 88, 172, etc., *vy marnv innav* 168; /g/: *vy ngovid* 4, *vy ng[o]vec* 16, *vy ngalw* 235.

C /p, t, k/ are denoted by *p*, *t*, *k*, and /b, d, g/ mainly by *b*, *d*, *g*, but three examples occur of /d/ medially between vowels denoted by *t*: *dillatog* 94, 116, *etivar* 235. /χ, θ, f/ are denoted by *ch*, *th*, *ff*, and /v/ by *v*-, -*v*- and -*f*- in free variation, and -*f*. *x* occurs in *glox* 93. /l/ and /λ/ are denoted by *l* and *ll* respectively. No distinction is made between /r̥/ and /r/. /rr/ occurs in *dorri* 38, 74, and *tyrr* 251. /s/ is denoted by *s*, and /m/ and /n/ by *m* and *n* respectively. /n/ and /nn/ are distinguished medially between penultimate and final syllables and finally in monosyllables, e.g. *ganv* 20, *llawenydd* 134; *ennyd* 129, *vnbennes* 67; *kan* 21, *poen* 36; *honn* 28, *hynn* 37. *n* occurs where *nn* would be expected in *synwyr* 154, *genyd* 245.

Initial lenition, except for /r̥/, is regularly shown. Aspiration of initial /p/, /t/, /k/ is shown as *ff*, *th*, *ch* respectively. Nasalization of initial consonants is shown as follows: /p/: *vy mhvmp synwyr* 196; /k/: *vy ngharedikaf* 1, *vy nghariad* 4, *vy nghlwyf* 63, 164; /b/: *vy mod* 97, 162, etc., *vy marny* 166; /d/: *vy narostwng* 121; /g/: *vy ngalw* 222, 227.

D /p, t, k/ are denoted by *p*, *t*(*t*), *k*. Examples of *tt* occur medially between vowels only, e.g. *lletty* 80, *hetta* 232, *attad* 227. /b, d, g/ are denoted by *b*, *d*, *g*, and /χ, θ, f/ by *ch*, *th*, *ff*. /v/ is denoted by *f* initially, medially between vowels, and finally, and by *v* medially after a cons., e.g. *bwystvil* 92, and *forvorwyn* 171. Final /v/ is lost in *vy ngredika* 1, *anfona* 5, *hagra* 31, *dravtha* 61, *arafa* 73, *mwia* 87, *kynta* 99, 138, 152, *vwya* 140, and *mwya* 140. /δ/ is denoted by *dd*. *x* occurs in *axawmpl* 58, *axiampal* 115, and *glwx* 93. /l/ and /λ/ are denoted by *l* and *ll* respectively. /r/ is denoted by *r* and occurs where *rr* would be expected in *dori* 38, 74. The distinction between initial /r̥/ and /r/ is shown as in B. A few examples of *r* occur initially where *rr* might be expected, e.g. *ac i ry i ben* 206, *rac* 3, *rwng* 47. /s/ is denoted by *s*, and /m/ and /n/ by *m* and *n* respectively. /n/ and /nn/ are rarely distinguished either medially between penultimate and final syllables or finally in monosyllables. Both are usually denoted by *n*. Exceptions are *gennych* 2, *hwnn* 46, 65, 93, *yrwnn* 92, *hynn* 40, *hwnnw* 88, *hynny* 53, 67, 112, 152, 165, 211, *hynne* 132.

Initial lenition is regularly shown. Aspiration of initial /p/, /t/, /k/ is shown as *ff*, *th*, *ch* respectively. Nasalization of initial consonants is shown as follows: /k/: *vy ngredika* 1, *vy ngariad* 4, *vy nglwyf* 63; /b/: *vy mod* 120, 162, etc., *vy marny* 166; /d/: *vy narostwng* 121; /g/: *vy ngalw* 222, *vy nalw* (error for *ngalw*) 227.

Orthographic agglutination of the unstressed aux. pron. is shown in *atochi* 2, *arnochi* 2, *vyochi* 3, *wrthyti* 14, *arnati* 39, *nakesti* 54, *genychi* 67, *rragoti* 86, *dy gariati* 87, *byosti* 91, *kyrchaisti* 91, *ir wyti* 104, *delaisti* 119, *ddylyti* 121, *o'th gariati* 123, *arnomi* 170, and *mynyti* 227.

(b) *Morphology and Syntax*

The language of A is MW; B, particularly in respect of orthography and phonology, has many features associated with Modern Welsh, e.g. /ð/ denoted by *dd*, the prep. 'to' and the uncoalesced form of the 3 sg. gen. pron. by *i*, and *ai* and *au* (corresponding to MW *ei*, *eu*) in monosyllables and final syllables. The original translation must have been made sometime prior to *c.*1400, the approximate date of the earliest surviving text, but how long before is uncertain. The language of CD is Early ModW with examples of failure to modernize. The following is not an exhaustive treatment of the grammar of these four texts but merely draws attention to certain select features. It should be used in conjunction with D. Simon Evans, *A Grammar of Middle Welsh* (*GMW*) (Dublin, 1964).

Noun

Gender: The following nouns vary in gender as between texts: *natur* (f. B, m. C, m. D with the exception of *y drydedd natyr* 71); *amser*, *exampl/sampl*, *troed* (f. C, m. BD); *ssarff* (f. B, m. C; D has *bwystvil* which is treated as f.). The context makes it clear that *dygerdav* 194 B, *digerfa* 188 C, *Teiger* 188 J is a female tiger and these words are consequently treated as f. in the texts.

Adjective

Number: The pl. of 'balch' is *beilch* in 123 B and *bailchon* in 121 C, *beilchion* in 121 D.

Pronoun

Aux. 3 pl.: Two forms occur in B, *wy* with conjugated preps.: *vddunt wy* 131, *ohonvnt wy* 244, and *hwynt* with gen. prons.: *ev kywyddoliaeth hwynt* 180, *a'i llygait hwynt* 242. Only the conjunct. form *hwythav* occurs with verbs in B: *piganhwythav* 243, *kyvodant hwythav* 248.

Accus. inf. 3 sg.: After *pei* the syllabic form occurs in A: *kanys pei as kaple6ch* 15; CD have *pe*+non-syllabic form: *kans pes kablech* 65. The corresponding *kans pae kaplech* 65 B is probably an error.

Stressed possessives: One example occurs in A and one in B. In both cases the usage is substantival: 1 sg. *y meu* 51 A, 2 sg. *y tav* (*di*) with aux. pron. 50 B.

Verb

Pres. indic. 3 sg. rel. of 'bod': C has the form *a sydd* regarded by Henry Lewis as rel. pron. *a*+*sydd*.[1] It is more likely, however, to be an orthographical variant of *ysydd*.

Pret. 3 sg.: *-es* occurs in *kymhorthes* 192 B, *dotes* 214 B; *-is* in *delis* (with vowel affection *a* > *e*) 213 B; an ablaut form in *dywa6t* 55 A. The form *-odd* appears in *bwriodd* 198 B, *tyvodd* 100 D, and *-oedd* in *daloedd* 208 C, *tyvoedd* 100 C.

Pluperfect of 'bod': Dialectal variants occur for the 2 sg.: *bysyd* 163 C, and 3 sg.: *bysai* 162 C, *byse* 162 D.

Constituent Order

In the main clause of a positive statement, marked or unmarked, the verb is never found in absolute initial. The following variants occur in respect of the constituent order:

(i) noun subj.+rel. pron. *a*+vb in agreement: *y gwr a gyll i lef* 42 B; *a deu ereill a ant* 40 A;

[1] Henry Lewis, 'Modern Welsh Versions of the Seven Wise Men of Rome', *RC* xlvi (1929), 52.

(ii) pron. subj. + rel. pron. *a* + vb in agreement: *mi a vynnaf anvon* 4 B; *ti a'm kyrchaisst* 95 B; *6ynt a vynnynt* 25 A;

(iii) noun obj. + rel. pron. *a* + inflected form of vb (+ subj.): *a'r lle clyttaf a gaffont* 37 A;

(iv) vn. obj. + rel. pron. *a* + inflected form of *gwneud* (+ subj.): *kanv yn arw gadarn druanaidd i lef a wna* 22 B; *kans* (*kanys* A) *hebrgovi* (*hebyrgofi* A) *a wna* 56 B, 6 A; *i garv yn vawr a wna hi* 80 C; *A chanv a wnant* 178 B; *a'i hely a wnair* 260 B. The narration in this text is in the 'present' and this could possibly account for the fact that the examples of this construction are comparatively few (cf. *GMW* §180 (b) (3) and T. Arwyn Watkins, *SC* xii/xiii (1977/8), 391; for Proinsias Mac Cana's comments on this, see *SC* xiv/xv (1979/80), 183);

(v) adv. + part. *y* AB, *i* BCD (*yd* A, *ydd* B, *idd* BCD, *ir* BD before a vowel) + vb (+ subj.): *yna y kan ef* 21 B; *a herwyd natur y bleid y dylyaf i golli vy llef* 1 A; *Ac ar hynny yd edrycheis i* 7 A; *A rrywur ydd edrychais innav* 57 B; *ag yna idd a ef ywch i pennav* 236 C; (cf. *kynn belled ac ir adnaper arni* 82 B); *ac yna i kria ac ir ychneidia yn dost* 225 D. In B and C an alternative form, *i* + aspiration, occurs before vowels: *kans pan glywo ef aroglav y vorwyn, y daw ef . . . ac y daw yr heliwr . . ., ac i hadnebydd hynny* 208 B; *ag yna idd a ef ywch i pennav, ag i hegyr ar i ddwyfron* 236 C; *ag o'r gwaed hwnnw i hira ef hwynt* 237 C;

(vi) part. *ef a* + vb (+ subj.): *ef a da6 yr adar jeueigk* 37 A; *ef a orwed deu o'r rei jeueingk* 39 A; *Ef a gyfflypir yn llyfr awduriaid* 43 B.

Verb-noun Subject

The subj. in the following vn. clauses follows a transitive vn. and is governed by the prep. *o*: *ac er gwybod ohonod* 121 B, *gwedy* (*gwedi* D) *gwybod ohonad* (*ohonod* D) 119 CD; *am j bigo ef ohonvnt wy* 244 B; *yr roi ohonaf inneu y meu ytti* 51 A; *glybod o neb henny* 74 B; *a chyn kaffel ohoni ddiossc i hessgidiav* 112 B.

In the C text clause corresponding to 74 B, the subj. precedes the vn. and is governed by the prep. *i*: *i neb glywed hynny* 74 C (see J. E. Caerwyn Williams, *Celtica* xiv (1981) 67–82, for this development), and the CD clause corresponding to 112 B is verbal: *a chyn i kaffo hi i diosg* (*kaffo hi ddiosc yr ysgidie* D) 112 CD.

Relative Clause

When the rel. of a positive rel. clause is subj. or obj., its form is usually *a*.[1]

The rel. as subj. of inflected vb: *i gariad a vo rrwng gwr a gwreic* 43 B; *a'r serch a'r kariad a dyvoedd* (*dyfodd* D) *rof j a thi* 100 CD.

The rel. as obj. of inflected vb: *kyntaf dim a gyrch hi arnaw i lygad* 140 B.

In the following *a'r a* occurs: *ac nad oes neb, er pelled o iwrthvnt, a'r a'i klywo* 180 B.

In C *a'r a* is replaced by *ag a*: *ag nad oes neb ag a'i klywo, er pelled a vo oddy wrthynt* 176 C.

o'r a / *a'r a* also occur in the following examples where the rel. is obj. of a vn.: *nat oes dim o'r a dylyo g6r sercha6l y wneuthur* 48 A; *popeth a'r a welo hi i wnevth*[*ur*] 105 B.

In the second of these examples *a'r a* is replaced by *ag*/*ac a* in CD: *pob peth ag* (*ac* D) *a welo hi* (*vn* D) *arall yn y wnaethur* 106 CD.

There are a number of examples of a special antecedent preceding *a*: *Kanys natur arall yssyd, yr honn a gefeis i o anyan yr eos* 4 A; *i gna y sarff, yr hwnn a elwir glox* (*glwx* D) 92 CD; *val y gallwyf torri vy newyn, yr hwnn yssydd yn peri ym ddywedud hynn* 36 B.

The prepositional rel. clause is introduced by the rel. part. *y* in *i gariad y bo gobaith ynddo* 24 B.

The part. is preceded by a special antecedent in *o anyan yr eos, yr h6nn y kefeis exemplar ohona6* 5 A; *y ssarff a elwir glux, vr honn y mae natur iddi* 90 B.

Negative rel. clauses (all subj. or obj.) are introduced by *ny*/*ni*: *nat oes dim o'r a dylyo g6r sercha6l y wneuthur nys g6nel6yf i yrot ti* 48 A; *ky*[*ff*]*lypv dyn noeth i'r hwnn ni char dim* 1:6 B.

In the following the *ni* is preceded by a special antecedent: *y pryf a elwir dygerdav* (*digerfa* C) . . . *yr honn ni* (*hon ny* C) *bydd llidioc* (*llidiog* C) 193 B, 188 C.

Noun Clauses

There is one example of a preposed positive non-verbal constituent being preceded by *pan yw*: *Peth eglur yw pan yw parabl yw* 9 B.

In all other cases *mae*/*mai* is the form that occurs: *ac diav yt mae*

[1] See 'Verb' for the form of the pres. indic. 3 sg. rel. of *bod*.

ar gerdd y dylassid wneuthur hynn 37 B; *a bid diav* (*ddie* D) *gennyd mae* (*mai* D) *ar gerdd i dylyswn j wnaethur hynn* 40 C.

In the following the preposed constituent is negated: *A mi a gigle gan eraill nat hoff gennyt vy mot yn gynn yssmalhaet ac ydd wyf arnat* 225 B.

The positive noun clause is of the verb-noun type when the meaning is 'present': *yny dybyger vod y ddaear a'r awyr yn dyvod ynghyd* 34 C; *ac vn o'i natturiav ef yw hwnn, bod i wddf kyn ssyched ac* . . . 69 B; *ef a welir vy mod i yn varw* 172 B; or 'past': *gwedy gwybod ohonad vy mod j gwedy ymwisgo o'th gariad ti* 119 C, *er gwybod ohonod vy mod i wedyr wyssgo o'th gariad ti* 121 B.

The verbal type occurs when the meaning is 'future' or 'conditional': *heb dybygv yt y deleut* [*vod*] *yn wrthgroch wrthyf* 134 B; *A mi a dybygwnn y byddwn vyw* 238 B.

Neg. noun clauses are always verbal and introduced by *na*(*t*), *na*(*d*): *Kans natur assen yw na mynn brevv byth* 32 B; *A mi a dybygaf nat oes ym chwaith kyngor* 229 B.

Copula Sentence

The constituent order in a main-clause positive copula sentence is predicate + copula + subj.: *Y pelikan, ederyn rryvedd yw hwnnw* 239 B; see T. Arwyn Watkins and P. Mac Cana, *BBCS* xviii (1958–60), 1–25; *GMW* § 145 N. 3.

Method of Editing

THE full texts of B, C, and the A fragment are printed in sequence. Variants from D are given in the apparatus beneath C, the two lacunae in D being supplied by J (Dafydd Jones, *Cydymaith Diddan*). Lacunae in B, resulting from the defectiveness of the manuscript or the faintness of the text, are indicated by empty square brackets; missing letters or words are supplied when they are obviously reconstructable. Scribal errors and omissions in ABC are corrected. Passages of the faded B-text, inked over by Gruffudd Hiraethog, are only noted in the footnote apparatus when the original reading has been altered. Punctuation and the division into sections is editorial.

Words are usually separated according to the modern practice, but there are exceptions. Orthographically agglutinated aux. pronouns have not been separated from the preceding inflected vb or prep., e.g. *dylavtithav* 133 B, *rragoti* 86 D, and the orthographically coalesced rel. pron. *a* (with a following *a*) and the rel. part. *y* (with a preceding *y*) have also not been separated, e.g. *yr heliwr aeth* 198 B, *Velly'm delyaisst* 103 B. The equivalent French text, taken from Cesare Segre's established text (with significant FG variants) is printed after the Welsh texts. I am responsible for dividing it into the twenty-one sections to correspond with the Welsh.

WELSH TEXTS

Text B

I Vyn ngeredikaf gedymddeithes, ydd wyf i yn[a] anvon anerch a chariad atochi, a bid hyssbys genyd vod gennyf gyvle aniwed arnad rac mor drugaroc vvosst wrthyf tra vvm yn menegi yt vy ngovid. Am hynny, mi a vynnaf anvon yt lythr, ac ynddo ydd anvonaf ddev beth yn yssgrivenedic, nid amgen, parabl a lliw, achos na allaf wasstatvod yn y lle yn y['m][b] gwelych vn gyndrychol, namyn dangos yn gyndrychol yt arwydd o'r llythr hwnn ryw gof o jwrthyf drwy liw a thrwy barabl. Peth eglur yw pan yw parabl yw, kans pob rryw yssgr[iv]enn[c] a ddangossir i bod yn barabl, kans pob rryw jaith drwy barabl y de[e]llir[d] hi, ac yr awr y darlle[e]r,[e] hi a ymchwel yn barabl ac, o'r tu arall, lliw. [p. 195] Kans ni [ ][f] llythr onid trwy [ ].[f] Wrth hynny, y ddav beth hynny yn vn ydd wyf i yn i [h]anvon[g] iti am nad oes ym ras kael[h] kyvlwr yn ddiogan i ymddiddan a chwi, ac nid oedd wiw gennyt tithav warandaw nac ysstyriaw ar vy ng[o]vec[i] i. Ac am hyny y dangossaf i iti vy ngovid ar gyfflyprwydd adar ac aniveiliaid, ac y bydd raid ymddiddan yn gadarnach no[c][j] y gwnaethpwyd hyd hynn.

II Megys am natur y keilioc, kans pan gano, i natur yw [kanv][a] yn nes i'r dydd noc haner nos, yna y kan ef yn vynych, a phan gano yntav haner nos, kanv yn arw gadarn druanaidd i lef a wna, kans y plygain yssydd gymyssgedic

I[a] MS *yni*. [b] MS *yn y*. [c] MS *yssgrenn*. [d] MS *dellir*. [e] MS *darller*. [f] Torn leaf. [g] MS *i anvon*. [h] MS *kael kael*. [i] MS *ngvec*. [j] *c* obliterated. II[a] MS *kanv* omitted.

a'r dydd a'r nos ac a gyfflybir i gariad y bo gobaith ynddo. Ac am nad oes imi chweith gobaith j ymgyrheuddud a'th drugaredd di, yr wyf megys mewn hanner nos, a phan vv ddim o'r gobaith ynof ydd oddwn megis mewn plygain ac yn kanv yn vynychach, ac yr awr honn y bydd raid ym ganv yn gadarnach.

III Kans dyn anobeithvs a vydd kadarn i lef, ac anioddevawdr, ac a gyfflibir i'r anifeil kadarnaf i lef a hakraf i lef o'r byd, nid amgen noc i'r assen. Kans natur assen yw na mynn brevv byth ond pann fo newyn arni yn ormodd ac na wypo ple i kaffo[a] kael [p. 196] [ ][b] bydd raid i minnav [ ][c] hynn j ddywedud ac j weddiaw, kans nid ydwyf yn ymgerheuddud a'th drugaredd di, val y gallwyf torri vy newyn, yr hwnn yssydd yn peri ym ddywedud hynn, ac diav yt mae ar gerdd y dylassid wneuthur hynn pes medressid.

IV Eussus, peidio a chanv a ddyleaf i, a mi a ddywedaf yt paham, o achos nattur y blaidd. Nattur y blaidd yw, o gwyl gwr evo yn gyntaf, y blaidd yna a gyll i rym a'i hyder. Os evo a wyl y gwr yn gyntaf, y gwr a gyll i lef, a'i ddywedud, a'i hyder. Ef a gyfflypir yn llyfr awduriaid y natur hwnnw i gariad a vo rrwng gwr a gwreic, kans pan vo kariad gwedy adeiliad rryddynt ill dev, os y wraic a gar y gwr yn gyntaf, o gwna hi arwyddion kariad tuac ato, yna [k]yn[a] ddwyssed ac i hydnapo y gwr hyny, hi a gyll i hyder o nakav y gwr. Os y gwr a gar y wraic yn gyntaf, hithav a vydd balchach yna. [p. 197] Ac [ ][b] garedic, a[m][c] na elleis i vod heb ddywedud vy meddw[l][d] yni wypwn y tav di yn gyntaf. Am hynny i nakeisst di vyvi, ac oherwydd natur y blaidd, mi a ddylewn golli vy llef, ac am hyny, gwae vi na wneuthvm y llythr hwnn drwy gan ac yn ffyrf o ymadrodd.

III[a] Words obscured by inking over as *ple li kaffo*. [b] Three lines too faint to read. [c] Two lines too faint to read. IV[a] *k* obscured by inking over. [b] One line too faint to read. [c] *m* uncertain. [d] *l* obliterated.

V Kans achos arall a gevais i[a] o natur yr eos, yr hwnn y kymerais exampl ohonno. Kans yr eos a gar j gerdd e hvn yn gymaint ac i bydd marw o dra chanv, kans hebrgovi a wna na bwyd na diod o dra chwant kanv. A rrywur ydd edrychais innav ar hyny rac vy marw, a mi a welaf mae ychydic a dal i'r kywddolion ev kanv. A phan [vv][b] orav y kenais jnnav, gwaethaf vv imi, ac am hyny y peidiais jnnav a chanv, a mi a draethaf hynn drwy lythr ac ymadrodd mal y gallo pawb i ddeall[c] yn hawdd, a'i ddarllain, ac ysstyriaw vy nghlwyf innav. Ac i chwithev, ddarlleodronn, am y llythr hwnn ydd wyf i yn i adolwc i chwi na chaploch[d] y llythr hwnn, kans pes[e] kaplech, over vyddai imi vy llavvr a'm[f] hamkann.

VI [p. 198] [ ]edd[a] gennyd, [o][b] chyfflypir nattur [gwraic i n]attur[c] blaidd. Kans y mae llawer etto o natturiav ar y blaidd, ac vn o'i natturiav ef yw hwnn, bod i wddf kyn ssyched ac na allo troi oni thry i holl gorff. Natur arall yw iddo na mynn kymryd yssgavaeth yn agos y'w loches. Trydedd natur yw, pan ddel o vewn kail vn aravaf ac y gallo, o damweinia i wryssgenn[d] dorri dan i droed val y typio ef glybod o neb henny, ef a ddeily arno e hvn, ac a vrath y troed o lid. A chwbl o'r naturiav hynn yssydd mewn gwraic, kans oherwydd y kyntaf, ni ddichon hi roi i chariad onys dyrydd j gyd o gwbl kyd gallo hi adel bod genthi. Ail natur yw, o damweinia bod yn haws genthi garv ymhell oddiaithr i llety noc yn agos i'w llety, ac os ymhell y kar hi, hihi a'i kar yn vawr val na allo ymgelu, ac os yn agos y kar hi, hi a'i kar ac a ymgel val nad adnaper arni. Trydedd yw, o damweinia iddi vyned mewn parablev kynn belled[e] ac ir adnaper arni,

V[a] MS *i hwnn* wrongly added after *gevais i*. [b] MS *vv* omitted. [c] Word inked over as *ddyall*. [d] MS *chalpoch*. [e] Word inked over as *pae*. [f] MS *ac am*. VI[a] Torn leaf; half a line missing. [b] *o* uncertain. [c] Torn leaf. [d] MS *wryssgenn nav*. [e] Word inked over as *helled*.

hi a veidr dial arni e hvn, ac ymgelv o barablev ereill, a brathv i thavod, am vyned gyn hytred o'r blaen ac y[dd][f] aethoedd, val y gwnaeth y blaidd. Ac velly, ni vedrais ymoglyd [p. 199] rragod ti [ ]riad[a] [ ][h] ydd oeddyd yn hygar gwrtais wrthyf.

VII Ac [ ]bvosst[a] vy mod i'th orvod y buosst kyn valched a [chyn][b] drahaussed ac i kyrchaisst vi y'm lladd yn vn natur ac y gwna y ssarff a elwir glux, vr honn[c] y mae natur iddi, pan welo ddyn noeth, hi a ffy, a phan welo ddyn a dillad amdanaw, hi a'i kyrch. Yn y modd hwnnw y gwnaethosst dithav a minnav, kans pan ddevthum i gyntaf i ymgydnabod a thi, ti a vvosst a bychic o gywilydd arnad, a phan wybuosst arnaf innav dy garv, ti a'm kyrchaisst yn gyn aruthred ac y bu aruthur gennyd vi. Vr ymgyvydnabod kyntaf a vv rrof a thydi a ellir i gyfflypv i'r dyn noeth, a'r kariad gwedy hynny a adeiliwyd rrof a thydi a ellir i gyfflypu i'r dyn a dillad amdanaw. Ac velly y try y kyvydnabod kyntaf a vv rrom, ac yna, mi a levessais dywedud iti kwbl o'm meddwl, a gwedy darvod imi wissgo o'th gariad ti, ni levessais ddywedud wrthyd ddim o'm meddwl.

VIII Velly'm delyaisst [ ][a] vi y'm lladd oblegyd vy nackav, ac velly'm dallais[st][b] [me]gys[b] i dallai yr helywr kall yr ab. Nat[ur][b] [p. 200] [ ][c] elle[ ][c] popeth a'r a welo hi i wnevth[ur][d] [ ]r[e] y natur hono y daw yr heliwr kywreint drwy gelvyddyd hyd y prenn yn lle bo yr ab, ac yno, ef a eisstedd gyverbyn a hi, ac a dynn essgidiav o'i vynwes nev j dan i wregys, ac a'i gwissc am i draed yn lle gwelo hi, ac yna, ef a ymaith, ac a edy yno ddwy essgid a vo kymhessur i'r ab. Ac yna, yr ab a red ar haflwydd, ac a wissc

[f] *dd* obscured by inking over. [g] Torn leaf; half a line missing. [h] Torn leaf; words missing and remaining text too faint to read. VII[a] Torn leaf. [b] Word too faint to read. [c] MS *hwnn.* VIII[a] Letters missing from repair. [b] Torn leaf. [c] Torn leaf; half a line missing. [d] *ur* uncertain. [e] Half a line too faint to read.

yr essgidiav o natur ddrwc, a chyn kaffel ohoni ddiossc i hessgidiav, ef a ddaw yr heliwr ati, ac yna, hi a gais y prenn val y gwnaeth gynt, ac nis gall hi, kans ydiw i hessgidiav am i t[h]raed,[f] ac velly y daeth hi i'r exampl hwnn yssydd yn kadarnhav ky[ff]lypv[g] dyn noeth i'r hwnn ni char dim a'r dyn[h] arall dilladoc [i'r hwnn a gar].[i] Kans megys na ellir daly yr ab tra vo droednoeth, ac i gellir i daly pan vo[j] j hessgidiav am i thraed, a[c] velly,[k] ni ellir daly y gwr a gatwo kariad. [Wrth] exampl yr heliwr[l] am yr ab y gwelaf jnnav y ffordd y deliaisst dithav vyvi, ac er gwybod ohonod vy mod i wedyr wyssgo o'th gariad ti, ni ddylevt ti vy ruth[r]o[m] i drwy eiriav beilch ssarrvc, na'm daly, na'm disstrywiaw, namyn bod yn llawen wrthyf, a hyny yn llawenach yr awr hon no phan vvm noeth o'th gariad.

IX [p. 201] Kans velly y gw[ ].[a] Natur y gigvran, pan vo [i h]adar[b] hi [heb][b] plu arnvnt, am nad ynt tebic nac y'w mam nac [y'w][b] tad, ni wyr Dduw nac y'w mam nac y'w tad[c] ddw[c] [ ][b] na diod vddunt yni vont wissgedic o blu a thebic y'w [mam][d] ac y'w tad, a gwybydd di i gennyf i, yn lle gwir, nad oes vddunt wy ddim ymborth yny vo plu arnvnt onid gwlith, ac yr awr y bo plu arnunt, ev mam a'i tad a'i magant. Ac vell[y],[e] arglwyddes, y dylavtithav wneuthur amdanaf jnnav tra vvm heb dybygv yt y deleut [vod][f] yn wrthgroch wrthyf. Ac yr awr y tybygais yt oblegyd vod dy blu o'th arbed arnaf y dylut vod yn llawenach wrthyf, a'm meithrin, a'm karv. A gwell y dyleir kyfflybu mewn kariad i natur y gigvran no natur yr ab, kans ar y gigvran y mae natur arall a ellir i gyfflybu i gariad. Kans pan

[f] MS *i traed.* [g] MS *kylypv.* [h] MS *ar ddyn.* [i] Text defective; sense demands the addition of a clause after *dyn arall dilladoc* comparing the clothed man to the man who loves. [j] MS *yn droednoeth* written after *pan vo* and afterwards deleted. [k] MS *a velly.* [l] MS *Exampl yr heliwr.* [m] MS *rutho.* IX[a] Torn leaf; half a line missing. [b] Torn leaf. [c] Text confused. [d] MS *mam* omitted. [e] MS *vell.* [f] MS *deleut yn.*

gyvarffo kigvran a chelain ar y ffordd nev ar y maes, kyntaf dim a gyrch hi arnaw i lygad, a ffordd yno i tynn hi yr emennydd, a pha mwyaf a gaffo, mwyaf a gais. Val hynny y gwna kariad, kans kyvydnabod y kariad a vydd drwy y llygad, ac ni ddaliai gariad byth oni bai drwy edrychiad.

X Ac velly y kyfflybir natur y llew [p. 202] [ ][a] i ddyn vyned heb i law, pan vo yn bwyta, ac edrych arnaw, achos bod wyneb dyn ac arwydd ssantoliaeth ynddaw oblegyt i wnevthur o gyffylybrwydd i wyneb Duw e hvn, ef a ar y llew i ofn, ac o achos natur y llew yssydd vwch i galonn no neb, ef a gywilyddi[a][b] am vod ofn arnaw, ac a ddwc rrvthr i'r dyn. A chwegwaith y gallai ddyn vyned heb i law ef heb wneuthur drwc iddaw oni bai edrych arnaw. Ac am hynny ydd wyf i yn dywedud mae tebic yw kariad i'r llew, kans ni red kariad ar neb onid trwy edrychiad, ac am hynny, kynta kyvadnabod yw llygad, a thrwy fford[d][c] honno i tynnir emennydd allan. Kans amenydd gwr a gyfflybir y ssynnwyr.

XI Ac yn enwedic y ffordd honno y kolleis bedwar ssynnwyr a'm gobaith, ac ydd euthvm mewn anobaith[a] am nad ydwyt ti yn mynnv edrych arnaf megys y mae natur yr ederyn a elwir kolendr. Natur[b] yr edn hwnn yw, pan ddyker gairbronn dyn klwyfvs, od edrych yr ederyn yn i wyneb yn vnion, arwydd y bydd byw, os yntav a dry i ben oddi wrtho, arwydd y bydd marw, megys [p. 203] [ ][c] ti a vynassut tirioni wrth[yf][d] ymhob lle, ac er pan ddywedais i y klevyd yssydd arna[f][d] a'm llygait ers hyny hyd heddiw, ni bv wiw gennyd ti edrych y'm llygaid i nac y'm hwyneb. Ac am hynny y bwriaisst di vi mewn anobaith, ac am hynny y dylyir vy marnv innav yn varw, kans nid oes obaith j gael trugaredd gennyd ti, kans anobaith yssydd angav i gariad,

X[a] Torn leaf; half a line missing. [b] *a* obscured by repair. [c] MS *fford*. XI[a] MS *onid yw arnaf* wrongly added after *anobaith*. [b] Word inked over as *Natyr*. [c] Text too faint to read. [d] Torn leaf.

kans nad oes mewn angav chwaith gobaith bywyd. Velly, nid oes obaith lle ni bo trugaredd am gariad.

XII Gan hynny, ef a welir vy mod i yn varw. Ac ni wnn ar bwy mae'r pechod, ai arnaf i ai arnad tithav, ygadvydd arnam yn dav, megys yr hwnn a gymer i angav drwy y vorvorwyn. Ac y mae tair amryw vorvorwyn, nid amgen, dwy ohonvnt yssydd a'r llaill hanner yn wyr a'r llall yn byssgod, a'r drydedd yssydd a'r naill hanner yn wraic a'r llall yn ederyn. A chanv a wnant, yr vn a gan o briod lef,[a] a'r llall a gan gida thelyn, a'r llall a gan gyda phibav, a chyn geredikеd yw ev kywyddoliaeth hwynt ac nad oes neb, er pelled o iwrthvnt, a'r a'i klywo, na vo raid iddo ddyvod i warandaw ar ev ssain.[b] A phan ddel y dyn yn agos atvnt, ef a gwssc,[c] a phan wypo y vorvorwyn i vod ef yn kyssgv, hi a ddaw, ac[d] i lladd yn i gwssc. Ac am hynny, ef a dybygir bod yn bechod [p. 204] [ ][e] a bod pechod ar y dyn hevyd am i chredv hithav. Velly i tybygaf jnnav amdanom ninnav bot arnat ti bechot am vy lladd i drwy dwyll, a bot arnaf jnnav bechot am gredu i tithav. Eussus, ni lavassaf addef vy meddwl iti, ac am hynny, bit arnaf i y pechot oll, ac velly i diveeisst di vi y'm kwssc drwy warandaw dy gan di j gyd.

XIII A hynny, ti a'm diveaisst i o'th wiliat ti, a'm edrychiad i a'th gymhorthes di o'm daly i. A gwell y twyllaissti vy edrychiad i y'm daly noc y twyllir y pryf a elwir dygerdav drwy j hedrychiad yn y drych, yr honn ni bydd llidioc er lletrata i chynavon, o chyvervydd a hi ddrych ar y ffordd. Kans ymddigryfhav a wna o welet j chyssgot yn y drych, a thybiaid mae vn o'i chynavon yw, ac am hynny ydd abergova llid. Yr heliwr aeth a'i chenav, ac a vwriodd y drych ar y ffordd er i ssomi hithav, ac i ymryddhav i genthi.

XII[a] MS *A chanv a wnant yr vn aken o briod lef ddwy ohonvnt* is corrupt; hence emendation, see Notes. [b] Word inked over as *sain*. [c] Word inked over as *gwsc*. [d] Word inked over as *ag*. [e] Torn leaf; one line missing.

Velly, o edrych arnad tithav y'm dileisst yni gollais gan nwyf vy mhvm ssynnwyr.

XIV Ac o'i haissiav hwythav y deliaisst [p. 205] di vyvi [ ]e[a] drwy glybod a gwelet o aroglav [ ][a] delid i megys yr vnigkorn wrth arogla[v][b] y vorwyn. Kans natur yr vnigkorn yw nad oes yn y byt anivail anos i hely na'i ddaly noc ef, ac vn korn a vydd ynghnywillyn i dal, ac nid oes yn y byd anivail a levys ssylvv ragddaw, na dyn, aithr morwyn jevangk lan wyry. Kans pan glywo ef aroglav y vorwyn y daw ef i ddaresstwng iddi, ac i dyrydd i benn yn i harffet, ac y daw yr heliwr kyvrwys, ac i hadnebydd hynny, ac y dyrydd vorwyn ar j ffordd pan el y'w hely, ac y daw yntav, ac y dyrydd i benn yn i harffetoc ac y kwssc, ac yna, yr helwyr a'i daliant yn i gwssc. Yn y modd hynny y delis kariat vinnav, ac y dotes y vorwyn ar vy ffordd, ac ydd evthvm jnnav, ac y kyssgais, ac o'r kwssc hwnnw y'm delit, ac y kollais y tri ssynnwyr gore ar vy helw drwy gyssgv, megys yr hy[ ][b] a ddelit drwy gan y vorvorwyn, ac y deli[ ].[b]

XV [p. 206] [ ][a] dylasswn jnne[v][b] rac kyssgu [ ][b] kariat tithav pob perigl a gwneuthur val y gwna y garanod. Natur y garanot yw na gysscant yni ddel llawer i'r vn lle onaddvnt, ac vn a wilia tra vo y llaill yn kyssgv. Ac velly gwna pob vn onaddvnt ar gylch.[c] A'r vn a vo yn gwilio a gymer mae[n][d] rrwng i ddwy goes rrac ofn dissgyn kyssgv ar[n]aw,[e] kans be kyssgai, y maen a ssyrthiai, ac yntav a ddeffroai. Ac velly y dylasswnn jnnav bod gennyf ryw ysstryw o gallter ac ymoglut rac ym gyssgv. Kans maen a arwyddoka kallter, ac am na bv gallter gennyf, ni wnn pa gyngor yssydd ym.

XVI A mi a dybygaf nat oes ym chwaith kyngor nac ychwaith meddiginiaeth, oni bai vy ngalw ohonot trwy

XIV[a] Torn leaf; half a line missing. [b] Torn leaf. XV[a] Torn leaf; half a line missing. [b] Torn leaf. [c] MS *glych*. [d] MS *mae*. [e] MS *araw*.

gariat trachefn mal y gwna y llew am i gynavon. Kans kynavon y llew a enir yn veirw, ac yn [vei]rw[a] y byddant hyd ymhenn y tr[i][b] diav [p. 207] [ ][c] y daw ev [ ][d] penn [ ][a] a rrac maint i vchenait ef [ ][a] bywyt ynddvnt. Hynn a ellir i dde[ ][a] gariat, pe tithav a vynnai vy ngalw jnnav drwy gariat ac ymddiddan a mi, velly y kyvodwnn jnnav yn vyw o'r marwol haint yssydd arnaf.

XVII A mi a dybygwnn y byddwn vyw, pe gwnelut ti a myvi val y gwna y pelika[n].[a] Y pelikan, ederyn rryvedd yw hwnnw. I natu[r][b] ef yw garv i veibion adar yn gymaint ac y daw yn rry vynych i ymwelet ac wynt, ac ydd eheta yn i kylch, ac y kywrdd i essyll ef a'i llygait hwynt, ac y piganhwythav ef, a chyn gravlonet ydiw yr edn hwnnw ac namyn gwnavr eniwet iddo, ac o lid am j bigo ef ohonvnt wy, yntav a'i lladd hwythav. A phan ddarffo iddo ev lladd, edivar vydd gantho, ac yna y daw vwch ev penn, ac ydd egyr ar i ysstlys, ac a'r gwaet hwnnw ydd ir ef hwynt, ac y kyvodant hwythav yn vyw o varw. Val hynny, [p. 208] [ ][c] dydi gyntaf [ ]n[b] megys kyw ac y'th bigais o [ddy]wedut[b] wrthyt vy ngovid. Ac yna, ti[th]av[b] a'm lleddaisst jnnav y varw, y gyvrw angav ac a berthyn ar gariat. Eussus, pe tydi a vynnai egori dy ysstlys a rroi ym dy galonn yssydd o vewn yt, velly, trwy ewyllys da y kyvotut ti vi yn vyw o varw, a gore meddeginiaeth ar vy haint i oedd gael dy gariat ti, ac ewyllys dy galonn. A mi a gigle gan eraill nat hoff gennyt vy mot yn gynn yssmalhaet ac ydd wyf arnat, ac os drwc gennyt ti hynny, dyro jmi dy galonn, ac velly y gelly di ymryddhav o'm yssmalhawch i.

XVIII Kans velly y gwna yr enivail a elwir kasstrin. Ar vn o['i][a] bedwar troet y mae meddigynaeth, a'i hely a wnair yn chwannoc o achos y troet hwnnw. A ffo a wna yntav hyd

XVI[a] Torn leaf. [b] MS *tr*. [c] Text missing from repair. [d] Torn leaf; half a line missing. XVII[a] *n* obliterated. [b] Torn leaf. [c] Torn leaf; half a line missing. XVIII[a] MS *vn o bedwar*.

hwya ac y gallo, a phan ddiffykio, ef a wyr o natur na helit ef[b] ond o achos y troed hwnnw. Ef a gymer [p. 209] [ ][c] velly y diangk yntav. Velly [ ][c] arglwyddes amdanaf jnnav, pa [ ][c] dy air tec di [ ][c] ti a vwrriaisst air tec [ ],[c] ac yna y twyllaisst vyvi.

Ac velly y tervyna y [ ].[c]

[b] MS *ef ef*. [c] Most of leaf missing.

Text C

Llyma lyfr a elwir Llyfr Ovydd

I Vy ngharedikaf gariadferch, idd wyf j yn danfon annerch a chariad atoch, a bid hysbys gennych vod gennyf j gyfle aniwed arnad ti rag mor drigarog a vyost di wrthyf j tra vym j yn manegi vy nghariad a'm dolur iti. Ag am hynny, mi a ddanfonaf iti lythr ag yndo ddav beth yn ysgryvenedig, nid amgen, parabl a lliw, am na baiddaf j ddyvod lle kaffwyf j ymddiddan a thi, ond mi a ddanfonaf atad ti arwydd kywir drwy barabl a lliw, kans pob ryw ysgryven a ddangosir i bod yn barabl, kans pob ryw jaith trwy barabl i deallir, kans pan ddarllenir pob llythyr, ef a ymchoel yn barabl, ag o'r ty arall yn lliw, am nad ymddengys llythyr ond trwy liw. Ag am hynny, mi a ddanfonaf atad ti ddav beth yn vn, am nad oes imi ras i gaffael yn ddiogan gyflwr ymddiddan a thi, a hevyd idd wyf j yn tybiaid nad oedd wiw gennyd wrando arnaf j na thosturio wrthyf. Ag am hynny, mi a ddangosaf iti gyfran o'm klwyf a'm dolur ar gyfflybrwydd adar ag anevailaid, am vod yn raid

D: heading *llyma lythyr anerch o ueith Ouydd yn anfon at i gariad.*
I 1 *Vy ngredika.* 1 *ir wf i yn anfon anerch.* 2 *atochi.* 2–3 *genyf i gyfle o aniwed arnochi.* 3 *rac.* 3 *drigaroc vyochi.* 3 *wrthyf i.* 3–4 *fym i.* 4 *vy ngariad a'm dolyr i chwi.* 4 omit *Ag.* 4–5 *am hyny mi anfona lythyr ac ynto ef.* 5 *ysgrifenedic.* 6–7 *o achos na beiddiaf ddyfod lle kaffwyf ddyfod i ymddiddan.* 7 *namyn mi a ddanfonaf.* 8 *kowir.* 8 *trwy.* 8 *pob ysgrifen.* 10 *dyellir.* 10 *yr awr i darllenir y llythr.* 10 *ymchwel.* 11 *ac.* 11–12 *kans nid ymddengys llythr ond yn lliw.* 12–13 *Ac am hyny mi anfona atad y ddav beth yn vn.* 13–14 *i gael ymddiddan ac i ddangos ynghyflwr wrthyti.* 14 *hefyd ir wyf i.* 15 *genyd.* 15 omit *j.* 15 *thostirio.* 16 *ac am hyn.* 16 *yt.* 16–17 *gyfran o'm kyflwr o gyfflybrwydd adar ac ynyfeiliaid.* 17 *oherwydd bod yn rraid.*

ymddiddan yn gadarnach rag llaw nag i gwnaethbwyd o'r blaen.

II Megis am natur y kailog, am vod i naturiaeth ef ganv yn nes[a] i'r dydd nag i hanner nos, kans yna i kan ef yn deg ag yn vynych, ag velly, pan gano [fo. 99] ef hanner nos i kan ef yn arw gadarn yna, megis i mae pylgain yn agos i'r dydd ag yn gymysgedig ag ef, ag velly y nos a gefflybir i gariad heb obaith yndo, ag am nad oes imi bellach obaith i ymgyrhaeddyd a'th drigaredd di idd wyf j megis am hanner nos, kans pe bai gennyf j ddim gobaith, mi a vyddwn megis y pylgain yn kanv yn deg ag yn vynych, a'r awr honn i bydd raid imi ganv yn arw gadarn.

III Kans peth anobaithol a vydd kadarn a garw i lef, ag ef a gefflybir i'r anevail kadarnaf a hakraf i lais yn yr holl vyd, a hwnnw yw'r asen. Kans natur yr asen yw na vynn ef vrefy byth yny vo newyn mawr arno, ag na wypo pa le i gallo gael bwyd, ag yna i rydd ef ryw fravad yny dybyger vod y ddaear a'r awyr yn dyvod ynghyd. Ag velly i bydd raid i minnav gymeryd poen a thristwch arnaf yn vwy ymhell o hynn allan i ddwedvd ag i weddio, kans nid odwyf j yn

[a] MS *ynes.*

18–19 *rrac llaw nac i gwneythbwyd hyd hyn.*

II 20 *natyr y kelioc.* 20 *Kans i natyr ef yw kany.* 21 *nac i haner nos.* 21 *ymric y dydd i kan ef yn dec.* 22 *a ffan gano ef am haner nos.* 23–4 *ac val i kymysgo y plygain a'r dydd i kan ef yn dekach.* 24 *ac velly y nos a gyfflybir.* 25 *ynto.* 25 *ac velly am nad oes ymi.* 25 omit *bellach.* 25–6 *obaith imgyrhayddyd a'th gariad ti.* 26 omit *j.* 26 *haner.* 27 *a ffe bai ddim gobaith genyf i.* 27 *fyddwn.* 27–8 *megis mewn plygain ac yn kany.* 28 *dec ac.* 28 *hon.* 29 *rraid ymi gany megis yn arw gadarn.*

III 30 *anobeithiol.* 30 *fydd garw gadarn i lef.* 30–1 *a hyn a gyfflybir.* 31 *ynifail.* 31 *hagra.* 32 *nid amgen noc i'r asen.* 32 *natyr.* 32–3 *na fyn brefy.* 33 omit *byth.* 33 *oni.* 33 *ac na.* 34 *ac yno i rrydd ef.* 34 *frefad.* 34 *yni dybyker.* 35 *ddaiar a'r wybyr yn dyfod.* 35 *Ac.* 35–6 *rraid i mine gymryd.* 37 *hyn.* 37 *ddwedyd ac.* 37–8 *nid wyf yn ymgyrhayddyd.*

ymgyrhaeddyd a'th drigaredd di, megis i gallwyf j dorri vy newyn arnad, yr hwnn a sydd yn peri imi ddwedvd val hynn, a bid diav gennyd mae ar gerdd i dylyswn j wnaethur hynn.

IV Ond mi a baidaf a chanv, kans mi a ddwedaf iti paham, o achos natur y blaidd. Kans natur y blaidd yw, os gwr a'i gwyl ef yn gyntaf, y blaidd a gyll i rym a'i hyder. Os y blaidd a wyl y gwr yn gyntaf, y gwr a gyll i rym a'i [fo. 99v] nerth, a hwnn a gyfflybir yn llyfr yr awduriaid i natur kariad a vo rwng gwr a gwraig, kans pan vo kariad gwedy adailiad ryddynt yll dav, os y wraig a gar y gwr yn gyntaf, y wraig a gyll i hyder o'i nakav ef, o gwna hi arwyddion kariad tiag ato ef val i hadnapo y gwr i bod hi yn y garv ef. Os y gwr a gar y wraig yn gyntaf, hithav a vydd balchach a thrawsach ymhell. Ag am hynny, arglwyddes garedig, am na ellais j vod heb ddangos vy meddwl iti yn gyntaf, ag am hynny i nakaist dithav vinnav, ag oherwydd natur y blaidd, mi a ddelywn golli vy nerth a'm parabl, ag am hynny, gwae vi na wnaethym y llythyr hwnn drwy gan ag yn ffyrf ymadrodd.

V A hevyd achos arall a gevais j o natur yr eos, yr hwnn i kymerais j sampl ohano. Kans yr eos a gar i gerdd i hvn yn gymaint ag na chymero ef na bwyd na diod o dra chwant ar

38 *i dori.* 39 *arnati.* 39 *yr hwn y sydd yn peri ymi ddwedyd.* 40 *ddie.* 40 omit *gennyd.* 40 *mai.* 40–1 *dlyswn wneythyr hyn.*

IV 42 *Eithr.* 42 *beidaf.* 42 *ytt.* 43 *oherwydd natyr y blaidd.* 43 omit *Kans.* 43 *natyr.* 44 *haner i rym a'i hyder.* 46 *awdyriaid.* 46 *natyr.* 46 *fo.* 47 *gwraic.* 47–8 *gwedi tyfy rryngyn yll day.* 48 *os gwraic a gar gwr.* 48 *wraic.* 49 *y'w nakav ef.* 49–50 omit *tiag ato ef.* 50 *megis ir adnapo.* 50 *yn i gary ef.* 51 *wraic.* 51 *hithe a fydd.* 51 omit *a thrawsach.* 52 *Ac am hyny.* 52 *garedic.* 52 *na elles i.* 53–4 *ac am hynny i nakesti vi oherwydd.* 54 *natyr.* 55 *ddylwn.* 55 *ac am hyny.* 55 *fi.* 55–6 *na wneythym y llyfr hwn.* 56 *ac.*

V 57 omit *A hevyd.* 57 *gefais i.* 57 *natyr.* 57 *hwn.* 58 *kymerais i axawmpl ohono.* 59 *gimint.* 59 *a ac na chymero ef.*

ganv hyd pan vo ef marw o newyn. A ry hir i bvm j heb ystyriaid hynny rag vy marw jnnav, a mi a draethaf hynn drwy lythyr ag ymadrodd val i gallo pawb i ddeall yn hawdd a darllain ag ystyriaid vy nghlwyf j a'm dolur, a hevyd i chwithav, y darlleawdwyr, na chanmoloch chwithav y llythyr hwnn, kans pes kablech, over a vyddai i minnav vy llavur.

VI Ag am hynny, vnbennes, na vyd ryvedd gennyd, o chefflybir natur gwraig i natur blaidd. Kans vn o'i naturiaethav [fo. 100] ef yw hynn, bod i vwnwgl ef kyn syched ag na allo ef droi ony thry i holl gorff ef o gwbl, a'u natur yw na vynn ef gymeryd vn ysgavael in agos y'w loches. Y trydydd natur yw, pan ddel ef i rodio yn ddirgel mewn koed ne le dyrys, ef a gerdd yn arava ag i gallo, ag o damchwaina i wrysgen dorri dan i droed ef val i tebyko ef i neb glywed hynny, ef a gny i droed o'i ddannedd yn ffest o ddigovaint wrtho i hvn. Ag velly, y kwbl o'r naturiaethav hynn a sydd ar wraig, kans oherwydd y kyntaf, ny ddychon hi roddi i chariad i neb onys rydd o gwbl, sef yw hynny, gadael bod genti. Yr ail yw, o damchwaina vod yn haws genti garv

60 *oni vo ef*. 60 *A rry hir i bym i*. 61 *hyny rac*. 61 *inav*. 61–2 *ac mi a dravtha hwn trwy lythyr ac ymadrodd*. 62 *ddyall*. 63 *a'i ddarllain ac*. 63 *vy nglwyf a'm dolyr*. 63–5 *adolwc i chwi, ddarllenyddion, na chabloch y llythr hwnn*. 65 *bes*. 65–6 *ofer a fyddav imi vy llythr*.

VI 67–8 *Ac am hynny, vnbenes, na fid ryfedd genychi, o chyflybir natyr merch i natyr blaidd. Kans mae llawer o natyrie ar y blaidd*. 68 omit *Kans*. 68–9 *natyriav*. 69 *hwnn*. 69 *vwnwc*. 69 omit *ef*. 69–70 *megis na*. 70 *oni*. 70 *i holl gorff o gwbwl*. 70 *ail natyr yw*. 71 *fyn*. 71 *gymryd*. 71 *ysgafel*. 71 *yn agos*. 71–2 *Y drydedd natyr*. 72 *pan el*. 73 *yn arafa ag i gallo i kerdda ef ac o disgin*. 74 *dori*. 74–5 *megis i tybio ef i glowed o neb*. 75 omit *hynny*. 75–6 *ef a gyfyd i droed ac a'i kny a'i ddanedd o dra dic wrtho i hvn*. 76–7 *Ac velly kwbwl o'r natyrie hyn a gyfflybir ar wraic*. 77 omit *kans*. 77–8 *y kyntaf yw ni ddigochon hi roi mo'i chariad onis rrydd*. 78 *gwbwl*. 78–9 omit *sef . . . genti*. 79 omit *yw*. 79 *damweinia*. 79 *gary*.

ymhell oddi wrth i llety nag yn agos, ag os ymhell i kar hi, i garv yn vawr a wna hi mal na allo hi ymgely o'i gariad ef, ag os yn agos i kar hi, hi a gar yn lledradaidd ag a'i kel ef val nad adnabydder erni. Y trydydd natur yw, o damchwaina yddi vyned mewn parablav kyn belled ag [i] hadnaper[a] erni, hi a vedr roi esgus drosti a chnoi i thavod i hvn mal i gwnaeth y blaidd am i droed. Ag velly, ny vedrais j ymweglyd ragod ti yr amser kyntaf, kans o'r dechrav, mwyaf oedd dy gariad ti ataf j, a'r amser hynny idd oeddyd ti yn hygar gwrtais wrthyf.

VII Ag velly, pan wyb[y]ost[b] di vy mo[d][c] j y'th garv di i byost di valch a thraws wrthyf j, ag i [fo. 100v] kyrchaist di vi y'm lladd hauach yr vn ffynyd ag i gna y sarff, yr hwnn a elwir glox, yr hwnn a sydd a'u natur, pan welo ddyn noeth, ef a ffy oddi wrtho, a phan welo ef ddyn dillatog, ef a'i kyrch ef yn llidiog. Ag velly i gwnaethost di a myvi, kans pan ddauthym j gyntaf i ymgydnabod a thi i byost di vwyn a boneddigaidd wrthyf j, a phan wybyost di vy mod j y'th garv di yn vawr j byost di valchach a thrawsach wrthyf j. Ag

[a] MS *ag hadnaper*. [b] MS *wybost*. [c] MS *mo*.

80 *i lletty noc*. 80 omit *ag*. 81 *yn vawr a wna megis na all hi*. 81 omit *ag*. 82 *kar ef*. 82 omit *hi a gar*. 82–3 *ac a'i kela megis nad ydnabydder erni*. 83 *natyr*. 83 *o disgin iddi*. 84 *parable*. 84 *ac ir adnaper*. 85 *feidr*. 85 *esgys*. 85 *i thafod*. 85 *megis i gwnaeth*. 86 *Ac*. 86 *ni fedrais i ymochelyd rragoti*. 87 *mwia*. 87–8 *dy gariati arnaf i*. 88 *amser hwnnw*. 88 *ir oeddyd ti*.

VII 90–1 *A ffan wybyost ymod i'th gary i byosti valchach a thrawsach*. 91 omit *wrthyf j*. 91–2 *ac i kyrchaisti vi*. 92 omit *hauach*. 92 *yn vn*. 92 *gwnaeth gwnaeth*. 92 *y bwystvil*. 92 *yrwnn*. 93 *glwx*. 93 *yr hwnn i mae natyr iddi*. 93–4 omit *pan welo . . . oddi wrtho a*. 94 *pan welo hi*. 94 *dilladoc*. 94–5 *hi a'i kyrch ef*. 95 *llidioc*. 95 omit *Ag*. 95 *gwneythost dithe a mine*. 96 *ddeythyn gyntaf imgydnabodath*. 96 omit *a thi*. 96 *byost vwyn*. 97–8 *wrthyf a ffan wybyost ymod i'th gary*. 98 *balchach vyost a thrawsach*. 98 omit *j*. 98 omit *Ag*.

velly, y kydnabod kyntaf ag a vy ryngom ni a ellir i gyfflybv i'r dyn noeth a'r serch a'r kariad a dyvoedd rof j a thi a ellir i gyfflybv i'r dyn dillatog, kans yr amser gyntaf, mi a levesais ddwedvd iti y kwbl o'm meddwl, ag velly, gwedy darfod imi ymwisgo o'th gariad ti, ny levesais j ddwedvd dim.

VIII Ag velly idd wyd ti y'm lladd j ag y'm dallv val i dalla'r helwr kywraint yr ap. Kans natur yr ap yw provi gwnaethur pob peth ag a welo hi arall yn y wnaethur, ag velly i daw yr helwr kywraint o'i ystyriaeth i hvn hyd gyverbyn a'r prenn i bo'r ap arno, ag yno, ef a eistedd yn gyverbyn a'r lle i gwelo yr ap, ag a wisg i ysgidiav ar i draed, ag ef a edy yno ysgidiav bychain a vo kymesur i'r ap, ag ef a oddyno. Ag yna i daw yr ap i'r llawr, a hi a gaiff yr ysgidiav hynny, ag a'i gwisg hwynt ar i thraed, a chyn i kaffo hi i diosg, ef a ddaw yr helwr eti, ag yno, hi a gais tringad [fo. 101] i'r prenn val i gwnai gynt, ond ny ad yr ysgidiav yddi dringad, ag velly i delir yr ap. Ag velly, y sampl honn a ellir i gefflybv i ddyn noeth a vo heb garv dim, a'r dyn dillatog a gefflybir i vn a vo yn karv. Am na ellir dala yr ap try vo hi yn

99 *y kydnabod kynta a fy rryngomi.* 99 *gyfflyby.* 100 *a dyfodd rrof i.* 101 *gyfflyby.* 101 *dilladoc.* 101 *kynta.* 101–2 *ni lyfesais ddwedyd wrthyd gwbwl omeddwl ac.* 102 *wedi.* 103 *ymwisgaw.* 103 *ni lyfesais i ddwedyd tim.*
VIII 104 *Ac.* 104 *ir wyti.* 104 omit *j.* 104 *ac i'm dally.* 105 *dalla yr heliwr kowrain.* 105–6 *natyr yr ab hi a braw wneythyr.* 106 *ac a welo vn arall yn i wneythyr ac.* 107 *heliwr kowraint.* 107 *ystriwiaeth.* 108 *goferbyn.* 108 *pren.* 108 *i obo yr ab.* 108–9 *ac ir eiste ef goferbyn a llygaid yr ab ac i gwisc ysgidie am i draed ac ysgidie bychain am i ddwylo.* 110 *ac i gad ef.* 110 *yr ysgidiav.* 110–11 *fo kymhesyr i draed yr ab ac ir af ef ymeth oddyno.* 111 *Ac yn y man.* 111 *i fo ddaw.* 111 *ab.* 111 *ac a gaiff.* 112 *ac a'i gwisg am i thraed.* 112–13 *kaffo hi ddiosc yr ysgidie.* 113 *heliwr kowraint.* 113–14 *ac yno i kais hi ddringo y pren megis i gwnai o'r blaen.* 114–15 *ac nis gaid yr ysgidie iddi ac i delir yr ab.* 115 *Ac velly yr axiampal hwn.* 116 *gyfflyby.* 116 *fo.* 116 *gary.* 116–17 *dilladoc a ellir i gyfflyby.* 117 *fo.* 117 *kary.* 117 *O achos na.* 117 *ab.* 117 *tra fo hi.*

droednoeth, ag velly, ny ellir dala yr vn a vo heb wisg kariad. Ag velly, wrth sampl yr helwr i delaist dithav vinnav gwedy gwybod ohonad vy mod j gwedy ymwisgo o'th gariad ti. Ag velly, ny ddelyyd ti vy narostwng j drwy airav bailchon, ond bod yn llawen wrthyf yn ragorawl yr awr honn na phan oeddwn j yn hoeth o'th gariad ti.

IX Kans velly i gwna y gigfran am i hadar. Kans natur y gigfran yw, pan vo i hadar hi heb plyf arnynt, am nad ynt yn debig y'w mam nag y'w tad, ny ddwg hi ddim trwydded yddynt yny vont yn wisgedig o blyf ag yn debig y'w mam a'i tad. A hynn a sy wir, nid oes yddynt ymborth o'r byd yr ennyd hynny ond gwlith wybrol, a phan vont yn llawn o blyf, i mam a'i tad a'i magant yn anwyl. Ag velly, arglwyddes, i delyyd tithav wnaethur a minnav bod yn anfwyn wrthyf kyn imi ymwisgo o'th gariad ti. Kans kyn hynny, megis kwan y gigfran, idd oeddwn heb plyf a chwedy [fo. 101^{v}] imi ymwisgo o'th gariad ti i delysyd ti wnaethur llawenydd a graeso ym mal i gwna y gigfran am i hadar. Ag velly, gwell i gellir kyfflybv mewn kariad natur y gigfran na natur yr ap, kans ar y gigfran i mae natur arall a ellir i gefflybv i gariad.

118 *ac.* 118 *ni.* 118 *y neb a gatwo i gariad yn gefrinach.* 119 *Ac velly yn axamal o'r heliwr i gwelaf i y ffordd.* 119 *delaisti fi.* 119–20 *gwedi gwybod ohonod.* 120 omit *j.* 120 *gwedi ymwisgo.* 120–1 *Ac am hyny.* 121 *ni ddylyti.* 121 *i.* 121 *eiri beilchion.* 122 *rragorawl.* 122 *yn yr awr hon.* 122–3 *ffan vym i yn noeth o'th gariati.*

IX 124–5 omit *Kans natur y gigfran yw.* 125 *blyf.* 125–6 *ydynt debic i'w.* 126 *nac.* 126–7 *ni ddwgant hwy na bwyd na dim ymborth yddynt oni vont wisgedic o blyf ac ydenydd a thebic y'w.* 128 *A hyn sy wir.* 128–9 *yr enyd hyny.* 129 *namyn.* 129 *a ffan von hwy yn wisgedic o blyf ac adenydd.* 130 *Ac velly, yr vnbenes.* 131 *dlysyd.* 131 *wneythyr.* 131 *minav.* 131 *wrthyf o'r blaen.* 132 *ymi.* 132 *gariati.* 132 *o flaen hynne.* 133 *kowion.* 133 *heb plyf idd oeddwn i.* 133 *a gwedi ymi.* 134 *o'th gariad di.* 134 *dlysyd.* 134 omit *ti.* 134 *wneythyr llywenydd.* 135 *chreso.* 135 *megis.* 135 *A hefyd gwell.* 136 *kyfflyby.* 136 *natyr* (twice). 136 *ab.* 136 *kans mae ar y gigfran natyr arall.* 137 *gyfflyby.*

Kans pan gyvarffo y gigfran a chelain, kyntaf dim ag a gyrcho hi i lygad ef, a ffordd hynny i tynn hi yr amhennydd i maes, a pha vwyaf a gaffo, mwyaf a gais. Ag velly i gwna kariad, kans dechrauad kariad a ddaw drwy edrychiad.

X Ag velly i kefflybir kariad ag edrychiad i natur y llew. Kans natur y llew yw, o damchwaina i ddyn vyned haibo heb i law ef, pan vo ef yn bwyta, ag edrych arno, am vod wyneb dyn ag arwydd santaiddrwydd arno am i Dduw i wnaethur ef ar gyfflybrwydd i wyneb i hvn, ef a gymer y llew i ofn ef, a hevyd y llew a sydd ywch i galon na neb, ag ef a gwilyddia am vod ofn arno, ag a ddwg rythyr i'r dyn, ag a'i lladd. A chwegwaith i gallai ddyn vyned yn ddiddrwg haibo yddo heb edrych arno. Ag am hynny idd wyf j yn[a] tybiaid mae tybig yw'r kariad i'r llew, kans ny red kariad ond trwy edrychiad, ag am hynny, kyntaf kydnabod yw edrychiad y llygaid, a ffordd honno i tynnir amhennydd dyn allan. Kans ymhennydd dyn a gefflebir i synwyr.

XI Ag yn vnwedig ffordd honno i kollais j bedwar synwyr a'm [fo. 102] gobaith, ag i dauthym j mewn anobaith,

[a] MS *yn yn*.

138–9 *gafarffo y gigfran ar y ffordd a chi, kynta dim a gyrch hi vydd i lygad ef*. 139 *kono*. 139 *tyn hi imenydd allan*. 140 *a ffwy vwya a gaffo hi, mwya a gais*. 140 omit *Ag*. 141 *dechreyad*.

X 142 *Ac hefyd*. 142 *kyfflybir*. 142 *ac*. 142 *i natyr*. 143 *Kans natyr*. 143 *damweinia*. 143 *i vn vyned heibiaw*. 144 omit *heb i law ef*. 144–5 *o achos bod wyneb*. 145 *ac*. 145 omit *arno*. 145 *o achos i Ddyw*. 146 *wneythyr ar gyfflybrwydd*. 146 *fo gymer*. 147 *hefyd*. 147 *y sydd*. 147 *no*. 147 *ac ef*. 148 *ac a ddwc rythr*. 148 *ac a'i*. 149 *vn vyned heibio yn ddiddrwc*. 150 omit *yddo heb edrych arno*. 150 *Ac am hyny ir wyf i*. 151 *mai tebic yw kariad*. 151 *ni*. 152 *ac*. 152 *kynta*. 152–3 omit *y llygaid*. 153 *a ffordd hyny*. 153 *tynir ymenydd gwr*. 153–4 *Kans ymenydd gwr*. 154 *gyfflybir*.

XI 155 *Ac yn vnwedic*. 155 omit *ffordd honno*. 155 *kollais i*. 155–6 *bedwar o'm pymp synwyr*. 156 *ac i deythym i*.

am nad wyd ti yn mynny edrych arnaf j, megis j mae natur yr aderyn a elwir kalendr. Kans natur yr aderyn hynny yw, pan ddyker geyrbron dyn klaf, od edrych yr aderyn yn gymwys yn wyneb y dyn klaf, arwydd i bydd byw y dyn, os yntav a dry i olwg haibo, arwydd i bydd marw y dyn. Ag velly, arglwyddes, y'm gwelir jnnav, ag ony bysai vy mod j y'th garv, ti a vysyd yn tirioni wrthyf j, ag velly, er pan ddwedais j vy nghlwyf wrthyd, ny by wiw gennyd edrych arnaf. Ag am hynny i bwraist di vi mewn anobaith, ag am hynny i delyir vy marny j i varw, am nad oes gobaith imi gael trigaredd gennyd, kans anobaith yw angav kariad.

XII Ag am hynny, ef a vernir vy mod j yn varw. Ag velly, ny wnn j ar bwy i mae y pechod, au arnaf j au arnad ti, kans ef a allai vod peth arnom ni yn dav, mal y dyn a gymer i angav trwy y vorvorwyn. Kans i mae tair amryw vorvorwyn, dwy onaddynt a sydd a'r naill hanner yn wyr a'r llall yn bysgod, a'r drydydd a sydd a'r llaill hanner yn wraig a'r llall yn aderyn. Ag velly, kanv yn dda a wna dwy onaddynt, kans

157 *wyti.* 157 *myny.* 157 *arnaf megis i mav.* 157 *natyr.* 158 *yderyn.* 158 *kalendyr.* 158 *Kans natyr kalendr yw.* 159 *pan ddyker ef garbron.* 159 *erych.* 159 *yderyn.* 159–60 *yn gymwys yn i wyneb.* 160–1 *os ynt.* 161 *olwc.* 161 *heibi.* 161 *Ac.* 162 *i'm.* 162 *ine.* 162 *ac oni byse.* 162–3 *vy mod i'th garv.* 163 *fysyd.* 163 *wrthyf ac.* 164 *ddwedais vy nglhwyf.* 164 *ni.* 164 *genyd.* 165 *Ac am hynny i byest vi.* 165–7 *ac o'r achos honn i dylir vy marny i yn varw kans nid oes gobaith o gael.* 167 *genyd ti kans anobaith yw kariad megis ange.*

XII 168 omit *Ag.* 168 *hyny.* 168 omit *ef a vernir.* 168 *vy mod i yn varw a chwedi ange.* 168 *Ac.* 169 *ni wn i ar bwy mae'r.* 169 *ai arnaf i ai arnad tithe.* 170 *ac ir wyf yn tybiaid vod pechod arnomi.* 170 *megis yr hwn.* 171 *drwy.* 171 *forvorwyn.* 171–2 *Kans i maent dair amryw vorforynion a dwy.* D breaks off here with *a dwy* because of a missing leaf. Variants for the missing portion are supplied by Dafydd Jones's *Cydymaith Diddan* (J). 172 *o honynt.* 172–3 omit *a sydd . . . a'r drydydd.* 173 omit *a.* 173 *naill.* 174 *ac felly canu.* 174 *o honynt.* 174 omit *kans.*

vn a gan gyda thelyn, a'r llall gyda phib. A chyn velysed yw i kerdd hwynt ag nad oes neb ag a'i klywo, er pelled a vo oddy wrthynt, na ddel i [fo. 102v] wrando ar i sain hwy. Ag velly, pan ddel yn agos atynt, ef a gwsg, a phan wypo y vorwyn i vod ef yn kysgi, hi a ddaw ato, ag a'i lladd ef yn y gwsg. Ag velly, ef a debygir vod yn bechod i'r vorwyn i ladd ef yn y gwsg yn dwyllodrys, a bod ran o'r pechod ar y dyn am i chredy hithav. Ag velly idd wyf j yn tybiaid amdanom ni yn dav vod arnad ti bechod am vy lladd j trwy dwyll, a bod arnaf jnnav bechod am dy gredv dithav. Ond ny levasaf j ddwedvd vy meddwl iti o gwbl, ag am hynny, bid arnaf y pechod oll, kans wrth wrando ar dy gan di i lleddaist di vi y'm kwsg.

XIII A hevyd megis i twyllir y pryf a elwir digerfa drwy edrychiad yn y drych, yr hon ny bydd llidiog er lledrata i chynawon, o chyverfydd drych a hi ar y ffordd. Kans llawenydd a digryvwch a gymer hi o weled i llvn yn y drych gan dybiaid vod vn o'i chynawon hi yno, ag yna i gollwng hi i digovaint yn angof, a'r helwr, a ddel i gaiso y kynawon, a

175 *un*. 175–6 *A chyn felused a sydd i cherdd ac nad oes neb ar ai Clywo*. 176 *fo*. 177 *oddi wrthynt*. 177 *wrando ei Cân hwynt*. 177–8 *ac felly*. 178 *pan ddel un*. 178 *attynt*. 178 *Wybyddo*. 179 *Fôrforwyn*. 179 *ei fod*. 179 *Cysgu*. 179 *atto ac*. 179 omit *ef*. 179 *yn i*. 180 *Ac felly fe debygir fod*. 180–1 *ir Forforwyn ladd Dyn yn i gwsg*. 181 *dwyllodrus*. 181 *Ond y mae rhan*. 182 *chredu*. 182 *hithau*. 182 omit *Ag*. 182 *Felly y tebygafinneu*. 183 *ein Dau*. 183 *fod arnat ti*. 183 *yn fy llâdd i drwy*. 184 *arnat finneu*. 184 *gredu dithau*. 184–5 *eithr ni lyfesais i addef fy 'nghlwyf o gwbl iti*. 185 *ac*. 185–6 *bid y pechod arnaf i ôll*. 186 *Canys drwy wrando*. 186 omit *di*. 186–7 *y lleddaist di fi yn fy 'nghwsg*.

XIII 188 *hefyd*. 188 *fal y twyllir*. 188 *Teiger*. 188–90 *trwy edrych mewn drŷch yr hyn i bydd llidiog, pan ddel yr Heliwr i ladratta ei chenafon, ac os cyferfydd hi a drŷch ar y ffordd*. 190 omit *Kans*. 191 *digrifwch mawr*. 191 *gymmer ef*. 191 *ei lun i hunan*. 192 *gan dybied ma'i un o'i Chenafon hi sydd yno*. 192 *ac*. 192 omit *yna*. 192–4 *gollwng ef ei ddigofaint dros gof, a phan ddel yr Heliwr i geisio'r Cenafon, ef a fwrw y drŷch*.

vwrw drych ar y ffordd er i thwyllo hi a'u siomi try vo ef yn myned a'r kynawon ymaith. Ag velly, wrth edrych arnad tithav, ti a'm divwynaist j hyd yny gollais j vy mhvmp synwyr.

XIV Ag am hynny i delaist di vi drwy aroglav, megis i delir yr vnikorn drwy aroglav morwyn jevank, am nad oes yn y byd vn anevail mor [fo. 103] anodd i ddala ag ef, ag vn korn a sydd yddo ynghenol i dalken, ag nid oes na dyn nag anevail a vaiddo i aros ond morwyn jevank lan wyry. Kans pan glywo ef aroglav y vorwyn a'u mwyn serchawgrwydd, ef a ddaw eti, ag ef a ry i benn yn y harffed hi, ag yna i kwsg ef, a'r helwr kall a edwyn hynny, a phan el ef i hela i gosod ef vorwyn ar i ffordd ef, ag yna i daw yr vnikorn, ag i dyry i benn yn y harffed hi, ag a gwsg, ag yna i dala'r helwr ef. Ag yn y modd hynny i daloedd kariad vinnav am roi y vorwyn ar vy ffordd. Ag yna i kollais y tri synwyr gorav ar vy helw drwy dwyll megis yr vnikorn.

XV Ag am hynny i delyswn j baido a'r kariad hynny ag ymweglyd rag kysgv, megis i gwna y garanod. Kans natur y garanod yw na chysgont yny ddel llawer onaddyn i'r vn lle,

194–5 *er mwyn ei thwyllo trâ fo ef yn mynd.* 195 *Cenafon.* 195 *ac felly.* 195–7 *os edrychi arnaf, tithau i'm gyrraist agos i golli fy 'mhym Synwyr.*

XIV 198 *Ac felly y deliaist fi trwy arogli.* 198–9 *y delir.* 199 *Unicorn.* 199 *aroglau.* 199 *Ifanc.* 199 *Canys nid oes.* 200 *un anifail.* 200 *mo'r anhawdd.* 200 *i ddal ac ef.* 200–2 *ac un Corn sydd ynghanol ei Dalcen, ac nid oes Dyn nac Anifail a eill i aros ef.* 202 *eithr.* 202 *Ifanc lân.* 202 *wyryf.* 202 *Canys.* 203 *aroglau morwyn.* 203 *ai.* 203 *Serchogrwydd.* 204–5 *i daw atti, ac i rhydd i ben atti iw Chwilio am lau, ac yno i Cwsg ef.* 205 *Heliwr Cywraint.* 205 *êl efe.* 205–6 *ef a esyd y Forwyn ar y Fordd.* 206 omit *ef.* 206 D resumes with *ac i daw ynte ac i ry.* 207 *ben ar i harff*[*ed*]. 207 *ac a gwsc.* 207 omit *ag.* 207 *yna i daw yr heliwr kowraint a'i deila ef drwy dwyll.* 207–8 *Ac velly i dela kariad vinav o achos rroi'r.* 209 *ar y ffordd.* 209 *Ac yna i kollais ine.* 209 *y iii synwyr.* 210 *inikorn.*

XV 211 *Ac.* 211 *dlyswn ine beidio.* 211 omit *hynny.* 211–12 *ac ymochlyd rrac kysgy.* 212 *natyr.* 213 omit *yw.* 213 *chysgant.* 213 *yni.* 213 *llawer ohonynt ynghyd i'r vn lle.*

ag yna i gwila vn try vo y llaill[a] yn kysgi. Ag velly i gwna pob vn onaddynt ar gylch. Ag yna, yr vn a vo yn gwilad a gymer maen krwn rwng i dwy troed rag ofn yddi gysgy, kans pan ddamch[w]aino[b] yddi gysgv, y maen a syrthia i'r llawr, ag yna i dyffro hithav. Ag velly i delyswn minnav vod gennyf ryw ddeall i rwystro ym gysgv, am vod hynny yn arwyddokae synwyr, ag am na bvm j synwyrys.

XVI Nid oes meddiginaeth ym yn y byd [fo. 103v] ony bai iti vy ngalw j atad drwy gariad val i gwna y llew am i gynawon. Kans kynawon y llew a enir yn vairw, ag yn vairw i byddant hyd ymhenn tri diav. Ag yna i daw i tad ywch i pennav, ag ef a gria mor groelon ywch i pennav hwynt, mor groelon ag i daw bywyd yndynt, a hynn a ellir i gefflybv at gariad, kans pei mynyd tithav vy ng[a]lw[c] jnnav atad trwy gariad yn gariadys, mi a gyvodwn o varw i vyw.

XVII A hevyd, pei gwnelyd ti a mi val i gwna y pelikan am i adar, mi a debygwn i byddwn vyw, am vod natur y pelikan i garv i adar yn kymaint ag i daw ef [i] ymweled[d] ag

[a] MS *lleraill.* [b] MS *ddamchaino.* [c] MS *nglw.* [d] MS *daw ef ymweled.*

---

214 *ac yno vn ohonynt a wilia.* 214 *tra fo.* 214 *lleill.* 214 *kysgy.* 214 *Ac.* 215 *ohonynt.* 215 *A'r vn a fo yn gwilied.* 216 *maen krwn o rychwant.* 216 *rrwng i ddwy goes.* 216 *rrac ofn disgin kysy arno.* 216–17 *kans o danweinia iddaw gysy.* 217 *syrth.* 218 omit *ag.* 218 *yno dyffroi a wna ynte.* 218 *Ac.* 218 *dlyswn ine.* 219 *genyf.* 219 *ryw gallineb i rwstro.* 219 *gysgy.* 219–20 *Kans i mae yn arwyddoka kallder.* 220 *ac am na by gallder genyf.*

XVI 221 *meneginiaeth a'm helpo.* 222 *attad dwy gariad.* 223 *gnawon.* 223 *O achos knawon.* 223 *veirw ac yn veirw.* 224 *ymhen.* 224 *y tri diwrnod.* 224 *Ac yno i daw.* 225 *penav.* 225–6 *ac yna i kria ac ir ychneidia yn dost ac mor greylon a fydd i lef ywch i pene i daw bowyd ynddynt.* 226 *hyn.* 226 *gyfflyby.* 227 *kans bai mynyti vy nalw ine.* 227–8 *drwy gariad ac ymddiddan a mi.* 228 *myfi a gyfodwn o veirw yn vyw.*

XVII 229 *hefyd.* 229 *bai.* 230 *dybygwn i kodwn o veirw yn vyw.* 230–1 *Kans natyr y pelikan yw kary.* 231–2 *yn gimint ac i daw ef imweled a hwy.*

hwynt yn ry vynych, ag ef a heda yn y kylch yn kynesed yddynt ag i kyhwrdd i adanedd ef a'i llygaid hwynt, ag yna i pigant hwy ef yny gaffo ef ddolur, ag yn y dolur hwnnw i lladd ef hwynt yn vairw. Ag etivar a vydd ganto ef hynny, ag yna idd a ef ywch i pennav, ag i hegyr ar i ddwyfron, ag i gollwng ef waed i galon, ag o'r gwaed hwnnw i hira ef hwynt, ag i kyvodant o vairw i vyw. Ag velly, pan adnabvm j di yn gyntaf idd oeddwn j megis kyw gan ddwedvd rann o'm dolyr. Ag yna, ti a'm lleddaist j yn varw o'r gyfryw angav ag a berthyn ar [fo. 104] gariad. Ond pei agoryd ti dy galon trwy wyllys da, ti a'm kyvodyd j o varw i vyw, kans gorav meddiginaeth y'm haint j oedd gael dy gariad ti a wyllys dy galon. A mi a glywaf gan rai nad yw yn dda genyd vy mod j mor ysmala ag wyf j, ag os drwg yw gennyd hynny, dyro imi dy galon y'm llawenhav.

XVIII Kans velly i gwna yr anevail a elwir castrin. Kans ar vn o'i draed ef i mae rinwedd a chyvarddonav mawr, a'i hela ef a wnair yn chwannog er mwyn y droed honno. A ffo

232 *rry.* 232–3 *ac i hetta ef kyn nesed yddynt.* 233 *ac i kyffwrdd ef.* 233 omit *i adanedd ef.* 233 *ac.* 234 *pigant ef ac a'i dolyriau ac.* 234 D breaks off here with *y dolyr hwnw* because of a missing leaf. Variants for the missing portion are supplied by Dafydd Jones's *Cydymaith Diddan* (J). 235 *efe.* 235 *feirw.* 235 *ac yna edifar a fydd ganddo ef.* 236 *ac i daw ef uwch eu pennau ag a egur.* 236–7 *ag a ollwng waed ei galon.* 237–8 *ac ar gwaed yr îrâ ef ynt hwy.* 238 *ac i codant o feirw yn fyw.* 238 *Ac felly.* 238–9 *adnabum i Di gyntaf.* 239 omit *idd oeddwn j megis kyw.* 239 *ddywedyd.* 239–40 *rhan o'm dolur.* 240 *Ac.* 240 *lleddaist i.* 240–1 *yn farw o'r cyfryw Angeu ac a berthyn i Gariad.* 241–2 *eithr pe bae i Tî egori dy galon.* 242 *drwy 'wllys.* 242 *codit o farw yn fyw.* 243–4 *Canys goreu meddyginiaeth ar lês fy haint a fyddae gael dy galon gariad Tî, ac 'wllys dy galon.* 244 *Ac mi glywaf.* 244–6 *nad ydyw hôff gennyt fy mod i mo'r Ysmala ac i'r wyf; onid ydyw, dyro.* 246 *i'm Ysmalhau.*

XVIII 247 *Canys felly i gwna'r Anifail.* 247 *Oblegid.* 248 *un.* 248 *y mae Cyferddonau (Cyfrwyddonau) mawr.* 249 *a wneir o achos ei draed yn ynghwaneg.* 249 *ffoi.*

a wna yntav yr hyd i gallo, a phan vo ef ymronn deffygio, ef a wyr na helid ef ond er mwyn y droed honno, ag yna i tyrr ef y droed honno ymaith o'i ddannedd, ag a'i gad hi ar y ffordd val i kaffer hi. Ag yna i ffy ef ar i dair troed. Ag velly, pan gaffo yr helwyr y droed honno, nid ymlidiyr ef ymhellach, ag velly i diank ef. Ag velly, arglwyddes, i gwnaethost dithav a minnav, kans pan wybyost di vy mod j yn dyvod, ti a vwraist air teg imi y'w gael, ag a ddiengaist dithav, ag velly i twyllaist di vi.

Ag velly terfyna.

250 *yntau*. 250 omit *yr*. 250–1 *a phan fo ef ar ddiffygio, fe a wyr na Helir mono ond o achos y Troed hwnnw*. 251 omit *ag*. 252 *y Troed hwnnw*. 252 omit *ymaith*. 252 *ai*. 252 *gedu ef*. 253 *fel*. 253 *Caffer*. 253 omit *hi*. 253 *Ac*. 253 *i ffu ar i dri throed*. 253 *Ac felly*. 254 *Heliwr*. 254 *Troed*. 254 omit *honno*. 254 *ymlid*. 255 *ac felly y dianc ef*. 255–6 *Cyfflybiaeth i hynny Arglwyddes y gwnaethost Dithau, a minnau*. 256 *Canys pan Wybuost fy mod i*. 257 *dyfod*. 257 *fwriaist*. 257 *têg*. 257–8 *iw gael ar y ffordd, ac i diengaist Dithau*. 258 *ac y Twyllaist Di finnau yn yr un môdd*. 259 omit *Ag velly terfyna*. J adds *Ovid Fardd*.

Text A

IV // vym, am na welut vi yn gyntaf a herwyd natur y bleid y dylyaf i golli vy llef, ac am hynny na wneuthum y llythyr h6nn[a] dr6y gan namyn ar ffuryf ymadra6d.

V Kanys natur arall yssyd, yr honn a gefeis i o anyan yr eos, yr h6nn y kefeis exemplar ohona6. Canys yr eos a gar y gan e hun yn gymeint ac y bo mar6 yn kanu, kanys hebyrgofi a wna y v6yt a'e dia6t o ch6ant canu. Ac ar hynny yd edrycheis i rac vy mar6, a mi a welaf mae bychydic a dal y'r kywydolyon eu kan. Kanys pan vu oreu y keneis i, g6aethaf oll vu ym, ac am hynny y peideis a'r kan ac y treytheis hynn o lythyr dr6y ymadra6d, mal y gallo pa6b y deall yn berffeith, a'e darllein, ac ystyrya6 vy nghl6yf[a] inneu a'm galar. Ac y ch6itheu, darlleodron, y llyth[yr][b] h6nn yd 6yf yn adol6c y6ch na chaploch weith y llythyr, kanys pei as kaple6ch, ouer vydei ym vy llauur.

VI A mi a goll6n heuyt vy neges, ac na vit ryued heuyt gennyt ti, o chyffelybeis natur g6reic y anyan bleid. Kanys y mae llawer etto o naturyeu ar y bleid, ac vn o'e naturyeu y6 h6nn, nyt amgen, vot t6f y gorff yn gyn//

XIX [fo. 527]// y'th ganlyn, kanys tydi yssyd vam her6yd caryat ymi, a g6ybyd di, yn lle gwir, nat oes a allo ymi na da na didan6ch onyt tydi. Ac ny mynn6n allel o neb ch6eith solaus ym onyt a allut ti ac a wnelut. A mi a gefeis dywedut y gan lawer vn mae ffol oed ym ossot vy mryt a'm[a] med6l arnat ti, ag atuyd y rei a dywedynt 6rthyf hynny, 6ynt a vynnynt pei triky6n y gyt ac 6ynt6y. A ha6s ympell oed ym gael trugared a meithrin ganthunt 6y no chennyt ti.

IV[a] MS *h6ñ*. V[a] MS *vȳghl6yf*. [b] MS *llyth*. XIX[a] MS *nā*.

XX Eissyoes, pei tydi a vynnei vy meithrin i, mi a vyd6n gystal ederyn 6rthyt ac y byd yr adar a elwir chuinng.[a] Natur y chuinng[a] y6, kyhyt o amser ac y bo y chuing yn meithrin y veibyon adar, kyhyt arall y hynny y byd y veibyon yn meithrin y chuinng[a] pryt na allo dim[b] o dra heneint.

XXI Ac velly y g6na adar yr up neu'r epopus. A phan welont yr adar jeueingk y rei hen yn dechreu b6r6 eu pluf o dra heneint, 6ynt a gyrchant anyal6ch a diffeith, lle ny bo sathyr na da na dynyon, a'r lle clyttaf a gaffont. Ac yna, ef a da6 yr adar jeueigk [fo. 527^{v}] ac a blufyant a'e gyluineu k6byl o'r holl bluf y ar y rei hen. Ac yna, ef a orwed deu o'r rei jeueingk y gyt ac vn o'r rei hen y gynnal g6res ynda6, a deu ereill a ant y gynnull[a] ymborth udunt. Ac uelly y magant 6y eu mam ac eu tat yny vo pluf newyd arnunt, a'e goll6ng y ehedec yn iach ieueingk.[b] Velly, argl6ydes, kyn gywiret vydaf inneu yt titheu ac y mae natur yr adar vry, os tydi a vynn vy meithrin i yn gyntaf yny v6yf was cryf a'm kynghori,[c] sef y6 hynny, vyng gadel[d] attat a'm kynnal y gyt a thi, megys gwir gedymdeith ytt. A g6ybyd di, yn lle gwir, nat oes dim o'r a dylyo g6r sercha6l y wneuthur nys g6nel6yf i yrot ti, a thydi a wdost hynny. Eissyoes, nyt kyn hoffet [gennyt][e] ti magyat da ymi ac ytt dy hun. Ac ef a welir ytti heuyt na heydeis i gaffel dy garyat ti yr roi ohonaf inneu y meu ytti, kanys balchd[er][f] y6 gennyt vy mot mor drahaus a hynny.[g] A pha ny bei dy valchd[er][h] di, ny byd6n i yn gyn wannet ac yn gyndr6c vy stat ac yd 6yf. Ac am hynny y dywa6t Ouidinus na dicha6n bot yn vn eistedua balchd[er].[f]

XX[a] MS *chuiñg.* [b] MS *dī.* XXI[a] MS *gyñull.* [b] MS *ieueīgk.* [c] MS *kȳghori.* [d] MS *vȳggadel.* [e] *gennyt* omitted in MS. [f] MS *balchd'.* [g] MS *hyñy.* [h] MS *valchd'.*

FRENCH TEXT

I [S 3. 1–8. 9] Toutes gens desirent par nature a savoir. Et pour chu ke nus ne puet tout savoir, ja soit che ke cascune cose puist estre seüe, si covient il ke sacuns sache aucune cose, et che ke li uns ne set mie, ke li autres le sache; si ke tout est seü en tel maniere qu'il n'est seü de nullui a par lui, ains est seü de tous ensamble. Mais il est ensi ke toutes gens ne vivent mie ensamble, ains sont li un mort avant ke li autre naissent, et cil ki ont esté cha en ariere ont seü tel cose ke nus ki ore endroit vive ne le conquerroit de son sens, ne ne seroit seü, s'on ne le savoit par les anchiiens.

Et pour chu Diex, ki tant aime l'omme qu'il le velt porveoir de quant ke mestiers lui est, a donné a homme une vertu de force d'ame ki a non memoire. Ceste memoire si a .ij. portes, veïr et oïr, et a cascune de ces .ij. portes si a un cemin par ou on i puet aler, che sont painture et parole.

Painture sert a l'oel et parole a l'oreille. Et comment on puist repairier a le maison de memoire et par painture et par parole, si est apparant par chu ke memoire, ki est la garde des tresors ke sens d'omme conquiert par bonté d'engien, fait chu ki est trespassé ausi comme present. Et a che meïsme vient on per painture et per parole. Car quant on voit painte une estoire, ou de Troies ou d'autre, on voit les fais des preudommes ki cha en ariere furent, ausi com s'il fussent present.

Et tout ensi est il de parole. Car quant on ot .i. romans lire, on entent les aventures, ausi com on les veïst en present. Et puis c'on fait present de chu ki est trespassé par ces .ij. coses, c'est par painture et par parole, dont pert il bien ke par ces .ij. coses poet on a memoire venir.

Et jou, de qui memoire vous ne poés partir, bele tres douce amie, ke la trace de l'amour ke j'ai eü a vos ne peire adés, si ke je n'en porroie estre si garis ke au mains n'i parust la sorsanure de la plaie, com biel ke je m'en seüse contenir, valroie adés manoir en la vostre memorie, s'il pooit estre. Et pour chu vous envoi je ces .ij. coses en une. Car je vous envoie en cest escrit et painture et parole, pour che ke, quant je ne serai presens, ke cis escris par sa painture et par sa parole me rende a vostre memoire comme present.

Et je vous monsterai comment cis escris a painture et parolle. Car il est bien apert k'il a parole, par che ke toute escripture si est faite pour parole monstrer et pour che ke on le lise; et quant on le list, si revient elle a nature de parole. Et d'autre part, k'il ait painture si est en apert par chu ke lettre n'est mie, s'on ne le paint.

Et meesmement cis escris est de tel sentence k'il painture desire. Car il est de nature de bestes et d'oisaus ke miex sont connissables paintes ke dites.

Et cis escris est ausi com l'arierebans de tous chaus ke je vous ai envoié dusques a ore. Car ausi comme uns rois, quant il va guerroier fors de son roialme, il en maine de ses melleurs hommes une partie, et s'en lasse encore gringnor partie a sa terre garder; mais quant il voit qu'il ne se puet soufire a tant de gent com il a mené, si parmande tous chiax qu'il a laissiés et fait son ariereban: ausi me covient il faire. Car se je vous ai maint bel mot que dit que envoié, et il ne m'ont mie tant valut ke mestiers me fust, il me covient en cest darrain escrit faire men ariereban, et dire del miex ke je sai, pour savoir se vous le prenderiés en grei. Car ja ne m'amissiés vous, si sont che coses la ou iels se doit molt deliter a veoir et orelle a oïr et memoire a remenbrer.

Et pour chu ke cis escris est mes arierebans, et ausi ke mes darrains secours ke je puisse mander, si covient ke je i parole plus forment k'en tous les autres.

II [S 8. 9–9. 11] Ausi c'on conte de la nature del coc: car li cos, de tant com il cante par nuit plus pres de la vespree ou de la jornee, de tant chant il plus sovent; et de tant com il cante plus pres de la mienuit, si cante plus efforciement et plus engrosse sa vois.

La vespree et la jornee, ki a nature de jour et de nuit mellee ensamble, si senefie l'amour dont on n'a del tout essperance ne del tout desesperance (—ne . . . desesperance FG), et la mienuis signifie l'amour del tout desesperee. Et dont, puis ke je n'ai nule esperance del monde (—del monde FG) des ore mais de vostre bone volenté avoir, si est ausi comme mienuit, et quant jeu en oi aucune esperance, se fu ausi comme a vespree: si cantai adonques plus sovent, et ore le me covient faire plus forment.

III [S 10. 1–9] Et la raison de ce que li desessperés a plus fort vois si est prise, je quit, en la beste del monde ki plus s'esforce de braire et ke (—plus s'esforce . . . et ke FG) plus a laide vois et orrible, c'est li asnes salvages. Car sa nature si est qu'il ne recane onques, fors quant il a tres erragie faim et il ne puet trover en nule maniere (—en nule maniere FG) de quoi il se puist soeler. Mais adont met il si grant paine a racaner qu'il se desront tous.

Et por chu me covient il, quant je ne puis en vous trover merci, metre grengnor paine c'onques mais, ne mie a forment canter, mais a forment et atangnamment dire.

IV [S 10. 9–12. 3] Car le canter doi jou bien avoir perdu, si vous dirai par quel raison. Le nature del leu (selonc la nature dou lu. Sa nature FG) si est teile ke, quant uns hom le voit avant qu'il voie l'omme, li leus en pert toute se force et son hardement; et si li leus voit l'omme primerains, li homme en pert sa vois, k'il ne puet mot dire (quant il voit j homme ainz que li hons le voie, li homme pert la vois, k'il ne peut mot dire (sonner ne dire F). Et se li hons uoit le lou auant li lous pert sa force et son hardement FG) (+Ce est escrit es liures dautorite FG, Ce est escrit en (ou K) liure de autorite KM).

Ceste nature si est trovee en amour d'omme et de feme. Car quant il a amour entre aus deus, se li hom puet percevoir par la feme meïsmes premerains k'ele l'aint, et k'il sace tant k'il li face reconoistre, elle a puis perdu le hardement d'escondire. Mais pour chu ke jou ne me puc[h] tenir ne souffrir de vous dire men corage avant ke je seüse riens del vostre, m'aveis vous eschivé. Che vous ai oï dire aucune fois. Et puis ke je sui primerains veüs, selonc le nature del leu j'en doi bien perdre le vois. C'est une raisons par quoi cis escris n'est mie fais en cantant, mais en contant.

V [S 12. 4–13. 2] Et une autre raisons de ce meïsme si est prise en la nature del crisnon (rossignoil FG) dont je me sui molt pris garde (—dont . . . garde FG). Car sa nature si est ke li kaitis aime tant sen canter k'il se muert en cantant, tant en pert sen mangier et tant s'en laie a pourcachier. Et por che me sui jou pris garde ke li chanters m'a si pau valu ke je m'i puisse tant fïer ke j'en perdisse nis moi, si ke ja li chanters ne m'i socourust; nomeement a chou ke je esprovai bien ke a l'eure ke je miex cantai et ke je miex dis en cantant, adont me fu il pis.

S 14. 4 . . . et le vous envoiai en maniere de contreescrit.

VI [S 15. 3–17. 2] Et ne vous mervelliés mie se j'ai l'amor de feme comparé a le nature del leu. Car encore a li leus molt d'autres natures par quoi il i a molt grengnor samblance. Car une de ses natures si est k'il a le col si roide k'il ne le puet flechier s'il ne torne tout sen cors avoec. Et l'autre nature si est k'i ne prendra ja proie pres de sa leviere, se lonc non. Et le tierce si est ke quant il entre en une berkerie au plus coiement qu'il puet, s'il avient ke aucuns rainceaus brise desous son pié ki noise face, il s'en venge a sen pié meïsme et le mort molt anguisseusement.

Toutes ces .iij. natures sont trovees en amour de feme. Car elle ne se poet doner, se toute ensamble non: c'est selonc le primiere nature. Et selonc le seconde si est ke s'il avient k'elle aime un homme, quant il ert loins de li si l'amera trop durement, et quant il ert pres, si n'en fra ja samblant. Et selonc le tierce nature si est ke s'elle va si avant de parolle ke li homme se perchoive k'ele l'aint, tout ausi ke li leus se vaingne par sa bouce (–par sa bouce FG) de son pié, si set elle trop bien par force de paroles recovrir et ramanteler chu k'ele a trop avant alei.

VII [S 17. 2–19. 3] Car volentiers voet savor d'autrui chu k'ele ne veut mie c'on sache de lui, et d'omme k'elle quide k'il l'aint se set elle tres fermement garder. Ausi comme li wivre, ki est de tel nature ke quant elle voit .i. homme nu, si en a paour et le fuit sans soi aseürer de rien; et se elle le voit vestu, si lui court sus ne ne le prise nïent.

Tout en tel maniere avés vous fait de moi, bele tres douce amie. Car quant je m'acointai a vous, si vous trovai d'une douce maniere a un poi de vergoingne telle com il convient, ausi (–com il . . . ausi FG) com se vous me resongnissiés .i. petit pour la novelté; et quant vous seüstes ke je vous amoie, si me fuistes si fierre com vous volsistes, et me corustes auques sus de paroles. La novelle acointance si est comparee a l'homme nu, et l'amours confremee a l'homme vestu. Car ausi com li hom naist nus, et puis se vest quant il est parnorris, ausi est il nus d'amours en le primierre acointance et decovers, si k'il li ose bien dire tout son corage. Mais aprés, quant il aime, il est si envolopés k'il ne s'en set issir, et se coevre del tout, si k'i n'ose riens dire de son pensé, ains se doute adés c'on ne le puist reprendre.

VIII [S 19. 3–21. 7] Et est ausi pris comme li cinges cauchiés. Car la nature del cinge si est k'il velt contrefaire quanques il voit faire. Si ke li sage veneor, ke per engien le voellent prendre, esspient k'il soient en tel lieu que li cinges les puist veoir (quil uoient le singe et que li singes les uoie F, que il les uoient G). Et dont se caucent et descaucent devant aus, et puis se partent l'iluec, et si laient uns solers a le mesure del cinge, et se vont esconser en aucun lieu. Lor vient li cinges, et velt ausi faire, et prent ses sollers, si les cauce par sa malaventure. Mais anc[h]ois k'il les puist descauchier, saut li venerres, si li cuert sus. Et li cinges cauchiés ne poet fuir, ne en arbre monter ne (—en arbre monter ne FG) ramper, si est pris.

Cis exemples conferme bien c'on doit comparer l'omme nu a celi ki n'aime mie, et le vestu a celui ki aime. Car ausi comme li cinges est delivres tant k'il est nus piés, ne n'est pris devant la k'il se cauce, ausi n'est li hom en prison devant k'il aime par amours. Et par cest example est confirmés cil de la wivre, et par ces .ij. voies voi jou bien le raison par quoi m'aveis fait pior samblant puis ke vous seüstes ke je vous amoie, ke devant: et pour chu ke li cinges n'est pris devant la k'il est cauchiés, et par chu ke li wivre cort l'omme seure quant elle le voit vestu.

Et si me samble il ke vous deüsiés faire le contraire, et ke mellour samblant deüse avoir de vous quant vous me veïstes vestu de vostre amour, ke quant j'en fuisse nus.

IX [S 21. 7–23. 8] Car tel est la nature del corbel, ke tant ke si corbelot sont sans plume, pour chu k'il ne sont noir (—pour chu . . . noir FG) et k'il nel resamblent (ne resemblent pere ne mere FG), ja ne les regardera ne ne pastera (—ne ne pastera FG), ains ne vivent se de rousee non, dusques tant k'il sont vestu de plume, k'il resamblent leur pere (et sachiez quil ne vivent fors (que G) de rousee, dusques adont kil (iusqua tant que il G) sont vestu de plume, si quil pueent resembler pere et mere FG).

Ensi m'est il avis ke vous deüsiés avoir fait, bele tres douce amie, ke quant je fuisse nuis de vostre amour, si ne vous causist de moi, et quant je en fuisse vestus, ke je portasse un escuchon de vos armes, si me deüsiés chierir et nourir en vostre amour quoi k'ele fust tenre et novelle, si com on norrist .i. enfant au doit. Et miex deüst vaintre en amour (—en amour FG) la nature del corbel ke cele de le wivre, ne cele del cinge.

Car corbeaus a encore autre nature, ke sor toutes riens resamble a nature d'Amour. Car sa nature si est ke quant il trove .i. homme mort, la primiere cose k'il en mangüe che sont li oeil; et par illuec en trait le chervelle, et com plus en trove, miex en trait. Ausi fait Amours. Car es primierres acointances est li hom pris par ses iex, ne ja Amors ne le prisist, s'i n'i eüst esgardé.

X [S 23. 9–25. 3] Car Amors fait ausi com li lions: quant li lions mangüe sa proie, s'il avient c'uns hom past d'encoste li, s'il le regarde, por che ke figure d'omme porte ausi comme unes ensanges de sengnorie, de tant com il est fais a l'ymage et a le samblance le Siengneur des siengneurs (—de tant . . . siengneurs FG), si covient ke li lions resongece son vis et son regart; mais por che k'il a naturel hardement, si a honte d'avoir paour, si court sus a l'homme, si tost com il le regarde. Et cent (vij FG) fois porroit passer li hom encoste le lion, ja li lions ne se moveroit por tant com li hom ne le regardast. Dont di je ke Amors resamble le lion, car ausi ne keurt Amours sus a nullui, s'il ne le regarde.

Dont prent Amours l'omme es primierres acointances par les iex, et par illuec pert li hom se cervelle. Le cervelle de l'homme signefie sens.

XI [S 28. 1–29. 6] Et ceste desesperance si est selonc la nature de la carandre. C'est uns oiseaus ke quant on le porte devant .i. malade, s'il regarde le malade droit enmi le vis c'est signes ke li malades garira, et s'i se torne d'autre part k'il ne le voille regarder, on juge k'il covient le malade morir.

Et pour chu me samble il, bele tredouce amie, ke puis ke il vous poise ke jou onques vous proiai et ke volentiers eüsiés amee m'acointance et ke volentiers m'eüsiés tenu compangnie, por ke jou ne parlasse de chu dont j'estoie malades, ke vous n'eüstes onques talent de moi regarder, malade, enmi le vis. Dont me doit on jugier por mort. Car par che m'avés mis en tel desconfort (desesperance FG) com il apartient a parfaite (–parfaite FG) desesperance (desconfort damors FG) sans nule atente de merci. Et c'est li mors d'amours. Car ausi com en mort n'a point de recoivrir, ausi n'a il point d'esperance de joie d'amour la ou on n'atent merci.

XII [S 29. 7–31. 4] Dont sui je mors, c'est voirs. Et ki m'a mort? Jou ne sai, ou vous ou jou, fors ke ambedoi i avons coupes. Ausi com de celi cui le seraine ocist, quant elle l'a endormi par son chant. Car il sont trois manieres de seraines, dont les .ij. sont moitié femes et moitié poisson, et le tierce moitié feme et moitié oseaus. Et cantent toutes .iij.: les unes en buisines, les autres en harpes et les tierces en droites vois; et est lor melaudie tant plaisans, ke nus hom ne les ot, tant soit loins, k'il ne lui conviengne venir. Et quant il est pres, si s'endort; et quant la seraine le trove endormi, si l'ocist (si l'ocient en dormant FG). Si me samble ke le seraine i a grans coupes quant elle l'ocist (+en dormant et FG) en traïson, et li hom grans coupes quant il s'i croit. Et si je sui mors par itel ockoison, et vous et jou i avons coupes. Mais je ne vous ose susmetre traïson, si n'en metrai les coupes se sour moi non, et dirai ke je mismes me sui mors.

XIII [S 40. 9–42. 6] M'aida dont le veüe a prendre? Oïl, miex fu je pris par mon veoir ke tigres n'est al mireoir, ke ja tant ne sera corchie de ses faons, s'on li emble, ke s'ele encontre un mireoir qu'il ne li covingne ses iels aerdre. Et se delite tant a regarder la grant beauté de sa bone taille, k'ele oblie a cachier chiax ki li ont emblé ses faons, et s'areste illuec comme prise. Car li sage veneor i metent le mireoir tout a enscient pour aus delivrer de li. (—ke ja tant ne sera . . . delivrer de li, +Donc (dont G) il auient que li saiges venierres fet quant il li a emblez ses faons si met mireors enmi sa (la G) uoie tout ensius comme il sen vet (uont G) et quant la tygre voit quele (que il G) a ses faons perduz si sen court ausius comme tout enragiee. et les suit toute la trace. et lors quant ele voit le mireour si sareste et se regarde. et se delite tant fort a soi (ali G) regarder quele en oublie ceus a Cacier qui enportent ses faons et sareste ilec comme prise FG.)

Dont je di ke se je fui pris a oïr et a veoir, ke che ne fu pas mervelle se je i perdi mon sens et ma memoirie. Car oïrs et veoirs sont les .ij. portes de memorie, si com il a esté devant dit, et si sont .ij. des plus nobles sens de l'homme. Car li hom a .v. sens: veïr, oïr, flarier, gouster et touchier, si com il a esté devant dit.

XIV [S 42. 7–44. 5] Et par le flairier meïsme fui je pris, ausi com li unicornes ki s'endort au douc[h] flair de la virginité a la damoisele. Car tele est sa nature k'i n'est nule beste si cruels a prendre, et a une corne enmi le front ke nule armure ne contretient, si ke nus ne l'ose coure sus ne atendre fors virgene pucele. Car quant il en sent une au flair, il s'agenoille devant lui et (—il s'agenoille devant lui et FG) si se humelie doucement ausi com por servir. Si ke li sage veneor ki se nature seivent metent une pucele en son trespas, et il s'endort en son geron; et lors, quant il est endormis, si vienent li veneor ki en veillant ne l'osent requerre, si l'ochient (l'ocient (occist G) en dormant FG).

Tout ensi s'est Amours vengié de moi. Car j'avoi esté li plus orguelleux hom vers Amours ki fust de mon eage, et me sambloit ke je n'avoie onques veü feme ke je vausisse mie avoir tout a ma volenté par si ke jou l'amasse ausi durement comme j'ai oï dire c'on amoit. Et Amors, ki est sages venerres, me mist en mon cemin une pucele a qui douc[h]our jou me sui endormis et mors de tel mort com a Amor apartient, c'est desperance sans atente de merci.

[S 45. 4–46. 2] Et por che di jou ke jou fui pris a ces .iij. sens: a oïr, a veïr et a flarier; et se je parfusse pris as autres .ij. sens: a gouster en baisant et a touchier en acolant, dont parfusse jou a droit endormis. Car adont dort li hom, quant il ne sent nul de ses .v. sens. Et de l'endormir d'amors vienent tout li peril. Car a tous les endormis suit la Mors, et a l'unicorne ki s'endort a la pucele et a l'homme ki s'endort a le seraine.

XV [S 46. 3–47. 10] Mais se je me vausisse estre gardés de cest peril (touz ces perilz FG), il me covenist avoir fait ausi com la grue ki les autres gaite. Car quant grues vont ensamble, tous jours en veille li une ke ke les autres dorment, et font la veille sacune a son tour. Et cele ki gaite, por chu (de paor FG) k'ele ne s'endorme, si prent petites pieretes en (entre EFGL) ses piés, por qu'ele ne puist fermement ester ne fermement endormir. Car grues dorment en estant; et quant ele ne puet fermement ester, si ne puet dormir.

Je di ke ausi deüse jou avoir fait. Car le grue ki les autres gaite c'est porveance, ki doit garder toutes les autres virtus de l'ame, et li pié sont la volentés. Car ausi com on va par les piés, ausi va l'ame par la volenté d'une pensee en autre, et li hom d'un fait en autre. Dont met li grue les pierres en ses piés, qu'ele ne puist fermement ester, et pour che k'ele ne s'endorme, quant le porveance tient si courte le volenté ke li autre sens ne s'i fient mie tant qu'il soient deceü. Et ki ensi eüst fait, si n'eüst eü garde.

XVI [S 54. 1–55. 3] Ausi di jou de moi, bele tredouce amie, ke jou croi (—bele . . . croi FG) ke aucune medicine (—medicine FG) est par quoi vous me poés resusciter, mais jou ne sai quele la medicine (quele ele FG) est, fors tant ke par la nature d'une beste saice on le nature d'une autre.

Et on set bien ke li lions resuscite son lioncel, et seit on bien comment. Car li lionceaus naist mors, et au tierc[h] jour si ruit li peres sor lui, et ensi le resuscite. Ausi me samble il ke se vous me voliés rapeller a vostre (—vostre FG) amour, ke che me porroit bien estre recouvriers a resussiter de tel mort com est la mors d'amors dont je sui mors.

XVII [S 55. 4–57. 8] Et tout ausi est il del pellican. Car on set bien ke li pellicans resussite ses faons, et seit on bien comment. Car li pellicans est uns oiseaus ki merveille aime ses poichins, et tant les aime k'il se jue trop volentiers a aus. Et quant il voient ke loer pere se jue a eaus, si s'en fient tant k'il i osent bien ausi juer, et tant li volent devant le vis, k'il le fierent de lor eilles es iex. Et il est de si orguelleuse maniere k'il ne puet soffrir c'on lui mesface rien, si s'en coresche, si les ochist. Et quant il les a ochis, si s'en repent. Lors lieve s'eile et oevre sen costé a son bec, et del sanc qu'il en trait si arouse ses pouchins qu'il a ochis, et ensi les resuscite il.

Aussi, bele tres douce amee, quant ge fui vos noviaus acointes, que la nouveletés de l'acointanche m'avoit fait aussi com vostre pouchin, si me feïstes si biau sanllant qu'il me fu avis que j'oseroie bien parler a vous de c[h]ou qui plus me devoit plaire (que ie vous dis ce donc plus mestoit F, que ie vous dis ce dont ie estoie malades G). Et vous me prisastes si pau avers vous, que c[h]ou que ge vous dis ne vous plot mie: si m'en avés ochis de tel mort com Amours apartient. Mais se vous voliés vostre douc[h] costé ouvrir, tant que vous m'eussiés arousé de vostre bone volenté, et douné le biau douc[h] cuer desirré qui dedens le costé gist, vous m'ariés resuscité. Quar c'est la sovrainne medechine de moi aidier que de vostre cuer avoir.

Et se ne fust ore se pour c[h]ou non, que ge vous ai aucune fois oï dire k'il vous anuioit de c[h]ou que ge vous prioie, et que volentiers me tenissiés compaingnie se ce ne fust, si me deüssiés vous vostre cuer douner pour estre delivre de mon anui.

XVIII [S 57. 8–58. 8] Aussi com li castoires fait. C'est une beste qui a un membre sour lui qui porte medechine, si le cace on pour celui menbre avoir. Et il fuit tant com il puet; mais quant il voit qu'il ne puet plus guencir, si a paour que on ne l'ochie. Et toutes voies a il tant de sens de sa nature (–de sa nature FG), qu'il set bien c'on ne le cace se pour celui membre non: si gete les dens et l'esrace et le laisse caoir enmi la voie (a terre FG); et quant on le treuve, se le laisse on aler, quar on ne le cace se pour c[h]ou non.

Aussi, bele tres douce amee, se ma proiere vous anoie tant com vous dites, vos vous em porriés assés biau delivrer par vostre cuer douner, quar ge ne vous sieuc[h] se pour c[h]ou non.

XIX [S 84. 9–85. 9] Ne por chu ne le di jou mie ke jel vausisse trover, ains le di pour chu ke j'ai trové ki m'a dit: 'Fole seroit le feme ki en vous metroit son cuer, car vous estes pris aillors de si vraie prise k'ele perdroit quant qu'ele metroit en vous'. Et par aventure ceste parole ou le vaillant m'ont plusors dit, et telles ki volentiers me retenissent, s'elles ne doutassent ke je les deüsse guerpir a la vois de ma vraie mere. (–Ne por chu . . . vraie mere FG). Mais puis qu'ensi est que vous ne autre ne volés cest euf couver, il puet bien estre perdus par longue demouree. Et perdus fust il piecha, se ne fust un pau de soulas que j'ai de restorement et de joliveté de corage qui de nature me vient, a coi ge me conforte.

XX [S 86. 9–87. 3] Et se vous me voliés nourir, bele tres douce amee mere (–mere FG), ge vous seroie aussi bons fiex come li faon de la chuigne et de la huple sont a leur meres. Quar autrestant de tans com la chuingne met a ses chuingnos nourir, autrestant de tans (–de tans FG) remetent li chuignot (metent il FG), quant il sont parcrut, a leur mere renorir.

XXI [S 87. 3–89. 2] Et aussi li faon de la huple. Quar quant ele est mal empenee, jamais ne mueroit ele a par li, aussi com autre oisel font, ains vienent li hupelot, si li esrachent a lour bes les vies pennes et puis si le keuvent et norrissent tant qu'ele est toute rempenee. Et bien metent autrestant de tans a li couver et (—a li couver et FG) a li nourrir, com ele mist a aus, quant ele les couva (—quant ele les couva FG).

Bele (Ausi vos di ge bele FG) tres douce mere (amie FG), aussi bons fix vous seroie jou mout volentiers (—mout volentiers FG). Quar (—Quar FG) se vous me voliés couver et norir, c'est a dire retenir com ami, si com il a esté devant dit que li ponrres estoit li prendres et li couvers li retenirs, sachiés qu'il n'est riens a quoi loiaus amis se doie assaier que ge ne feïsse pour vous. Mais se vous ne prisiés tant ma nourreture come la vostre, et qu'il vos sanlle que ge ne vous aroie mie assés guerredonné por vostre amour se ge vous avoie douné la moie, a chou respont jou qu'il n'est riens c'amours ne face ivel. Quar en amours n'a ne val ne tertre, ains est aussi ounnie coume mers sans ondes. Dont uns poitevins dist que riens ne vaut l'amours qui ensi ondoie; et pour c[h]ou dist Ovides que amours et segnourie ne puent demourer ensanlle en une caiere.

NOTES

These notes deal mainly with forms and passages which mis-translate, obscure, abbreviate, or differ from the original French. In each case, page and line reference is made to the corresponding French passage in Cesare Segre's edition and is accompanied by an English translation. French passages not translated are noted and briefly summarized. Attention is also drawn to certain stylistic devices and scribal practices in the Welsh, and some editorial emendations to the Welsh text are explained.

1–19 **B,** 1–19 **CD:** The first section corresponds to de Fornival's introduction (S 3. 1–8. 9). However, the translator has only selected certain passages for translating, so that the main argument of the original is obscured.

6 **B:** achos na allaf wasstatvod yn y lle; the Welsh has rendered the French temporal clause *quant je ne serai presens* (S 6. 6), 'when I shall not be present', as a clause of reason. 6–7 **CD** have changed the sense completely: am na baiddaf j . . . a thi.

9 **B,** 8 **CD:** *Et je vous monsterai . . . painture et parolle* (S 6. 9), 'And I shall show you how this writing has painting and words', which should follow drwy liw a thrwy barabl **B,** drwy barabl a lliw **CD,** is not translated.

13–17 **B:** Wrth hynny . . . vy ng[o]vec i, 12–15 **CD:** Ag am hynny . . . na thosturio wrthyf; no equivalent in French.

17–18 **B,** 16–17 **CD:** Ac am hyny . . . aniveiliaid differs from the French *Et meesmement cis escris . . . ke dites* (S 7. 4–6), 'And moreover this writing is of such significance that it desires painting. For it is in the nature of animals and birds that they are more recognizable painted than spoken of'.

18 **B,** 17 **CD:** passage (S 7. 7–8. 8), which should follow aniveiliaid/anevailaid, is not translated. In this, the writer compares his writing, now his last recourse in winning his beloved's affections, to a rearguard sent by a king to reinforce his army fighting far away.

21 **B,** 21 **CD:** yn nes i'r dydd noc (nag i **CD**) haner nos (+ ymric y dydd D); a misrendering of *pres de la vespree ou de la jornee* (S 8. 10–9. 1), 'nearer to dusk or to day'.

23 **BD:** y plygain, 23 **C:** pylgain 'dawn, cock-crow, matins'; the French has *La vespree et la jornee* (S 9. 4), 'the dusk and the dawn'.

34–5 **CD:** ag yna i rydd ef ryw fravad yny dybyger vod y ddaear a'r awyr yn dyvod ynghyd; *Mais adont met il si grant paine a racaner qu'il se desront tous* (S 10. 5–6), 'But then he goes to so much trouble to bray that he shatters everything'. The image in the Welsh occurs also in an Early ModW version of 'Iarlles y Ffynhawn', see R. L. Thomson, 'Iarlles y Ffynhawn: the Version in Llanstephan MS 58', *SC* vi (1971) 70; see also NLW MS 13075, f. 1v for another copy (unedited). The passage is missing from **B** so it is not possible to say whether or not the image was in the original Welsh translation.

36–8 **B:** val y gallwyf . . . pes medressid, 38–41 **CD:** megis i gallwyf . . . wnaethur hynn; no equivalent in French.

40–4 **B,** 43–7 **CD:** o gwyl gwr evo (os gwr a'i gwyl ef **CD**) . . . gwr a gwreic: *quant uns hom . . . d'omme et de feme* (S 11. 2–5), 'when a man sees him before he sees the man, the wolf as a result loses all his strength and boldness, and if the wolf sees the man first, the man loses his voice thereby, so that he cannot say a word. This nature is found in the love of man and woman'. The order of clauses in Welsh reflects that of the established French text not that of FG where the order is reversed.

43 **B:** Ef a gyfflypir yn llyfr awduriaid, 46 **CD:** a hwnn a gyfflybir yn llyfr yr awduriaid; only FGKM have a basis for this reading, see above p. xxvii.

47 **B:** hi a gyll i hyder o nakav y gwr, 48–9 **CD:** y wraig a gyll i hyder o'i (y'w **D**) nakav ef; *elle a puis perdu le hardement d'escondire* (S 11. 8), 'she has lost the boldness to deny [it]'; *d'escondire* is ambiguous. It can equally refer to the woman's act of denying the man or to her denying that she loves him. The Welsh renders it as if it meant the former.

47–9 **B,** 50–2 **CD:** Os y gwr a gar y wraic yn gyntaf . . . garedic; no equivalent in French.

52–3 **B,** 55–6 **CD:** ac am hyny, gwae vi na wneuthvm y llythr hwnn drwy gan ac yn ffyrf o (— o **CD**) ymadrodd, 2–3 **A:** ac am hynny na wneuthum y llythyr h6nn dr6y gan namyn ar ffuryf ymadra6d; *C'est une raisons par quoi cis escris n'est mie fais en cantant, mais en contant* (S 12. 2–3), 'That is one reason why this writing is not made in song but in story-form'; whereas **A** renders the French correctly, **BCD** have obscured the sense by using ac instead of namyn before yn ffyrf (o) ymadrodd, and inserting gwae vi (fi **D**), for which there is no equivalent in French.

54 **B,** 57 **CD,** 5 **A:** yr eos; only FG have *rossignoil* 'nightingale' (S 12. 5) as opposed to *crisnon* 'cricket' in the other French texts, see above p. xxvi. The nightingale is also found in *Le Bestiaire d'amour rimé*, see A. Thordstein, op. cit., lines 207–12. For the nightingale in medieval European literature, see J. M. Telfer, 'The Evolution of a Mediaeval Theme', *Durham University Journal* xlv (1952–3) 25–34.

54–5 **B:** yr hwnn y kymerais exampl ohonno, 57–8 **CD:** yr hwnn i kymerais j sampl ohano, 5 **A:** yr h6nn y kefeis exemplar ohona6; *dont je me sui molt pris garde* (S 12. 5), 'to which I have paid much attention'; the Welsh reflects the established French text, the equivalent being omitted in FG.

57–8 **B:** A rrywur ydd edrychais innav ar hyny rac vy marw, 60–1 **CD:** A ry hir i bvm j heb ystyriaid hynny rag vy marw jnnav, 7–8 **A:** Ac ar hynny yd edrycheis i rac vy mar6; no equivalent in French.

58–61 **B,** 8–10 **A:** a mi a welaf . . . a chanv (a'r kan **A**); only **AB** render the French *Et por che me sui jou pris garde . . . abont me fu il pis* (S 12. 7–13. 2), although they render *ke li chanters m'a si pau valu* 'that singing has been of so little benefit to me' as mae ychydic (bychydic **A**) a dal i'r kywddolion ev kanv (kan **A**) with a slight shift of meaning, and omit to render the clause *ke je m'i puisse . . . socourust* 'that I might devote myself to it to such an extent that I might lose even myself in it, so that singing did not help me at all'.

61 **B,** 60 **CD,** 10 **A:** passage (S 13. 2–14. 4; 14. 4–15. 2), which should follow a chanv **B,** a'r kan **A,** newyn **CD,** is not translated. In this, the theme that singing at one's best brings ill-fortune to the singer is continued by reference to the swan, *li cingne,* which sings best in the year it is to die. The writer regrets his words to his beloved resulting in the loss of her company and would willingly re-eat them like the dog, *li chien,* which returns to its vomit and eats it.

61–6 **B,** 62–6 **CD,** 11–15 **A:** mal y (val i **CD**) gallo pawb (pa6b **A**) . . . vy llavvr a'm hamkann (llauur **A,** llavur **C,** llythr **D**); no equivalent in French.

16 **A:** A mi a goll6n heuyt vy neges; not found in **BCD** and no equivalent in French.

77 **B:** j gyd o gwbl; the adverbs j gyd 'all' and o gwbl 'wholly, all' are synonyms and one of the phrases should probably be deleted.

77 **B:** kyd gallo hi adel bod genthi, 78–9 **C:** sef yw hynny, gadael bod genti; no equivalent in French; the meaning is not clear; **D** omits the clause.

77–81 **B:** Ail natur . . . arni, 79–83 **CD:** Yr ail . . . erni; *Et selonc le seconde . . . ja samblant* (S 16. 6–8), 'And the second is that if it happens that she loves a man, when he is far away from her, she will love him very much, and when he is close by, she will not show it at all'; the Welsh paraphrases the French rather than translates it fully.

77 **D:** ni ddigochon seems to be the result of indecision as to whether to select digon or its alternate dichon, see F. O. Lindeman, *BBCS* xxix (1980–2) 507–12.

79 **B,** 80 **CD:** llety; no equivalent in French.

83–5 **B:** hi a veidr dial arni e hvn . . . val y gwnaeth y blaidd, 84–6 **CD:** hi a vedr roi esgus drosti . . . mal i gwnaeth y blaidd am i droed; *tout ausi ke li leus . . . a trop avant alei* (S 16. 10–17. 2), 'just as the wolf takes revenge on his foot with his mouth, so she knows very well how to cover up and disguise, by the power of words, the fact that she has gone too far'; although **B** is closer to the French than **CD,** the meaning is changed slightly. The French emphasizes the woman's knowledge of how to recover and conceal her feelings, like the wolf taking revenge on its foot. The Welsh merely states that the woman, like the wolf, takes revenge upon herself, conceals herself by means of other words, and bites her tongue for going so far as she has. The phrase am vyned . . . aethoedd in **B** has no equivalent in French.

85–7 **B,** 86–9 **CD:** Ac (Ag **C**) velly, ni vedrais . . . yn hygar gwrtais wrthyf; no equivalent in French.

88–9 **B:** Ac [ ]bvosst vy mod i'th orvod . . . y'm lladd, 90–2 **CD:** Ag velly, pan wyb[y]ost di vy mo[d] j y'th garv . . . y'm lladd hauach; this differs greatly from the French: *Car volentiers voet savor . . . fermement garder* (S 17. 2–4), 'For she would gladly know about another person what she does not wish to be known about herself, and she knows how to guard very securely against a man whom she thinks loves her'.

90 **B,** 92–3 **CD:** a elwir glux (glox **CD**); no equivalent in French for this word for the serpent.

90–1 **B,** 93 **D:** vr (yr **D**) hwnn y (i **D**) mae natur (natyr **D**) iddi; both **BD** have the m. form of the dem. pron. hwnn referring to sarff 'serpent' which is treated subsequently as a f. noun, hence the emendation to the f. form honn. In **C,** sarff is treated as a m. noun.

94 **B:** ti a vvosst a bychic o gywilydd arnad, 96–7 **CD:** i byost di vwyn a boneddigaidd wrthyf j (—j **D**); *si vous trovai . . . pour la novelté* (S 18. 2–4), 'so I found you of sweet manners with a little shame as is fitting, just as if you feared me a little because of the newness [of the acquaintance]'; none of the Welsh texts renders this passage fully. Instead, the two qualities found in the woman, her possessing a little shame and her sweet manners, are split between the texts, **B** preserving the former and **CD** the latter. This suggests that the original Welsh translation from which **BCD** descend combined both. The reference to the woman's fear of the writer because of the newness of the acquaintance is not translated.

95–6 **B:** ti a'm kyrchaisst yn gyn aruthred ac y bu aruthur gennyd vi; *si me fuistes . . . sus de paroles* (S 18. 5–6), 'then you were as fierce as you liked to me, and ran at me a little with words'; **B** fails to render *de paroles* 'with words', resulting in a shift of meaning. **CD** have altered the meaning completely: 98 **C:** j byost di valchach a thrawsach wrthyf j, 98 **D:** balchach vyost a thrawsach wrthyf.

99–100 **B:** Ac velly y try y kyvydnabod kyntaf a vv rrom, 101 **CD:** kans yr amser gyntaf does not render the equivalent French *Car ausi com li hom . . . en le primierre acointance et decovers* (S 18. 8–9), 'For just as man is born naked, and then dresses himself once he has grown up, so too is he naked of love at the first meeting and revelation'.

100–1 **B:** ac yna, mi a levessais dywedud iti kwbl o'm meddwl, 101–2 **C:** mi a levesais ddwedvd iti y kwbl o'm meddwl, 101–2 **D:** ni lyfesais ddwedyd wrthyd gwbwl omeddwl; *si k'il li ose bien dire tout son corage* (S 18. 10), 'so that he dares to utter all his mind'; the Welsh narrates in the 1 sg. whereas the French has the 3 sg. The neg. ni in **D** is an error for the pron. mi.

101 **B,** 102–3 **CD:** a (ag velly **CD**) gwedy darvod imi wissgo (ymwisgo **CD**) o'th gariad ti; *Mais aprés, quant il aime . . . et se coevre del tout* (S. 18. 10–19. 1), 'But afterwards, when he is in love, he is so covered that he is not able to go out, and conceals everything'; the Welsh is so abbreviated that it does not convey the sense of the original.

101–2 **B:** ni levessais ddywedud wrthyd ddim o'm meddwl, 103 **CD:** ny levesais j ddwedvd dim; *si k'i n'ose riens dire . . . le puist reprendre* (S 19. 1–3), 'so that he does not dare utter any of his mind, rather he fears constantly that he may be caught again'; the Welsh continues the narrative in the 1 sg. The clause *ains . . . reprendre* is not translated.

103 **B:** Velly'm delyaisst, 'thus you have caught me', 104 **B:** velly'm dallais[st], 'thus you have blinded me'; it was a common scribal practice in the 15th century and early 16th century to coalesce orthographically the rel. part. y with a preceding y; cf. also 222 **B:** Ac velly gwna. Orthographic coalescing of the rel. pron. a with a following a occurs in 110 **B:** ef a ymaith, 148–9 **B:** ef a ar y llew, 198 **B:** yr heliwr aeth, 110–11 **C:** ef a oddyno.

108–9 **B:** o'i vynwes nev j dan i wregys; no equivalent in French.

117–20 **B:** Kans megys na ellir daly yr ab . . . a gatwo kariad, 117–18 **CD:** Am (O achos **D**) na ellir dala yr ap . . . a vo heb wisg kariad (a gatwo i gariad yn gefrinach **D**); *Car ausi comme li cinges est delivres . . . k'il aime par amours* (S 20. 6–9); 'For just as the ape is delivered when he is bare-footed, and is not caught before he puts shoes on, so the man is not imprisoned before he is truly in love'; the Welsh obscures the meaning of the French.

120–1 **B:** [Wrth] exampl yr heliwr . . . deliaisst dithav vyvi, 119 **C:** Ag velly, wrth sampl yr helwr i delaist dithav vinnav, 119 **D:** Ac velly yn axamal o'r heliwr . . . delaisti fi; a greatly abbreviated rendering of *Et par cest example . . . elle le voit vestu* (S 20. 9–21. 4), 'And by this example is confirmed that of the viper, and by these two ways I see well the reason why you have been outwardly less kind to me since you got to know that I loved you than before, both because the ape is not caught before it is shod, and because the viper runs up to the man when it sees him clothed'.

122–4 **B:** ni ddylevt ti vy ruth[r]o . . . disstrywiaw differs from the French *ke vous deüsiés faire le contraire* (S 21. 5), 'that you should do the opposite'. 121 **CD** have darostwng 'to humiliate' rather than ruthro 'to rush'.

128–9 **B:** ni wyr Dduw nac y'w mam nac y'w tad ddw[c] [ ] na diod vddunt; the text is so confused that the original translation cannot be restored.

133–7 **B:** 130–5 **CD:** Ac vell[y], arglwyddes . . . a'm karv (am i hadar **CD**) differs from the French *Ensi m'est il avis . . . enfant au doit* (S 22. 4–23. 1), 'Thus it seems to me that you ought to have done, very sweet, beautiful friend, that when I was naked of your love, you were not bothered at all about me, and when I was dressed in it and carried a scutcheon with your arms, then you should have cherished and nourished me in your love, tender and new as it might be, just as one nourishes a child by hand (*lit.* with the finger)'.

140 **B:** ar y ffordd nev ar y maes, 138 **D:** ar y ffordd; no equivalent in French.

143–4 **C**: haibo heb i law ef; the adverbs haibo and heb law are synonyms and one should probably be deleted.

149–51 **B:** ac o achos natur y llew . . . ac a ddwc rrvthr i'r dyn, 147–9 **CD:** a hevyd y llew a sydd . . . ag a ddwg rythyr i'r dyn, ag a'i lladd; *mais por che k'il a naturel hardement . . . si tost com il le regarde* (S 24. 4–5), 'but because it has natural boldness, so is it ashamed of being afraid, so it attacks the man as soon as he looks at it'; the clause *si tost . . . regarde* is not translated.

151 **B,** 149 **CD:** chwegwaith; no basis for this in French. FG have *vij fois* 'seven times'; other texts have *cent fois* (S 24. 5), 'a hundred times'.

156 **B,** 154 **CD:** passage (S 25. 3–28. 1), which should follow ssynnwyr **B,** synwyr **CD,** is not translated. In this, the weasel, *la mostoile*, which conceives by the ear and gives birth by the mouth, is compared to beautiful words of love which are conceived by the ear and delivered by the mouth. The weasel's nature of carrying its young for fear of losing them is compared to the great despair of love.

157–60 **B,** 155–8 **CD:** Ac yn enwedic y ffordd honno . . . yr ederyn a elwir kolendr; no equivalent in French. This is a transition or bridge passage to introduce the concept of despair which had been developed in the account of the weasel.

163–4 **B:** megys [ ] ti a vynassut tirioni wrth[yf] ymhob lle, 161–3 **CD:** Ag velly, arglwyddes . . . yn tirioni wrthyf j; an abbreviated rendering of *Et pour chu me samble il . . . tenu compangnie* (S 28. 6–8), 'And therefore it appears to me, very beautiful, sweet friend, that since it grieves you that I ever begged you and that willingly you would have loved my friendship, and that willingly you would have kept me company'.

164–5 **B:** ac er pan ddywedais i y klevyd yssydd arna[f] a'm llygait ers hyny hyd heddiw, 163–4 **CD:** ag velly, er pan ddwedais j vy nghlwyf wrthyd; *por ke jou ne parlasse de chu dont j'estoie malades* (S 28. 8–29. 1), 'because I did not speak of that which caused me to be ill'; the Welsh has rendered a negative clause of reason as a positive temporal clause.

178–9 **B:** A chanv a wnant yr vn aken o briod lef ddwy ohonvnt, a'r llall a gan gida thelyn, a'r llall a gan gyda phibav, 174–5 **CJ:** Ag velly, kanv yn dda a wna dwy onaddynt, kans vn a gan gyda thelyn, a'r llall gyda phib; *Et cantent toutes .iij.: les unes en buisines, les autres en harpes et les tierces en droites vois* (S 30. 1–3), 'And all three sing/play: the one on trumpets, the second on harps, and the third in her proper voice'; **B** is defective. The sense may be restored by regarding ddwy ohonvnt as intrusive, having crept in from the previous sentence, and by emending yr vn aken o briod lef to yr vn a gan o briod lef. The presence of dwy onaddynt/ohonynt also in **CJ** suggests that this intrusion goes back to (β) from which **B** and **CD(J)** descend. However, **CJ** have rationalized the difficulty by omitting reference to the third siren who sings with her proper voice, and by making dwy onaddynt/ohonynt refer only to two sirens, the one playing the harp and the other the pipe.

188–90 **B:** Eussus, ni lavassaf . . . dy gan di j gyd, 184–7 **CJ:** Ond (eithr **J**) ny levasaf j . . . y'm kwsg (yn fy 'nghwsg **J**) differs from the French *Mais je ne vous ose susmetre traïson . . . sui mors* (S 31. 2–4), 'But I do not dare to impute treachery to you, instead I will only put the blame upon me myself, and I shall say that I, myself, have killed myself'.

190 **B,** 187 **CJ:** passage (S 31. 5–40. 8), which should follow j gyd **B,** y'm kwsg **C,** yn fy 'nghwsg **J,** is not translated. In this, the writer argues in favour of taking precautions against being caught by hearing, as the asp, *aspis*, which guards the balm-tree, does against those who try to lull it to sleep in order to steal the balm. Sound has such force that it dispels many displeasing things, like the blackbird, *le merle*, which, although the ugliest bird to be kept in a cage, is more avidly guarded than any other bird because of its song. A long discussion follows on the five senses, seeing, hearing, smelling, tasting, and touching, represented respectively by *li liens*, a small white worm which can see through walls, the mole, *la taupe*, the vulture, *li voltiers*, the ape, *li singes*, and the spider, *li araingne*. Sound can compensate for any defect in the other senses, like the blind mole which can hear so clearly that nothing can surprise it. It is also one of four beasts which live on pure elements, namely, the mole on earth, the herring, *heren*, on water, the plover, *plovier*, on air, and the salamander, *salamandre*, on fire.

191–2 **B:** A hynny, ti a'm diveaisst i . . . o'm daly i; the French begins the account of the tigress with a question and answer: *M'aida dont le veüe a prendre? Oïl* (S 40. 9), 'Did sight then help me to be captured? Yes'.

192 **B:** a'th gymhorthes di o'm daly i; the use of the prep. o is unusual; o'm daly i means literally 'from catching me', but the sense requires 'to catch me'.

196–9 **B:** Kans ymddigryfhav a wna . . . i ymryddhav i genthi, 190–5 **CJ:** Kans (— Kans J) llawenydd a digryvwch a gymer hi (ef **J**) . . . a'r kynawon ymaith; *Et se delite tant a regarder . . . delivrer de li* (S 41. 2–42. 1), 'And delights so much in looking at the great beauty of her good shape, that she forgets to chase those who have stolen away her young, and she stops there as if caught. For the wise hunters put the mirror there deliberately to deliver her up to them; the Welsh and the French differ in the reasons why the tigress forgets the chase; in the former, she believes that her reflection is one of her cubs and in the latter, she merely stops to admire herself.

200–1 **B:** Velly, o edrych arnad tithav . . . vy mhvm ssynnwyr, 195–7 **CJ:** Ag velly, wrth edrych arnad tithav . . . vy mhvmp synwyr; a greatly abbreviated rendering of *Dont je di ke se je fui . . . si com il a esté devant dit* (S 42. 2–6), 'Then I say that I was caught by hearing and seeing, that it was no marvel if I lost my sense and my memory. For hearing and seeing are the two gates of memory, as has been said before, and they are two of the most noble senses of man. For man has five senses: seeing, hearing, smelling, tasting, and touching, as has been said before'.

205–6 **B:** ac vn korn a vydd ynghnywillyn i dal, 200–1 **CJ:** ag vn korn a (—a **J**) sydd yddo (—yddo **J**) ynghenol i dalken; *et a une corne enmi le front ke nule armure ne contretient* (S 43. 2–3), 'and it has a horn in the middle of its forehead that no armour can withstand'; *ke nule . . . contretient* is not translated.

208–9 **B:** y daw ef i ddaresstwng iddi, ac i dyrydd i benn yn i harffet, 204 **C:** ef a ddaw eti, ag ef a ry i benn yn y harffed hi, 204 **J:** i daw atti, ac i rhydd i ben atti iw Chwilio am lau; *il s'agenoille devant lui* (*—il . . . lui FG*) *et si se humelie doucement ausi com por servir* (S 43. 5–6), 'it kneels down before her and so abases himself gently as if to serve [her]'; only **B** renders *il s'agenoille . . . lui* as y daw ef i ddaresstwng iddi. **BCJ** misrender *et si se humelie . . . servir* as ac i dyrydd (ag ef a ry **C,** ac i rhydd **J**) . . . harffet (harffed hi **C,** atti **J**). **J** tries to make more sense by adding iw Chwilio am lau.

213–15 **B:** Yn y modd hynny y delis . . . y'm delit, 207–9 **CD:** Ag yn y modd hynny (Ac velly **D**) i daloedd (dela **D**) . . . vorwyn ar vy (y **D**) ffordd; a greatly abbreviated rendering of *Tout ensi s'est Amours . . . sans atente de merci* (S 43. 10–44. 5), 'In this way has Love taken revenge upon me. For I have been the most haughty man of my years (*lit.* age) with regards to Love, and it seemed to me that I have never seen a woman whom I wanted at all to have completely at my disposal so that I might love her as intensely as I have heard say that one did. And Love, which is the wise hunter, puts in my way a girl by whose sweetness I have fallen asleep and have died from such a death as belongs to Love; this is despair without expectation of mercy'.

215 **B,** 209 **CD:** passage (S 44. 6–45. 3), which should follow delit **B,** ffordd **CD,** is not translated. In this, the idea of being caught by smell is continued with reference to the beasts which are enticed by the sweet smell of the panther, *le panthere*, and die from it.

216 **B,** 209–10 **CD:** ac (+yna **CD**) y kollais . . . drwy gyssgv (dwyll **CD**); a greatly abbreviated rendering of *Et por che di jou . . . mul de ses .v. sens* (S 45. 4–7), 'And therefore I say that I was caught by these three senses, by hearing, seeing, and smelling, and if I should be caught by the other two senses, by taste in kissing and by touch in caressing, from which I should rightly be sent to sleep. For then the man sleeps, when he is not conscious of any of his five senses'.

217–18 **B:** megys yr hy[ ] a ddelit drwy gan y vorvorwyn, ac y deli[ ],

210 **CD:** megis yr vnikorn; a greatly abbreviated rendering of *Et de l'endormir d'amors . . . a le seraine* (S 45. 7–46. 2), 'And from falling into Love's sleep there come all dangers. For death follows all sleepers, both the unicorn which falls asleep because of the maiden, and the man sent to sleep by the siren'.

221 **B:** llawer i'r vn lle onaddvnt; the insertion of i'r vn lle between llawer and onaddvnt may be for stylistic purposes. A similar example occurs in 'Buchedd Catrin Sant', *BBCS* xxv (1972–4) 265: Ar g6r dr6c h6n6 a duc llauer y agheu or cristonogyon.

225 **B;** kans be kyssgai, y maen a ssyrthiai, ac yntav a ddeffroai, 216–17 **CD:** kans pan ddamch[w]aino (o danweinia **D**) yddi gysgv, y maen a syrthia i'r llawr, ag yna i dyffro hithav (yno dyffroi a wna ynte **D**); the French gives a different reason for the crane taking a stone: *por qu'ele ne puist fermement ester ne fermement endormir* (S 46. 7–47. 1), 'because of which it cannot stand firmly nor sleep soundly'.

225 **B,** 218 **CD:** *Car grues dorment en estant . . . si ne puet dormir* (S 47. 1–2), 'For cranes sleep standing, and when it cannot stand firmly, it cannot sleep', which should follow ddeffroai **B,** dyffro hithav **C,** dyffroi a wna ynte **D,** is not translated.

225–8 **B,** 218–20 **CD** Ac velly y dylasswnn . . . pa gyngor yssydd ym (synwyrys **C,** gallder genyf **D**); a greatly abbreviated rendering of *Je di ke ausi deüse . . . si n'eüst eü garde* (S 47. 3–10), 'I say that so too should I have done. For the crane which watches over the others is foresight, which must protect all the other virtues of the soul, and the feet are the will. For just as one goes by means of the feet, so too the soul goes by means of the will from one thought to another, and man from one deed to another. Hence the crane puts the stones in its feet so that it may not stand firmly, and so that it does not go to sleep, since foresight holds the will so short (i.e. as if on a short rein) that the other senses do not trust it to the extent of being deceived. And whoever were to have done this, he would not have been afraid'.

228 **B,** 220 **CD:** passage (S 48. 1–53. 9), which should follow yssydd ym **B,** synwyrys **C,** gallter genyf **D,** is not translated. In this is developed the idea of the need for foresight, symbolized by the tails of the peacock, *li paons*, and the lion, *li lions*. The classical story of Argus and Mercurius is related—how Mercurius lulled the cowherd Argus to sleep with his pipe and stole the cow the latter was guarding. The writer is dead and needs a medicine to resuscitate him like that used by the swallow, *l'aronde*, to revive its young.

229–31 **B:** A mi a dybygaf . . . am i gynavon, 221–3 **CD:** Nid oes meddiginaeth . . . am i gynawon; an abbreviated rendering of *Ausi di jou de moi . . . et seit on bien comment* (S 54. 1–5), 'So I say of me, beautiful, very sweet friend, that there is some medicine by which you can resuscitate me, but I do not know what the medicine is, except that by the nature of one animal may be known the nature of another. And it is well-known that the lion resuscitates its cubs and it is well-known how'.

234–7 **B:** Hynn a ellir . . . o'r marwol haint yssydd arnaf, 226–8 **CD:** a hynn a ellir . . . o varw i vyw (o veirw yn vyw **D**); an abbreviated rendering of *Ausi me samble il . . . je sui mors* (S 54. 6–55. 3), 'Thus it appears to me that if you wish to recall me by your love, that that could well be a [means of] recovery for me to resuscitate me from such a death as is the death of love from which I am dead'.

239 **B,** 230 **CD:** *Car on set bien . . . et seit on bien comment* (S 55. 4–5), 'For it is well-known that the pelican resuscitates its young and it is well-known how', which should follow y pelika[n] **B,** am i adar **CD,** is not translated.

240–1 **B:** y daw yn rry vynych i ymwelet ac wynt, 231–2 **CD:** i daw ef [i] ymweled ag hwynt (imweled a hwy **D**) yn ry vynych; the French has *k'il se jue trop volentiers a aus* (S 55. 6–7), 'that he very willingly plays with them'.

241–2 **B,** 232–3 **CD:** ac ydd eheta (ag ef a heda **C,** ac i hetta ef **D**) . . . a'i llygait hwynt; an abbreviated rendering of *Et quant il voient . . . de lor eilles es iex* (S 55. 7–9), 'And when they see that their father is playing with them, then they have such trust in him that they dare to play too, and fly up in his face to such an extent that they strike him in the eyes with their wings'.

243 **B:** a chyn gravlonet ydiw yr edn hwnnw ac; the French has *Et il est de si orguelleuse maniere* (S 55. 9–56. 1), 'And he has such a haughty manner that'.

248–50 **B:** Val hynny . . . wrthyt vy ngovid, 238–40 **CJ:** Ag velly . . . rann o'm dolyr; *Aussi, bele tres douce amee . . . qui plus me devoit plaire* (*que ie vous dis ce donc plus mestoit* (*dont ie estoie malades G*) *FG*) (S 56. 5–8), 'Thus, beautiful, very sweet friend, when I was newly acquainted with you, and the newness of the acquaintance had made me as it were your chick, you treated me so graciously that I thought that I would indeed dare to speak to you of that which must most please me (that I say to you that which was most necessary to me (with which I was ill G) FG)'; the Welsh follows G.

250 **B,** 240 **CD:** *Et vous me prisastes . . . ne vous plot mie* (S 56. 8–10), 'And you valued me so little as compared with yourself that that which I told you did not please you at all', which should follow vy ngovid **B,** dolyr **CD,** is not translated.

255–8 **B,** 244–6 **CJ:** A mi a gigle (glywaf **C,** Ac mi glywaf **J**) . . . o'm yssmalhawch i (y'm llawenhav **C,** i'm Ysmalhau **J**); *Et se ne fust ore se pour c[h]ou non . . . pour estre delivre de mon anui* (S 57. 5–8), 'And were it not for the fact that I had once heard you say that it peeved you that I was imploring you and that you would willingly keep my company otherwise, you would give me your heart in order to be free from my importuning'; **BJ** are correct in translating *anui* 'pain, torment, importunity' as yssmalhawch, ysmalhau, which Ifor Williams (*PKM*, 287) argued once meant 'importunity, persistence; to importune, persist'. Also 255–6 **B:** nat hoff gennyt vy mot yn gynn yssmalhaet ac ydd wyf arnat renders *k'il vous anuioit de c[h]ou que ge vous prioie*, where *anuioit* is the imperf. indic. of *enoier*, *enoiier* 'to annoy, beg, importune'. Later, ysmalwch, ysmala acquired the meanings of 'care; careful' and 'amusement; funny' (see Melville Richards, *BBCS* x (1939–41) 240–1), which accounts for the substitution of llawenhav 'to gladden, amuse' in **C,** probably regarded by Llywelyn Siôn as a synonym.

260 **B:** vn o['i] bedwar troet, 248 **CJ:** vn o'i draed ef; the Welsh renders *un membre* (S 57. 9) 'a member' as if it meant 'foot' rather than 'penis'. For an account of the medicinal value of the male beaver's sexual organs and its self-castration to escape the hunter, see F. McCulloch, op. cit., 95.

251–3 **CJ:** ag (—ag **J**) yna i tyrr ef . . . ar i dair troed (dri throed **J**), missing **B;** *si gete les dens . . . enmi la voie* (*a terre FG*) (S 58. 3–4), 'it plunges its teeth into it and tears it out and lets it fall into the middle of the road (on the ground FG)'; the Welsh reflects the established French text in rendering *enmi la voie* 'into the middle of the road' as ar y ffordd; FG has *a terre* 'on the ground'.

264–6 **B,** 255–8 **CJ:** Velly [ ] arglwyddes (Ag velly, arglwyddes **C,** Cyfflybiaeth i hynny Arglwyddes **J**) . . . y twyllaisst vyvi (i twyllaist di vi **C,** y Twyllaist Di finnau yn yr un môdd **J**) differs from the French *Aussi, bele tres douce amee . . . pour c[h]ou non* (S 58. 6–8), 'Thus, beautiful, very sweet friend, if my imploring displeases you as much as you say, you could quite well free yourself of it by giving me your heart, for I do not pursue you except for that'.

267 **B,** 259 **CJ:** Between the account of the beaver, with which **BCD(J)** end, and the account of the partridge, with which the **A** fragment resumes, the original French text (S 58. 8–84. 9) gives accounts of the woodpecker, *li espés*, the swallow, *l'aronde*, the hedgehog, *li yrechons*, the crocodile, *li cocodrille/cocatris*, the hydrus, hydra, *ydre*, the viper, *la vipre*, the she-ape, *la singesse*, the sawfish, *la serre*, the turtledove, *li torterele*, and the partridge, *la pertris*.

20–7 **A:** y'th ganlyn . . . no chennyt ti; a greatly abbreviated rendering of *Ne por chu ne le di jou . . . a coi ge me conforte* (The whole of this passage to *de ma vraie mere* is omitted in FG) (S 84. 9–85. 9), 'Nevertheless, I do not say at all that I deserve to find it, rather I say it because I have found someone who said to me "Foolish would be the woman who would set her heart on you, for you are caught elsewhere in such a true grasp that she would lose whatever she set on you." And as it happens many people have told me these words or the equivalent and if such as would gladly hold me back if they did not doubt that I should leave them at the voice of my true mother. But since it is so that neither you nor any other wish to incubate this egg, it may well be wasted by long delay. And it would have been lost a while ago had it not been for a little solace, which I had from the recovery and cheerfulness of feelings, which comes to me naturally, with which I comfort myself'.

The passage (S 82. 1–84. 9) immediately preceding this in the French describes how the partridge steals the eggs of other partridges and broods them, but the chicks, when they are hatched, on hearing the call of their true mother, fly to her and follow her. The writer is like the egg which his beloved has laid, but since there is no woman who would hatch him, and since he has some hope that his beloved will hatch him in the end, he will not leave her for another, but he is afraid that this delay will destroy him.

27 **A:** passage (S 85. 10–86. 8), which should follow chennyt ti, is not translated. In this is described how the ostrich, *l'ostrice*, covers its eggs in the sand, forgets them, and allows the warmth of the sand to incubate them. The writer compares himself to the egg which no-one has covered and which remains unhatched, because he is denied the pleasure of the heart which might sustain him, and which is like warmth.

34–7 **A:** A phan welont yr adar jeueingk . . . a'r lle clyttaf a gaffont; no equivalent in French.

37–9 **A:** Ac yna, ef a da6 yr adar jeueigk . . . y ar y rei hen; an abbreviated rendering of *Quar quant ele est mal empenee . . . tant qu'ele est toute rempenee* (S 87. 4–7), 'For when she is badly plumed, she would never moult by herself like other birds do, but the young come and pull out the old feathers with their beaks, and then they cherish and feed her till her feathers are regrown'.

39–43 **A:** Ac yna, ef a orwed . . . yn iach ieueingk differs from the French *Et bien metent autrestant . . . quant ele les couva* (—*quant ele les couva* FG) (S 87. 7–9), 'and indeed, they take as much time in caring for her and (—in caring for her and FG) feeding her as she took with them, when she incubated them (—when she incubated them FG)'.

44–7 **A:** os tydi a vynn vy meithrin . . . megys gwir gedymdeith ytt; *Quar se vous voliés couver et norir . . . et li couvers li retenirs* (S 88. 2–4), 'For if you wish to incubate and nurture me, that is, keep me as a friend, as it has been said before, that the laying is the taking and the incubating the keeping'; the passage *si com il a esté devant dit . . . li retenirs* is not translated.

49 **A:** a thydi a wdost hynny; no equivalent in French.

50–2 **A:** Ac ef a welir ytti heuyt . . . y meu ytti; *et qu'il vos sanlle . . . se ge vous avoie douné la moie* (S 88. 6–8), 'and if it seems to you that I would not have repaid you enough for your love if I had given you mine'; the Welsh reflects the reading of the established French text; the equivalent is omitted in FG.

52 **A:** *a chou respont jou qu'il n'est riens c'amours ne face ivel . . . qui ensi ondoie* (S 88. 8–11), 'to this I reply that there is nothing that love does not do equally. For in love there is neither valley nor hill; instead,

it is even like a sea without waves, concerning which a man from Poitiers said that the love which undulates is worth nothing', which should follow y meu ytti, is not translated.

52–4 **A:** kanys balchd[er] y6 gennyt . . . ac yd 6yf; no equivalent in French.

54–5 **A:** Ac am hynny y dywa6t Ouidinus na dicha6n bot yn vn eistedua balchd[er]; *et pour c[h]ou dist Ovides que amours et segnourie ne puent demourer ensanlle en une caiere* (S 88. 11–89. 2), 'and for this reason, Ovid said that love and lordliness cannot remain together in one seat'; **A** ends abruptly in the middle of this quote from Ovid. The full quote in Welsh was probably something like na dicha6n bot yn vn eistedua balchder a chariat. C. Segre (op. cit., XI) shows that the reference is to Ovid's *Metamorphoses* II, lines 846–7: *Non bene conveniunt, nec in una sede morantur / Maiestas et amor*, 'Majesty and love do not agree well, nor can abide long in the same seat', see F. J. Miller, ed., *Ovid: Metamorphoses*, London, 1916. Any remaining translation has not survived. The French (S 89. 2–102. 7) contains accounts of the eagle, *li aigles*, the dragon, *li draghon*, the elephant, *l'olifant*, doves, *colons*, the whale, *la balaine*, and the fox, *li gorpiex*. One text, BL Harley MS 273 (L), adds the scorpion, *li escorpion*.

VOCABULARY

The arrangement of the vocabulary follows the order of the Roman alphabet except that no distinction is made between *c* and *k* (both are placed under *c*), *i* and *j*, *u* and *v*. The symbol *6* is treated as *w*. Except where an initial mutation is petrified, words are listed under the radical consonant; these reflect the orthographical system of each text, so that words with *g-*, *ch-*, *ngh-*, the mutated forms of /k/, are restored as *k-* in ABCD and as *c-* in J. The first occurrence of each word is listed, where possible, under the B-form, followed by any orthographical variants in B and equivalent forms and variants in the other texts. Where B-forms do not occur, words are listed under their first occurrence in A, C, or D(J), respectively. The ModW dictionary form is supplied, where one exists, in brackets after each catch-word. Inflected verb forms are listed under the relevant verbal noun, nouns under the singular form, adjectives under the radical form, and inflected prepositions under the citation form. Catch-words are quoted in their ModW dictionary forms where no corresponding examples occur in the texts. Cross-references are given where it is considered necessary, as for example when there is a substantial difference in orthography or form. Cross-references are not normally given in the case of the following when they represent orthographical variants: *c/g*, *d/dd*, *f/v*, *m/mm*, *n/nn*, *p/b*, *r/rr/rh*, *s/ss*, *t/d*.

a 1. (*a*) (len.) rel. pron. affirm. 4BA, heading C, 7D; see *GMW* §§ 65–7.
2. (*a, ac*) (asp.) conj. and 2B, 1A, 2CD; **ac** 5B, 2A, 5D, **ag** 4C, 21 D.
3. (*â, ag*) (asp.) prep. with 15B, 7CD; **ac** 241B, 40A, 145D, **ag** 24C; **a** used after equat. 52A; **ac** 46B, 6A, 176J, **ag** 59C; **ac** used after superl. 72B, **ag** 73CD.

a, ant, see *myned.*

ab (*âb*) f. ape 105BD, **ap** 105CD.

abergova, see *hebrgovi.*

achos (*achos*) f. cause, reason 54B, 57CD; conj. because, for 146B, *achos na* 6B; see *o achos* and *GMW* § 259.

adain (*adain*) f. wing; pl. *adanedd* 233C, *adenydd* 129D, *ydenydd* 127D.

addef (*addef*) vn. confess, disclose 188B, 185J.

adeiliad (*adeiliad*) vn. build 45B, **adailiad** 47C; pret. impers. *adeiliwyd* 98B; for the formation of this vn., see *WG*, 390, *GMW* § 179.

adenydd, see *adain.*

aderyn, see *ederyn.*

adnabod vn. recognize, know; indic. pres. 3 sg. *edwyn* 205CJ; consuet.

pres. 3 sg. *adnebydd* 210B; pret. 1 sg. *adnabvm* 238C, *adnabum* 238J; subjunct. pres. 3 sg. *ydnapo* 47B, *adnapo* 50CD; subjunct. pres. impers. *adnaper* 81B, 84CD; subjunct. imperf. impers. *adnabydder* 83C, *ydnabydder* 83D; see *GMW* § 158.

adolwc (*adolwg*) vn. beseech 64B, 63D, **adol6c** 14A.

aeth, -oedd, see *myned.*

aflwydd (*aflwydd*) in *ar haflwydd* adv. unfortunately, unluckily 111B.

ag a rel. pron. 106C, **ac a** 106D; see Henry Lewis, *BBCS* x (1939–41) 200.

ag atuyd, see *ygadvydd.*

agoryd, see *egori.*

agos (*agos*) adj. near 71BD, 23C; equat. *kynesed* 232C, *kyn nesed* 232D; comp. *nes* 21BCD; see *GMW* § 42.

ai . . . ai (*ai . . . ai*) disjunctive part. either . . . or 173B, 169D, **au . . . au** 169C; see *GMW* §§ 253–4.

ail (*ail*) ord. second 77B, 79C, 70D.

aissiav (*eisiau*) m. absence, need 202B.

aithr (*eithr*) prep. except for 207B, **eithr** 202J; **eithr** conj. but 241J; *eithr ni* 184J; see *GMW* §§ 215, 256.

allan (*allan*) adv. out 156B, 153C, 139D, *o hynn* (*hyn D*) *allan* henceforth, thenceforth 36CD.

am (*am*) (len.) prep. about, on account of, regarding 2A, 4BCD; 1 sg. *amdanaf* 134B; 3 sg. m. *amdanaw* 92B; 1 pl. *amdanom* 186B, 182CJ; see *GMW* §§ 63(a), 203; conj. because, for 17C, 148D; *am na*(*d*) 14B, 1A, 6C, 13D.

amkann (*amcan*) m. and f. intention, purpose 66B.

amenydd, amhenydd, see *emennydd.*

amgen (*amgen*) in *nid amgen* (*noc*) namely 63CD, *nyt amgen* 19A; see *ny.*

amryw (*amryw*) pronom. many, diverse, various 175B, 171CD.

amser (*amser*) m. (m. and f. in C) time, period 30A, 87CD.

anerch (*annerch*) m. and f. greeting, salutation 2B, heading D, **annerch** 1C.

anfwyn (*anfwyn*) adj. unkind, ungentle, churlish 131CD.

angav (*angau*) m. death 170B, 167C, 171D, **ange** 167D, **angeu** 240J.

angof (*anghof*) m. without memory in *gollwng . . . yn angof* forget 192C.

anhawdd, see *anodd.*

anioddevawdr (*anioddefawdr*) adj. intolerable, unbearable 30B.

anivail (*anifail*) m. animal 205B, **anifeil** 31B, **enivail** 259B, **anevail** 31C, **ynifail** 31D, **anifail** 200J; pl. *aniveiliaid* 18B, *anevailaid* 17C, *ynyfeiliaid* 17D.

aniwed (*niwed*) m. harm 3B, 3CD, **eniwet** 244B; on the prosthetic vowel before *n*-, see Kenneth Jackson, *BBCS* xxx (1982) 45–9.

anobaith (*anobaith*) m. despair 158B, 156CD.

anobaithol (*anobeithiol*) adj. hopeless 30C, **anobeithiol** 30D.

anobeithvs (*anobeithus*) adj. hopeless 30B.

anodd (*anodd*) adj. difficult, hard 200C, **anhawdd** 200J; comp. *anos* 205B.

anvon (*anfon*) vn. send 1B, **anfon** heading D; indic. pres. 1 sg. *anvonaf* 5B, *anfona* 5D.

anwyl (*annwyl*) adj. dear, loving 130CD.

anyal6ch (*anialwch*) m. desert, wilderness 36A.

anyan (*anian*) m. and f. nature, temperament, quality 4A.

ar (*ar*) (len.) prep. on 16B, 7A, 40CD; 1 sg. *arnaf* 95B, 15CD; 2 sg. *arnat* 187B, 25A, 183J; *arnati* (agglutinated) 39D, *arnad* 3BC, 169D; 3 sg. m. *arno* 74B, 33CD, *arnaw* 141B; 3 sg. f. *arni* 33B, *erni* 83CD; 1 pl. *arnam* 174B, *arnom* 170C, *arnomi* (agglutinated) 170D; 2 pl. *arnochi* (agglutinated) 3D; 3 pl. *arnunt* 132B, 42A, *arnvnt* 127B, *arnynt* 125CD; see *aflwydd*, *kyfflyprwydd*, *cylch*, *helw*, *llês*, and *GMW* § 63(a).

a'r a, pron. or part. introducing rel. clause 105B, **ar ai** 176J, **o'r a** 48A; see *GMW* § 75.

araf adj. quiet, gentle; superl. *aravaf* 72B, *arava* 73C, *arafa* 73D.

arall (*arall*) pronom. another, other 12B, 4A, 11CD; pl. *ereill* 83B, 41A, *eraill* 255B; see GMW § 96(b).

arbed (*arbed*) vn. save, preserve 136B.

arffet (*arffed*) f. lap 209B, **arffed** 204C, **arff**[**ed**] 207D.

arffetoc (*arffedog*) m. and f. apron 212B.

arglwyddes (*arglwyddes*) f. lady 133B, 52CD, **argl6ydes** 43A.

aroglav (*aroglau*) m. smell, scent 203B, 198C, **aroglau** 199J, **arogli** (probably a printing error) 198J; see Ifor Williams, *Y Beirniad* viii (1918–20) 259.

aros (*aros*) vn. withstand, resist 202CJ; in MW it was followed by a direct object, see D. Simon Evans, *Buched Dewi*, 52 note.

aruthur (*aruthr*) adj. terrible, merciless, cruel 96B; equat. *aruthred* 96B.

arwydd (*arwydd*) m. and f. sign, symbol 8BCD; pl. *arwyddion* 46B, 49CD.

arwyddokae (*arwyddocáu*) vn. signify, denote 220C, **arwyddoka** 220D; indic. pres. 3 sg. *arwyddoka* 227B.

as syllabic form of inf. accus. pron. 3 sg. used after *pei* 15A; see *GMW* § 59.

asgell f. wing; pl. *essyll* 242B.

assen (*asen*) f. ass, onager 32B, **asen** 32CD.

a sydd, a sy, see *bod*.

at (*at*) (len.) prep. to, towards 226C, heading D; 1 sg. *ataf* 88C; 2 sg. *attat* 46A, *atad* 7CD, *attad* 222D; 3 sg. m. *ato* 179C, *atto* 179J; 3 sg f. *ati* 113B, *atti* 204J, *eti* 113CD; 2 pl. *atoch* 2C, *atochi* (agglutinated) 2BD; 3 pl. *atvnt* 182B, *atynt* 178C, *attynt* 178J; see *GMW* § 63(a).

au . . . au, see *ai . . . ai*.

awdur m. author; pl. *awduriaid* 43B, 46C, *awdyriaid* 46D.

awr (*awr*) in (*y*)*r awr hon*(*n*) adv. this hour, now 28BCD; *yr awr* conj. when 11B, 10D.

awyr (*awyr*) m. and f. air 35C.

axamal, axawmpl, axiampal, see *exampl*.

bae, bai, see *bod*.

baidd-af, -o, see *beiddio*.

balch (*balch*) adj. proud 91C; pl. *beilch* 123B, *bailchon* 121C, *beilchion* 121D; equat, *balched* 89B; comp. *balchach* 48B, 51CD.

balchder (*balchder*) m. pride 52A.

bardd (*bardd*) m. poet 259J.

barnv (*barnu*) vn. judge 168B, **barny** 166CD; indic. pres. impers. *bernir* 168C.

bei, see *bod*.

beiddio vn. venture, dare; indic. pres. 1 sg. *baiddaf* 6C, *beiddiaf* 6D; subjunct. pres. 3 sg. *baiddo* 202C.

beilch, beilchion, see *balch*.

bid, bit, see *bod*.

blaen, see *o flaen*.

blaidd (*blaidd*) m. wolf 40B, 43CD, **bleid** 1A.

bod (*bod*) vn. be 2BCD, **bot** 186B, 19A; indic. pres. 1 sg. *wyf* 1BC, 14D, *6yf* 14A, *wf* 1D, *ydwyf* 35B, *odwyf* 37C; 2 sg. *ydwyt* 159B, *wyd* 104C, *wyti* (agglutinated) 104D; 3 sg. *y mae* 68B, 17A, 181J, *i mae* 23C, 93D, *j mae* 157C, *i mav* 157D, *mae* 173B, 68D, *yw* 9B, 32C, 20D, *y6* 18A, *ydiw* 114B, *ydyw* 244J, *oes* 15B, 21A, 13CD; rel. *yssydd* 23B, *yssyd* 4A, *a sydd* 39C, 175J, *a sy* 128C, *y sydd* 39D, *sy* 128D, *sydd* 192J; 3 pl. *i maent* 171D, *ynt* 127B, 125C, *ydynt* 125D; consuet. pres. 1 sg. *bydaf* 44A; 3 sg. *bydd* 18B, 28CD, *byd* 29A; 3 pl. *byddant* 232B, 224CD; imperf. 1 sg. *oddwn* 27B, *oeddwn* 123C, 133D; 2 sg. *oeddyd* 86B, 88CD; 3 sg. *oedd* 16B, 15CD, *oed* 24A; pret. 1 sg. *bvm* 3B, 60C, *bym* 3CD; 2 sg. *bvosst* 3B, *buosst* 88B, *byost* 3C, 96D, *byosti* (agglutinated) 91D, *byest* 165D; 3 sg. *bu* 96B, 9A, *bv* 26B, *by* 99CD; 2 pl. *byochi* (agglutinated) 3D; plup. 2 sg. *bysyd* 163CD; 3 sg. *bysai* 162C, *byse* 162D; subjunct. pres. 1 sg. *b6yf* 45A; 3 sg. *bo* 24B, 6A, 33CD; 3 pl. *bont* 129B, 127CD, *bon*(*hwy*) 129D; imperf. 1 sg. *byddwn* 238B, 27CD, *byd6n* 28A; 3 sg. *byddai* 65BC, *bydei* 15A, *byddav* 65D, *byddae* 243J, *bai* 144B, 27CD, *bei* 53A, *bae* 241J; imper. *bid* 2BCD, *bit* 16A, 189B, *byd* 67C; see *GMW* § 144.

boneddigaidd (*boneddigaidd*) adj. gentle, amiable, polite, noble 97CD.

bon hwy, see *bod*.

bowyd, see *bywyd*.

brathv (*brathu*) vn. bite, pierce, wound 84B; indic. pres. 3 sg. *brath* 74B.

bravad (*brefad*) vn. bray 34C, **brefad** 34D.

brevv (*brefu*) vn. bray 33B, **brefy** 33CD.

bric (*brig*) in *ymric y dydd* at the break of day 21D.
bryt (*bryd*) m. mind, thought 24A.
bu/bv, -m, -osst, -ost, see *bod*.
b6r6 (*bwrw*) vn. throw, cast; *b6r6 eu pluf* moult 35A; indic. pres. 3 sg. *bwrw* 194CJ; pret. 2 sg. *bwriaisst* 167B, *bwrriaisst* 265B, *bwraist* 165C, *bwriaist* 257J; 3 sg. *bwriodd* 198B.
bwyd (*bwyd*) m. food 57B, 34CD, **b6yt** 7A.
b6yf, see *bod*.
bwystvil (*bwystfil*) m. beast 92D.
bwyta (*bwyta*) vn. eat 146B, 144CD.
by, -est, -m, -och, -ost, see *bod*.
bychan, adj. small, little; pl. *bychain* 110CD.
bychic (*bychig*) pronom. small, little in *bychic o gywilydd* a little shame 94B; see *GMW* § 112.
bychydic (*bychydig*) pronom. little, few 8A; see *ychydic*.
byd, bydd, -af, -ant, see *bod*.
byd (*byd*) m. world 32B, 32CD, **byt** 205B.
bys-ai, -e, -yd, see *bod*.
byth (*byth*) adv. ever, for ever 33B, 33C; see *GMW* § 247(e).
byw (*byw*) adj. alive, living 162B, 160CD.
bywyd (*bywyd*) m. life 170B, 226C, **bywyt** 234B, **bowyd** 226D.

cablu vn. revile, blame, reprove; subjunct. pres. 2 pl. *kaploch* 64B, 14A, *kabloch* 65D; imperf. 2 pl. *kaplech* 65B, *kaple6ch* 15A, *kablech* 65CD.
kadarn (*cadarn*) adj. strong, powerful 22B, 23CD; comp. *kadarnach* 19B, 18CD; superl. *kadarnaf* 31BCD.
kadarnhav (*cadarnhau*) vn. confirm, strengthen 116B.
cadw vn. keep; subjunct. pres. 3 sg. *katwo* 120B, 118D.
kaffel (*caffael*) vn. get, obtain 112B, 51A, **kaffael** 13C, **kael** 15B, 27A, 34CD; indic. pres. 3 sg. *kaiff* 111CD; pret. 1 sg. *kevais* 54B, 57C, *kefeis* 4A, *kefais* 57D; subjunct. pres. 1 sg. *kaffwyf* 7CD; 3 sg. *kaffo* 34B, 112CD; 3 pl. *kaffont* 37A; impers. *kaffer* 253C, *caffer* 253J; see *GMW* § 161.
kaiff, see *kaffel*.
kail (*cail*) f. sheepfold, flock of sheep 72B.
kailog, see *keilioc*.
kaiso (*ceisio*) vn. seek 193C, **ceisio** 193J; indic. pres. 3 sg. *kais* 113BCD.
kalendr, see *kolendr*.
kall (*call*) adj. wise, wily 105B, 205C.
kallineb (*callineb*) m. wisdom, prudence, understanding, craftiness 219D.
kallter (*callter*) m. wisdom, prudence, understanding, craftiness 226B, **kalldder** 220D.
kalonn (*calon*) f. heart 149B, **kalon** 147CD.

kan 1. (*can*) (nas.) num. before a noun, hundred 200B.
2. (*cân*) f. song 53B, 3A, 56CD; indic. pres. 3 sg., see *kanv*.

kanlyn (*canlyn*) vn. follow 20A.

canmol, -i vn. praise; subjunct. pres. 2 pl. *kanmoloch* 64C.

kans (*cans*) conj. since, because 10B, 8CD; *kans ydiw* 114B; *kans ni*(*d*) 13B, 37C, 11D, *kans ny* 151C, *kans nad* 170B; see *GMW* § 261.

kanv (*canu*) vn. sing, crow 21B, 20C, 60D, **kanu** 6A, **kany** 20D, **canu** 7A, 174J; indic. pres. 3 sg. *kan* 21BCD; pret. 1 sg. *kenais* 60B, *keneis* 9A; subjunct. pres. 3 sg. *kano* 20B, 22CD.

kanys (*canys*) conj. since, because 4A, **canys** 5A, 186J; *canys nid* 199J; see *GMW* § 261.

kapl-ech, -e6ch, -och, see *cablu*.

karedic (*caredig*) adj. kind, loving, dear 49B, 52D, **karedig** 52C; equat. *keredikеd* 180B; superl. *keredikaf* 1B, *karedikaf* 1C, *kredika* 1D.

kariad (*cariad*) m. love 2BC, heading D, **kariat** 214B, **kariati** (agglutinated) 87D, **caryat** 21A.

kariadferch (*cariadferch*) f. lady-love, sweetheart, mistress 1CD.

kariadys (*cariadus*) f. loving, affectionate, kind 228C.

karv (*caru*) vn. love 78B, 50C, 81D, **kary** 50D; indic. pres. 3 sg. *kar* 45B, 5A, 48CD.

kasstrin (*castrin*) m. beaver 259B, **castrin** 247CJ; borrowed from French *castoires* beaver (< Latin *castor*).

kedymddeithes (*cydymddeithes*) f. female companion 1B.

kedymdeith (*cydym*(*dd*)*aith*) m. companion 47A.

kefeis, see *kaffel*.

kefflebir, kefflyb-ir, -v, see *kyfflybu*.

kefrinach (*cyfrinach*) m. and f. secret 118D.

keilioc (*ceiliog*) m. cock 20B, **kailog** 20C, **kelioc** 20D.

ceisio, see *kaiso*.

kelain (*celain*) f. corpse, carcass 140B, 138C.

celu vn. hide, conceal, keep secret; indic. pres. 3 sg. *kel* 82C, *kela* 82D.

kelvyddyd (*celfyddyd*) f. art, craft, ruse, wile, trick 107B.

ken-ais, -eis, see *kanv*.

kenav (*cenau*) m. cub, whelp 198B; pl. *kynavon* 195B, *kynawon* 190C, *knawon* 223D, *cenafon* 190J.

kerdd (*cerdd*) f. song, poem, music 38B, 40CD.

cerdded vn. walk; indic. pres. 3 sg. *kerdd* 73C, *kerdda* 73D.

kev-ais, -eis, see *kaffel*.

chi, see *chwi*.

chuinng m. stork 29A, **chuing** 30A; borrowed from French *chuingne* stork (< Latin *ciconia*).

chwannoc (*chwannog*) adj. eager, keen, convetous, greedy 261B, **chwannog** 249C.

chwant (*chwant*) m. desire 57B, 59CD, **ch6ant** 7A.

chwegwaith (*chwegwaith*) adv. (num. *chwe* six + *gwaith* time) six times 151B, 149CD.

chweith (*chwaith*) adv. used in neg. sentences, any 25B, **chwaith** 170B, **ch6eith** 22A; *chwaith . . . nac ychwaith* neither . . . nor 229B.

chwi (*chwi*) indep. pron. 2 pl. 15B, **chi** 138D; aux. (agglutinated) in *arnochi* 3D, *atochi* 2BD, *genychi* 67D, *vyochi* 3D; see *GMW* §§ 54(a), 62(a).

chwilio (*chwilio*) vn. search 204J.

chwithev (*chwithau*) indep. conjunct. pron. 2 pl. 63B, **ch6itheu** 13A, **chwithav** 64C; see *GMW* §§ 54(c), 62(b).

kigle, see *klybod*.

kigvran (*cigfran*) f. raven 126B, **kigfran** 124CD.

kimint, see *mawr*.

klaf (*claf*) adj. sick, ill 159CD.

klevyd (clefyd) m. sickness, disease 165B.

klowed, see *klybod*.

klwyf (*clwyf*) m. wound, disease, sickness 63BD, 16C, **kl6yf** 12A.

klwyfvs (*clwyfus*) adj. painful, sore, sick 161B.

klybod (*clybod*) vn. hear, smell 74B, **klywed** 74C, **klowed** 74D; indic. pres. 1 sg. *klywaf* 244C, *clywaf* 244J; pret. 1 sg. *kigle* 255B; subjunct. pres. 3 sg. *klywo* 181B, 176C, *clywo* 176J.

clyd adj. sheltered, snug, warm, comfortable; superl. *clyttaf* 37A.

klyw-af, -ed, -o; clyw-af, -o, see *klybod*.

knawon, see *kenav*.

knoi (*cnoi*) vn. bite, chew 85CD; indic. pres. 3 sg. *kny* 75CD.

knywillyn (*cnewyllyn*) m. centre, nucleus, core 206B.

cod-ant, -it, kodwn, see *cyfodi*.

coeden f. tree; pl. *koed* 72CD.

koes (*coes*) f. leg 224B, 216D.

kof (*cof*) m. memory 8B; *gollwng . . . dros gof* forget 192J.

kolendr (*colendr*, *calendr*) m. heron 160B, **kalendr** 158CD, **kalendyr** 158D; borrowed from French *calandre* heron (< Latin *caladrius*).

kolli (*colli*) vn. lose 52B, 2A, 55CD; indic. pres. 3 sg. *kyll* 41B, 44CD; pret. 1 sg. *kolleis* 157B, *kollais* 200B, 196C, 209D; subjunct. imperf. 1 sg. *koll6n* 16A.

korff (*corff*) m. body 70BCD, 17A.

korn (*corn*) m. horn 206B, 201C, **corn** 201J.

kowion, see *kyw*.

kowir, see *kywir*.

kowrain(t), see *kywreint*.

kraeso (*croeso*) m. welcome 135C, **kreso** 135D.

kravlonet, see *kroelon*.

kredika, see *karedic*.

kredv (*credu*) vn. believe, trust 186B, 184C, **kredu** 188B, **kredy** 182C, **credu** 182J.

kreylon, see *kroelon.*

crio vn. cry; indic. pres. 3 sg. *kria* 225CD.

kroelon (*creulon*) adj. cruel 226C, **kreylon** 226D; equat. *kravlonet* 243B.

krwn (*crwn*) adj. round 216CD.

cryf (*cryf*) adj. strong 45A.

kwan, see *kyw.*

kwbl (*cwbl*) pronom. whole, total, all 75B, 76C, **k6byl** 38A, **kwbwl** 76D; *o gwbl* adv. entirely, totally, (not) at all 77B, 70C, 185J, *o gwbwl* 70D; see *GMW* § 108.

kwilyddia, see *cywilyddio.*

kwrtais (*cwrtais*) adj. courteous, modest, shy 87B, 88CD.

kwssc (*cwsg*) m. sleep 184B, **kwsg** 180C, **cwsg** 180J; indic. pres. 3 sg., see *kyssgu.*

kyd (*cyd*) conj. although 77B; see *GMW* § 262.

kydnabod (*cydnabod*) m. acquaintance 99CD.

cyfaredd f. medicine, remedy, potion; pl. *kyvarddonav* 248C, *cyferddonau*, *cyfrwyddonau* 248J.

cyfarfod vn. meet; consuet. pres. 3 sg. *kyvervydd* 195B, *kyverfydd* 190C, *cyferfydd* 190J; subjunct. pres. 3 sg. *kyvarffo* 140B, 138C, *kafarffo* 138D; see *GMW* § 153.

cyferddonau, see *cyfaredd.*

cyfflybiaeth (*cyffelybiaeth*) f. likeness, similarity 255J.

kyfflybu (*cyffelybu*) vn. compare 137B, **kyfflypu** 98B, **kyfflypv** 97B, **kyfflybv** 99C, **kefflybv** 116C, **kyfflyby** 99D; indic. pres. impers. *kyfflybir* 24BD, 46C, *kyfflibir* 31B, *kyfflypir* 43B, *kefflybir* 24C, *kefflebir* 154C; pret. 1 sg. *kyffelybeis* 17A.

kyfflyprwydd (*cyffelybrwydd*) m. likeness, similarity in *ar gyfflyprwydd*, *o gyffylybrwydd* in the likeness of 17B, 148B, *ar* (*o*) *gyfflybrwydd* 17CD.

cyffwrdd, cwrdd vn. meet, touch, contact; indic. pres. 3 sg. *kywrdd* 242B, *kyhwrdd* 233C, *kyffwrdd* 233D.

cyfodi, codi vn. rise, ascend; indic. pres. 3 sg. *kyfyd* 75D; 3 pl. *kyvodant* 248B, 238C, *codant* 238J; subjunct. imperf. 1 sg. *kyvodwnn* 236B, *kyvodwn* 228C, *kyfodwn* 228D, *kodwn* 230D; 2 sg. *kyvotut* 253B, *kyvodyd* 242C, *codit* 242J.

kyfran (*cyfran*) m. and f. portion, share 16CD.

cyfrwyddonau, see *cyfaredd.*

kyhwrdd, see *cyffwrdd, cwrdd.*

kyhyt, see *hir*

cylch (*cylch*) m. circle, turn in *ar gylch* in turns, by rotation 223B, 215CD; *yn i kylch* about them 241B, *yn y kylch* 232C; see *GMW* § 245(c).

kyll, see *kolli.*

kymaint, kymeint, see *mawr.*

kymer, kymer-ais, -o, -yd, cymmer, see *kymryd.*

kymhessur (*cymesur*) adj. commensurate, of equal size 111B, **kymesur** 110C, **kymhesyr** 110D.
cymorth vn. help, assist; pret. 3 sg. *kymhorthes* 192B.
kymryd (*cymryd*) vn. take, seize 71B, 36D, **kymeryd** 36C; indic. pres. 3 sg. *kymer* 174B, 146CD, *cymmer* 191J; pret. 1 sg. *kymerais* 55B, 58CD; subjunct. pres. 3 sg. *kymero* 59CD.
kymwys (*cymwys*) adj. proper, straight, direct 160CD.
cymysgu vn. mix, mingle; subjunct. pres. 3 sg. *kymysgo* 23D.
kymyssgedic (*cymysgedic*) adj. mixed, mingled 23B, **kymysgedig** 24CD.
kyn 1. (*cyn*) prep. before 132CD; conj. before 112BCD; see *GMW* § 264.
2. (*cyn*) precedes equat. of adj. 46B, 43A, 69CD, **cyn** 175J, **kynn** 82B; see *gyn* and *GMW* § 43.
kynavon, kynawon, see *kenav*.
kyndr6c, see *drwc*.
kyndrychol (*cyndrych(i)ol*, *cynddrych(i)ol*) adj. present, in one's sight or presence 7B.
kynesed, see *agos*.
kynghori (*cynghori*) vn. counsel, advise 46A.
kyngor (*cyngor*) m. counsel, advice 228B.
kynnal (*cynnal*) vn. hold, maintain, keep, sustain 40A.
kynnull (*cynnull*) vn. collect, gather 41A.
kynt (*cynt*) adv. earlier, formerly, before 114BC.
kyntaf (*cyntaf*) adj. first 41B, 1A, 44CD, **kynta** 154B, 99D.
cyrchu vn. approach, make for, attack; indic. pres. 3 sg. *kyrch* 92B, 94CD; 3 pl. *kyrchant* 36A; pret. 2 sg. *kyrchaisst* 89B, *kyrchaist* 91C, *kyrchaisti* (agglutinated) 91D; subjunct. pres. 3 sg. *kyrcho* 138C.
kyssgot (*cysgod*) m. reflection, likeness, shadow 196B.
kyssgu (*cysgu*) vn. sleep 219B, **kyssgv** 183B, **kysgv** 212C, **kysgi** 179C, **kysgy** 216C, 214D, **cysgu** 179J; indic. pres. 3 sg. *kwssc* 183B, *kwsg* 178C, *kwsc* 207D; 3 pl. *kysscant* 221B, *kysgant* 213D; pret. 1 sg. *kyssgais* 215B; subjunct. pres. 3 pl. *kysgont* 213C; imperf. 3 sg. *kyssgai* 225B.
kystal, see *da*.
kyvadnabod (*cyfadnabod*) m. recognition, acquaintance 155B, **kyvydnabod** 99B.
kyvarddonav, see *cyfaredd*.
kyvle (*cyfle*) m. chance, opportunity 3B, **kyfle** 2CD.
kyvlwr (*cyflwr*) m. condition, state, opportunity 15B, **kyflwr** 14CD.
kyvrw (*cyfryw*) pronom. such 251B, **kyfryw** 240C, **cyfryw** 240J; see *GMW* § 100(b).
kyvrwys (*cyfrwys*) adj. cunning, wily, crafty 210B.
kyw (*cyw*) m. chick 249B, 239C; pl. *kwan* 133C, *kowion* 133D.
kywddolion, see *cywyddol*.

kywilydd (*cywilydd*) m. shame, disgrace 94B.

cywilyddio vn. shame, be ashamed; indic. pres. 3 sg. *kywilyddi[a]* 150B, *kwilyddia* 148CD.

kywir (*cywir*) adj. correct, true 8C, **kowir** 8D; equat. *kywiret* 43A.

kywrdd, see *cyffwrdd*, *cwrdd*.

kywreint (*cywrain*, *cywraint*) adj. skilful, wise, cunning 107B, **kywraint** 105C, **kowraint** 107D, **cywraint** 205J, **kowrain** 105D.

cywyddol m. singer, poet; pl. *kywddolion* 59B, *kywydolyon* 9A.

kywyddoliaeth (*cywyddoliaeth*) m. and f. poetry, song, music 180B.

da (*da*) m. wealth, goods, goodness 21A; adj. good 253B, 50A, 174CJ; equat. *kystal* 29A; comp. *gwell* 137B, 135CD; superl. *gorav* 59B, 209CD, *gore* 216B, *goreu* 9A, 243J; see *GMW* § 42.

daear (*daear*) f. earth 35C, **daiar** 35D.

daeth, see *dyvod*.

dallv (*dallu*) vn. blind, deceive 104C, **dally** 104D; indic. pres. 3 sg. *dalla* 105CD; pret. 2 sg. *dallais[st]* 104B; subjunct imperf. 3 sg. *dallai* 104B.

daly (*dal*, *dala*) vn. capture, seize, take 118B, **dala** 117CD, **dal** 200J; indic. pres. 3 sg. *deily* (see *GMW* § 129) 74B, *dala* 207C, *deila* 207D, *dela* 208D; 3 pl. *daliant* 213B; impers. *delir* 115CD; pret. 2 sg. *delyaisst* 103B, *deliaisst* 121B, *dileisst* 200B, *delaist* 119C, *delaisti* (agglutinated) 119D, *deliaist* 198J; 3 sg. *delis* 213B, *daloedd* 208C; impers. *delid* 203B, *delit* 215B; subjunct. imperf. 3 sg. *daliai* 144B.

damchwain, damwain vn. happen, occur; indic. pres. 3 sg. *damweinia* 73B, 79D, *danweinia* (scribal error) 217D, *damchwaina* 73C; subjunct. pres. 3 sg. *damch[w]aino* 217C.

dan (*dan*) (len.) prep. under 73B, 74CD; see *GMW* § 237.

danfon (*danfon*) vn. send 1C; indic. pres. 1 sg. *danfonaf* 5CD.

dangos (*dangos*) vn. show 7B, 53C, 14D; indic. pres. 1 sg. *dangossaf* 17B, *dangosaf* 16CD; impers. *dangossir* 10B, *dangosir* 9CD.

dant m. tooth; pl. *dannedd* 75C, 252J, *danedd* 75D.

daresstwng (*darostwng*) vn. submit, bend or bow down 209B, *darostwng* 121CD.

darllain (*darllen*) vn. read 62B, 63CD, **darllein** 12A; indic. pres. impers. *darllenir* 10CD; subjunct. pres. impers. *darlle[e]r* 12B; see *GMW* § 179.

darlleawdr, darlleodr m. reader; pl. *darlleodronn* 63B, *darlleodron* 13A, *darlleawdwyr* 64C.

darllenydd m. reader; pl. *darllenyddion* 64D.

darvod (*darfod*) vn. 'past' aux. (see *GMW* § 154) 101B, **darfod** 102CD; subjunct. pres. 3 sg. *darffo* 245B.

dav (*dau*) num. m. two 14B, 5CD, **dev** 5B, **deu** 39A, **day** 48D, **dau** 183J; f. **dwy** 110B, 172CD.

dauthym, daw, da6, see *dyvod*.

deall (*deall*) vn. understand 62BC, 12A, **dyall** 62D; indic. pres. impers. *de[e]llir* 11B, *deallir* 10C, *dyellir* 10D.
dechrav (*dechrau*) m. beginning 87CD.
dechrauad (*dechreuad*) m. beginning 141C, **dechreyad** 141D.
dechreu (*dechrau*) vn. begin 35A.
dechreyad, see *dechrauad.*
de[e]llir, see *deall.*
deffroai, see *dyffroi.*
deffygio (*diffygio*) vn. fail, grow weary, weaken 250C, **diffygio** 250J; subjunct. pres. 3 sg. *diffykio* 262B.
deil-a, -y, see *daly.*
del, see *dyvod.*
del-a, -aist, -iais(s)t, -id, -ir, -is, -it, -yaisst, see *daly.*
deleut, dely-ir, -swn, -syd, -wn, -yd, see *dylyu.*
devthum, deythym, see *dyvod.*
di (*di*) aux. pron. 2 sg. 26B, 21A, 3C, 38D; see *ti.*
dial (*dial*) vn. avenge 83B.
dianc vn. escape; indic. pres. 3 sg. *diangk* 264B, *diank* 255C, *dianc* 255J; pret. 2 sg. *diengaist* 257CJ.
diav 1. see *dydd.*
2. (*diau*) adj. doubtless, certain 37B, 40C, **die** 40D.
dia6t, see *diod.*
dic (*dig*) m. anger, wrath 75D.
dichon, -i vn. be able, avail, enable; indic. pres. 3 sg. *dichon* 76B, *dicha6n* 55A, *dychon* 77C, *digochon* 77D.
didan6ch (*diddanwch*) m. pleasure, entertainment 22A.
diddrwg (*diddrwg*) adj. unharmed, uninjured 149C, **diddrwc** 149D; see *drwc.*
die, see *diav* 2.
diengaist, see *dianc.*
difa vn. destroy, kill, consume, devour; pret. 2 sg. *diveeisst* 190B, *diveaisst* 191B.
diffykio, diffygio, see *deffygio.*
difwyno vn. spoil, disfigure, destroy; pret. 2 sg. *divwynaist* 196C.
digerfa f. tigress 188C; see *dygerdav*, *teiger.*
digochon, see *dichon.*
digovaint (*digofaint*) m. anger 75C, *digofaint* 193J.
digryvwch (*digrifwch*) m. pleasure, joy, delight 191C, **digrifwch** 191J.
dileisst, see *daly.*
dilladoc (*dilladog*) adj. clothed, attired 117B, 94D, **dillatog** 94C.
dilledyn m. garment; pl. *dillad* 91B.
dim (*dim*) m. thing, something, anything 116B, 32A, 27CD; *ddwedyd tim* to say anything 103D; *dim o* with positive meaning (see *GMW* § 117) 27B; with neg. meaning (in conjunction with neg. part.) 102B, 48A; *mo'i* (< *dim o+i*, gen. pron. 3 sg. f.) 77D; 3 sg. m. *mono* 251J.

diod (*diod*) f. drink 57B, 59CD, **dia6t** 7A.

diogan (*diogan*) adj. irreproachable 15B, 13C.

diossc (*diosg*) vn. take off (clothing or footwear) 112B, **diosg** 113C, **diosc** 113D.

dirgel (*dirgel*) adj. secret, hidden 72CD.

dissgyn (*disgyn*) vn. fall, befall, happen 224B, **disgin** 216D; indic. pres. 3 sg. *disgin* 73D.

disstrywiaw (distrywio) vn. destroy 124B.

dithav (*dithau*) aux. conjunct. pron. 2 sg. 93B, 54C, **dithau** 184J, **dithe** 95D; see *tithav* and *GMW* §§ 54(c), 62(b).

diwrnod (*diwrnod*) m. day 224D.

dlys-wn, -yd, see *dylyu*.

dodi vn. put, place; pret. 3 sg. *dotes* 214B.

dolur (*dolur*) m. pain, wound, hurt, disease 4C, 240J, **dolyr** 240C, 4D; pl. *dolyriau* 234D.

dringo (*dringo*) vn. climb 113D; **tringad** 113C.

dros (*dros*) (len.) prep. over 193J; 3 sg. f. *drosti* 85CD; see *GMW* § 239.

drwc (*drwg*) m. harm 152B; see *diddrwg*; adj. bad, evil 112B, **drwg** 245C; equat. *kyndr6c* 54A; superl. *gwaethaf* 60B, *g6aethaf* 10A; see *GMW* § 42.

drwy (*drwy*) (len.) prep. through, by 9B, 8C, 56D, **dr6y** 3A; *drwy/trwy dwyll* through/by deceit 187B, 183CJ; *drwy/trwy gariat/gariad* through/by love 230B, 227CD; *drwy gelvyddyd* through/by skill 107B; see *trwy* and *GMW* § 240.

drych (*drych*) m. mirror 194B, 189CJ.

Duw (*Duw*) m. God 128B, 145C, **Dyw** 145D.

dwc, dwg, dwgant, see *dwyn*.

dwed-af, -ais, -vd, -yd, see *dywedud*.

dwy, see *dav*.

dwyfron (*dwyfron*) f. breast, chest, bosom 236CJ.

dwylo, see *llaw*.

dwyn vn. bring, bear; indic. pres. 3 sg. *dw[c]* 129B, *dwg* 126C; *ef a . . . dwc rrvthr (rythr D) i* he rushes, makes a rush at 150B, 147D, *ef a . . . dwg rythyr i* 147C; 3 pl. *dwgant* 126D; subjunct. pres. impers. *dyker* 161B, 159CD.

dwys adj. serious, solemn, earnest; equat. *dwyssed* 46B.

dy (*dy*) (len.) gen. pron. 2 sg. thy 95B, 50A, 87CD; see *GMW* § 56(a).

dyall, dyellir, see *deall*.

dyker, see *dwyn*.

dychon, see *dichon, -i*.

dydd (*dydd*) m. day 21B, 21CD; **diav** pl. following numerals 233B, 224C; see *GMW* § 51(b).

dyffroi (*deffroi*) vn. awaken 218D; indic. pres. 3 sg. *dyffro* 218C; subjunct. imperf. 3 sg. *deffroai* 225B.

dygant, see *dwyn*.

dygerdav f. tigress 194B; see *digerfa*, *teiger*.

dylyu vn. to be entitled to, to be obliged to; indic. pres. 1 sg. *dyleaf* 39B, *dylyaf* 2A; impers. *dyleir* 137B, *dylyir* 168B, *delyir* 166C, *dylir* 166D; plup. 1 sg. *dylasswn* 219B, *dylasswnn* 226B, *dylyswn* 40C, *delyswn* 211C, *dlyswn* 211D; 2 sg. *delysyd* 134C, *dlysyd* 134D; impers. *dylassid* 38B; subjunct. pres. 3 sg. *dylyo* 48A; imperf. 1 sg. *dylewn* 51B, *delywn* 55C, *dylwn* 55D; 2 sg. *dylevt* 122B, *dylavtithav* (agglutinated) 133B, *deleut* 134B, *dylut* 136B, *delyyd* 121C, *dylyti* (agglutinated) 121D; see *GMW* § 165.

dyn (*dyn*) m. man 30B, 93C, 94D; pl. *dynyon* 37A.

dyr-o, -y, -ydd, see *rroi*.

dyrys (*dyrys*) adj. wild, uncultivated 73CD.

dyvod (*dyfod*) vn. come 181B, 6C, **dyfod** 6D; indic. pres. 3 sg. *daw* 106B, 107CD, *da6* 38A; pret. 1 sg. *devthum* 93B, *dauthym* 96C, *deythym* 156D, *deythyn* (scribal error) 96D; 3 sg. *daeth* 115B; subjunct. pres. 3 sg. *del* 72BC, 213D; see *GMW* § 143.

Dyw, see *Duw*.

dywedud (*dywedyd*) vn. tell, say 35B, **dywedut** 250B, 23A, **dwedvd** 37C, **dwedyd** 37D, **dywedyd** 239J; indic. pres. 1 sg. *dywedaf* 39B, *dwedaf* 42CD; pret. 1 sg. *dywedais* 164B, *dwedais* 164CD; 3 sg. *dywa6t* 55A; subjunct. imperf. 3 pl. *dywedynt* 25A; m. speech, utterance 42B.

e, see *ei*.

'e inf. gen. pron. 3 sg. m. 7A; 3 pl. 38A; see *'i*, *'u*, and Introduction, pp. xxxiii–iv.

ederyn (*aderyn*) m. bird 160B, 29A, **aderyn** 158C, 174J, **yderyn** 159D; pl. *adar* 18B, 29A, 17CD; *adar yr up* hoopoes 34A.

edivar (*edifar*) adj. sorry, repentant 246B, **etivar** 235C, **edifar** 235J.

edn (*edn*) m. bird 160B.

edrych (*edrych*) vn. look 146B, 144CD; indic. pres. 2 sg. *edrychi* 195J; 3 sg. *edrych* 161B, 159C, *erych* (scribal error) 159D; pret. 1 sg. *edrychais* 58B, *edrycheis* 8A.

edrychiad (*edrychiad*) m. sight 144B, 141CD.

edwyn, see *adnabod*.

ef (*ef*) indep. pron. 3 sg. m. 74B, 10CD; aux. 21B, 20CD; see *GMW* §§ 54(a), 62(a).

ef a (*ef a*) (len.) affirm. part. 43B, 37A, 113CD; see E. P. Hamp, *BBCS* xxix (1980–2) 83–4 and *GMW* § 191.

efe (*efe*) aux. redup. pron. 3 sg. m. 205 J.

eglur (*eglur*) adj. clear, plain 9B.

egori (*egori*) vn. open 252B, 241J; indic. pres. 3 sg. *egyr* 246B, 236C, *egur* 236J; subjunct. imperf. 2 sg. *agoryd* 241C.

ehedec (*ehedeg*) vn. fly 43A; indic. pres. 3 sg. *eheta* 241B, *heda* 232C, *hetta* 232D.

ei 1. (*ei*) (len.) gen. pron. 3 sg. m. his 179J; (asp.) f. her 189J; see *i* 5, *y* 5, and *GMW* § 56(a).
2. (*eu*) gen. pron. 3 pl. their 177J; see *ev*, *i* 6, and *GMW* § 56(a).

ein (*ein*) gen. pron. 1 pl.; *ein Dau* both of us 183J; see *yn* 5.

eissyoes, see *eussus*.

eistedd vn. sit; indic. pres. 3 sg. *eisstedd* 108B, *eistedd* 108C, *eiste* 108D.

eistedua (*eisteddfa*) f. seat, chair, abode 55A.

eithr see *aithr*.

el, see *myned*.

emennydd (*ymennydd*) m. brain 142B, **amenydd** 156B, **amhennydd** 139C, **ymhennydd** 154C, **imenydd** 139D, **ymenydd** 153D.

enivail, see *anivail*.

eniwet, see *aniwed*.

ennyd (*ennyd*) m. and f. short space of time 129C, **enyd** 129D.

enwedic (*enwedig*) adj. especial particular 157B, **vnwedig** 155C, **vnwedic** 155D.

eos (*eos*) m. (f. in ModW) nightingale 54B, 5A, 57CD.

epopus m. hoopoe 34A; from Latin *epops*, *-opis* hoopoe.

er (*er*) prep. although, despite notwithstanding 121B, 176CJ, **yr** 51A; **er** in order to 199B, 194C; 2 sg. *yrot* for thy sake 49A; *er mwyn* prep. for the sake of 249C, 194J (see *GMW* § 246); *er pan* (len.) conj. since 164B, 163CD (see *GMW* § 273); *ers* prep. since 165B (see *GMW* § 147 (e)).

eraill, ereill, see *arall*.

esgus (*esgus*) m. and f. excuse, pretence 85C, **esgys** 85D.

essgid (*esgid*) f. shoe 110B; pl. *essgidiav* 108B, *ysgidiav* 109C, 110D, *ysgidie* 109D.

essyll, see *asgell*.

etto (*eto*) adv. again 68B, 18A; see *GMW* § 247(d).

ev (*eu*) gen. pron. 3 pl. their 59B, **eu** 9A, 236J; see *ei* 2, *i* 6.

evo (*efo*) indep. redup. pron. 3 sg. m. 41B; see *GMW* §§ 54–5.

eussus (*eisoes*) adv. nevertheless, however 39B, **eissyoes** 28A.

euthvm, evthum, see *myned*.

ewyllys (*ewyllys*) m. (also f. in ModW) will 253B, **wyllys** 242C, **'wllys** 242J.

exampl (*ecsampl*) m. example 55B, **exemplar** 5A, **axawmpl** 58D, **axiampal** 115D, **axamal** (scribal error for **axampal**) 119D, **sampl** f. 58C.

fe, see *fo*.

fel i, see *val*.

ffest (*ffest*) adj. fast, firm 75C.

ffo (*ffoi*) vn. flee 261B, 249C, **ffoi** 249J; indic. pres. 3 sg. *ffy* 91B, 94C, *ffu* 253J.

ffol (*ffôl*) adj. foolish 24A.

ffordd (*ffordd*) f. way, road, path, manner 121B, 139CD.
ffu, ffy, see *ffo.*
ffynyd (*ffunud*) m. way, fashion, manner 92CD.
ffyrf (*ffurf*) m. and f. form, manner 53B, 56CD, **ffuryf** 3A.
fo (*fo*) (len.) affirm. part. 111D; **fe** 180J.

gadel (*gadael*) vn. leave, let, allow 77B, 46A, **gadael** 78C; indic. pres. 3 sg. *gedy* 110BC, *gedu* 252J, *gad* 114C, *gaid* 114D; see *GMW* § 166.
gair (*gair*) m. word 265B, 257CJ; pl. *geiriav* 123B, *gairav* 121C, *geiri* (scribal error) 121D.
gairbronn (gerbron) prep. before, in front of, in the presence of 161B, **geyrbron** 159C, **garbron** 159D; see *GMW* § 209(a).
galar (*galar*) m. grief, sorrow, lament 13A.
gallel (*gallael*) vn. permit, be able 22A; indic. pres. 1 sg. *gallaf* 6B; 2 sg. *gelly* 257B; 3 sg. *gall* 114B, 81D, *geill* 202J; impers. *gellir* 97B, 99CD; pret. 1 sg. *gelleis* 49B, *gellais* 52C, *gelles* 52D; subjunct. pres. 1 sg. *gallwyf* 36B, 38CD; 3 sg. *gallo* 62B, 11A, 33CD; imperf. 2 sg. *gallut* 23A; 3 sg. *gallai* 151B, 149CD.
galw (*galw*) vn. call 230B, 222CD; indic. pres. impers. *gelwir* 90B, 29A, heading C, 93D.
gan (*gan*) (len.) prep. with, by 172B; with vn. to express simultaneous action with that of the main vb 192CJ; 1 sg. *gennyf* 2BC, *genyf* 2D; 2 sg. *gennyt* 16B, 27A, 245J, *gennyd* 67B, 15C, *genyd* 2B, 245C, 15D; 3 sg. m. *gantho* 246B, *ganto* 235C, *ganddo* 235J; 3 sg. f. *genthi* 77B, *genti* 79CD; 2 pl. *gennych* 2CD, *genychi* (agglutinated) 67D; 3 pl. *ganthunt* 27A; see *y gan* and *GMW* §§ 63(c), 208.
garan f. crane; pl. *garanod* 220B, 212CD, *garanot* 221B.
garbron, see *gairbronn.*
garw (*garw*) adj. rough 22B, 29CD.
ged-u, -y, see *gadel.*
gell-ais, -eis, -es, -ir, see *gallel.*
gelwir, see *galw.*
geni vn. be born; indic. pres. impers. *genir* 232B, 223CD; see *GMW* § 167.
gesyd, see *gossot.*
geyrbron, see *gairbronn.*
glan (*glân*) adj. pure, virtuous 208B, 202C, **glân** 202J.
glux m. name of serpent 90B, **glox** 93C, **glwx** 93D.
gobaith (*gobaith*) m. and f. hope 24B, 25CD.
goferbyn a, see *gyverbyn a.*
goll6ng (*gollwng*) vn. release, drop, let fall 42A; indic. pres. 3 sg. *gollwng* 237J; *gollwng . . . yn angof* (*dros gof* J) forget 192CJ.
golwg (*golwg*) m. and f. sight, look, gaze, glance 161C, **golwc** 161D.
gorav, gore, goreu, see *da.*
gormodd (*gormod*) pronom. excessive 33B.
gorvod (*gorfod*) vn. win, conquer, overcome 88B.

gorwedd vn. lie; indic. pres. 3 sg. *gorwed* 39A.
gossot (*gosod*) vn. put, place 24A; indic. pres. 3 sg. *gosod* 205C, *gesyd* 205J.
g[o]vec (*gofeg*) f. mind, sense, thought, intent, speech 17B.
govid (*gofid*) m. pain, affliction, distress 4B.
gras (*gras*) m. and f. grace, favour, goodwill 15B, 13CD.
grym (*grym*) m. strength, force, power 41B, 44CD.
gwae (*gwae*) m. and f. woe, in the nominal construction *gwae vi* (*fi D*) woe is me 52B, 55CD.
gwaet (*gwaed*) m. blood 247B, **gwaed** 237CJ.
gwaethaf, g6aethaf, see *drwc*.
gwan adj. weak; equat. *gwannet* 54A.
gwarandaw (*gwrando*) vn. listen 16B, **gwrando** 15CD.
gwas (*gwas*) m. boy, lad, servant, vassal 45A.
gwasstatvod (*gwastadfod*) vn. be permanent 6B.
gwddf (*gwddf*) m. and f. neck 69B.
gwdost, see *gwybod*.
gweddiaw (*gweddïo*) vn. pray 35B, **gweddio** 37CD.
gwedy (*gwedi*, *wedi*) perfective part. coalesced with gen. pron. 3 sg. m. 44B, 47C, **gwedi** 47D, **wedi** 102D; with perfective part. *r*(*y*), *wedyr* 122B; conj. after *a* and *a chwedy* 133C, *a chwedi* 168D; see *GMW* §§ 121, 186, 217.
gweith (*gwaith*) m. work 14A, **gueith** heading D.
gwelet (*gweled*) vn. see 196B, **gweled** 191CJ; indic. pres. 1 sg. *gwelaf* 58B, 8A, 119D; 3 sg. *gwyl* 40B, 44CD; impers. *gwelir* 172B, 50A, 162CD; imperf. 2 sg. *gwelut* 1A; subjunct. pres. 2 sg. *gwelych* 7B; 3 sg. *gwelo* 91B, 93CD; 3 pl. *gwelont* 35A.
gwell, see *da*.
gwilio (*gwylio*) vn. watch, guard 223B, **gwiliat** 191B, **gwilad** 215C, **gwilied** 215D; indic. pres. 3 sg. *gwilia* 222B, 214D, *gwila* 214C.
gwir (*gwir*) adj. true 47A, 128CD; *yn lle gwir* in truth, verily 21A, 130B.
gwisg (*gwisg*) m. and f. dress, clothing, apparel 118C.
gwissgedic (*gwisgedig*) adj. dressed, clothed, apparelled 129B, **gwisg-edig** 127C, **gwisgedic** 127D.
gwissgo (*gwisgo*) vn. dress 101B, **gwyssgo** 122B; indic. pres. 3 sg. *gwissc* 109B, *gwisg* 112CD, *gwisc* 109D.
gwiw (*gwiw*) adj. fitting, worthy 16B, 15CD.
gwlith (*gwlith*) m. dew 132B, 129CD.
gwn(n), see *gwybod*.
gwneuthur (*gwneuthur*) vn. do, make 38B, 48A, **gwnevthur** 106B, **gwnaethur** 40C, **gwneythyr** 40D; indic. pres. 3 sg. *gwna* 23B, 7A, 49CD, *g6na* 34A, *gna* 92C; 3 pl. *gwnant* 178B; impers. *gwnavr* 244B, *gwnair* 260B, 249C, *gwneir* 249J; imperf. 3 sg. *gwnai* 114CD; pret. 1 sg. *gwneuthvm* 52B, *gwneuthum* 2A, *gwnaethym* 56C, *gwneythym* 56D; 2 sg. *gwnaethosst* 92B, *gwnaethost* 95C, 256J, *gwneythost* 95D;

3 sg. *gwnaeth* 85BCD; impers. *gwnaethpwyd* 19B, *gwnaethbwyd* 18C, *gwneythbwyd* 18D; subjunct. pres. 1 sg. *g6nel6yf* 48A; imperf. 2 sg. *gwnelut* 238B, 23A, *gwnelyd* 229CD; see *GMW* §§ 141, 180(b)(3).

gwr (*gŵr*) m. man 41B, 43CD, **g6r** 48A; pl. *gwyr* 176B, 172C.

gwraic (*gwraig*) f. woman 45B, 47D, **gwreic** 44B, **g6reic** 17A, **gwraig** 47C, 173J.

gwregys (*gwregys*) m. girdle, belt 109B.

g6res (*gwres*) m. heat 40A.

gwrthgroch (*gwrthgroch*) adj. gruff, surly, rough, discourteous 135B.

gwryssgenn (*gwrysgen*) f. branch, stick, stalk 73B, **gwrysgen** 74CD.

gwybod (*gwybod*) vn. know 121B, 120CD; indic. pres. 1 sg. *gwnn* 172B, 169C, *gwn* 169D; 2 sg. *gwdost* 49A; 3 sg. *gwyr* 128B, 251CJ; pret. 2 sg. *gwybuosst* 95B, *gwybyost* 90CD, *gwybuost* 256J; subjunct. pres. 3 sg. *gwypo* 34B, 33CD, *gwybyddo* 178J; imperf. 1 sg. *gwypwn* 50B; imper. 2 sg. *gwybydd* 130B, *g6ybyd* 21A; see *GMW* § 157.

gwyl, see *gwelet*.

gwyry (*gwyry(f)*) adj. virgin 208B, 202C, **gwyryf** 202J.

gyda (*gyda*) (asp.) prep. in company with 179B, 175CJ, **gida** 179B; see *GMW* § 210.

gylfin m. beak, bill; pl. *gyluineu* 38A.

gyn precedes equat. of adj. 84B, 53A, **gynn** 256B, 19A; see *kyn* 2.

gyrru vn. drive; pret. 2 sg. *gyrraist* 196J.

gyverbyn a (*gyferbyn â*) prep. (asp.) opposite 108BC, **goferbyn a** 108D.

haeddu vn. deserve, merit; pret. 1 sg. *heydeis* 51A.

hagr adj. ugly; superl. *hakraf* 31BC, *hagra* 31D.

haibo (*heibio*) adv. past 143C, **heibio** 149D, **heibiaw** 143D, **heibi** (scribal error) 161D.

haint (*haint*) m. and f. malady, sickness 237B, 243CJ.

hanner (*hanner*) m. half 26B, 21C, 172J, **haner** 21BD.

hauach (*haeach*) adv. almost, very nearly, well nigh 92C; see *GMW* § 247 (m).

hawdd (*hawdd*) adj. easy 62BD; comp. *haws* 78B, 79CD, *ha6s* 26A; see *GMW* § 42.

heb (*heb*) (len.) prep. without 49B, 24CD; see *llaw* and *GMW* § 218.

hebrgovi ((*h*)*ebrgofi*) vn. forget 56B, *hebyrgofi* 7A; indic. pres. 3 sg. *abergova* 198B.

heda, see *ehedec*.

heddiw (*heddiw*) adv. today 165B.

heib-i, -iaw, -io, see *haibo*.

heliwr (*heliwr*) m. hunter, huntsman 106B, 105D, **helywr** 104B, **helwr** 105C; pl. *helwyr* 213B, 254C.

helpu vn. help; subjunct. pres. 3 sg. *helpo* 221D.

helw (*elw*) m. profit, gain, possession, protection in *ar vy helw* in my possession 216B, 209CD.

hely (*hela*) vn. hunt, chase, pursue 205B, **hela** 205CJ; indic. pres. impers. *helir* 251J; imperf. impers. *helit* 262B, *helid* 251C.

hen (*hen*) adj. old 35A.

heneint (*henaint*) m. old age 33A.

henny, see *hwnnw*.

herwyd (*oherwydd*) prep. according to, because of 1A, **her6yd** 20A; **oherwydd** 51B, 54C, 17D; see *GMW* §§ 219, 232(g), 268.

hetta, see *ehedec*.

hevyd (*hefyd*) adv. also 185B, 14C, **heuyt** 16A, **hefyd** 14D; see *GMW* § 247(d).

heydeis, see *haeddu*.

hi (*hi*) indep. pron. 3 sg. f. 11B, 82C, 84D; aux. 46B, 49CD; see *GMW* §§ 54(a), 62(a).

hihi (*hyhi*) indep. redup. pron. 3 sg. f. 79B; see *GMW* § 54(b).

hir (*hir*) adj. long 60CD; equat. *kyhyt* 30A; superl. *hwya* 262B; see *GMW* § 42.

hithav (*hithau*) indep. conjunct. pron. 3 sg. f. 48B, 51C, **hithe** 51D; aux. hithav 186B, 182C, **hithau** 182J; see *GMW* §§ 54(c), 62(b).

hoeth, see *noeth*.

hoff (*hoff*) adj. favourite, dear, agreeable, praiseworthy 256B, **hôff** 244J; equat. *hoffet* 49A; for the meaning 'praiseworthy', see I. Williams, *BBCS* ii (1923–6) 39–41.

holl (*holl*) pronom. all, whole 70B, 39A, 31CD; see *GMW* § 107.

hon, honn, see *hwnn*.

honno, hono, see *hwnnw*.

hvn (*hun*) self with preceding gen. pron. 2 sg. *dy hun* 50A; 3 sg. *e hvn* 55B, *e hun* 6A, *i hvn* 58CD; *i hunan* 191J; see *GMW* § 98.

hwnn (*hwn*) dem. pron. sg. m. this 8B, 39C, 46D, **h6nn** 3A, **hwn** 39D, **yrwnn** (agglutinated with def. art.) 92D; f. **honn** 28BC, 4A, **hon** 125B, 28D; neut. and pl. **hynn** 19B, 11A, 37C, **hyn** 16D; see *GMW* §§ 91–4.

hwnnw (*hwnnw*) dem. pron. sg. m. that 43B, 32C, 88D, **hwnw** 234D; f. **honno** 155B, 153C, **hono** 106B, 139D; pl. **hynny** 4BC, 2A, 67D, **hyny** 17B, 4D, **henny** 74B, **hynne** 132D; see *GMW* §§ 91–4.

hwy (*hwy*) indep. pron. 3 pl. 232D; aux. 177C.

hwya, see *hir*.

hwynt (*hwynt*) indep. pron. 3 pl. 247B, 232C, 235J; aux. 180B, 112C, 233D; see *GMW* §§ 54(a), 62(a).

hwythav (*hwythau*) aux. conjunct. pron. 3 pl. 202B.

hyd (*hyd*) (len.) prep. until 19B, 224CD; as far as 107BCD; *hyd pan* (len.) conj. until, so that 60C; *hyd . . . y* conj. as far as, as long as 261B, *hyd i* 250J, *yr hyd i* 250C; *hyd yny* conj. until 196C; see *GMW* §§ 220, 269.

hyder (*hyder*) m. and f. boldness, courage, valour 41B, 44CD.

hydr adj. brave, courageous, strong; equat. degree *hytred* 84B.

hygar (*hygar*) adj. amiable, amicable, dear, loving 87B, 88CD.
hyn, hynn, see *hwnn*.
hynne, hynny, hyny, see *hwnnw*.
hyssbys (*hysbys*) adj. known, evident 2B, **hysbys** 2CD.

i 1. (*i*) (len.) prep. to, for 15B, 13C, 7D, **j** 25B, 6C; 1 sg. *imi* 25B, 13CD, *jmi* 257B, *i minnav* 34B, 35C, *i mine* 35D; 2 sg. *iti* 14B, 4C, 53D, *i Tî* 241J, *i Di* 239J, *i tithav* 188B; 3 sg. m. *iddo* 71B, *iddaw* 152B, 217D; 3 sg. f. *iddi* 82B, 93D; 2 pl. *i chwi* 64B, 4D, *i chwithev* 63B, *i chwithav* 63C; 3 pl. *vddunt* 129B, *udunt* 41A; see *y* 1 and *GMW* §§ 63(d), 221.
2. (*y*) affirm. part. preceding verbs 34B, 9CD, **j** 98C; **idd** 1C, 26D, **ir** 82B, 1D, **i'r** 245J; see *y* 2 and *GMW* § 190.
3. (*y*) (len.) predicative part. 166C; see *y* 3, *yn* 3, and T. Arwyn Watkins, *BBCS* xix (1960–2) 295–315.
4. (*i*) aux. pron. 1 sg. 1BD, 2A, **j** 1C; see *GMW* § 62(a).
5. (*ei*) (len.) gen. pron. 3 sg. m. his 20BC, heading D, **j** 55B; with *hun* self *e hvn* himself 55B, *e hun* 6A; (asp.) f. her 10B, 9CD, **j** 118B; with *hun* self *e hvn* herself 83B; see *ei* 1, *y* 5, *hvn*.
6. (*eu*) gen. pron. 3 pl. their 112C, 130D; see *ei* 2, *ev*.
7. see *yn* 1.
'i inf. pron. 3 sg. m. gen. (len.) 41B, 44CD, f. 197B, 192C, 77D; accus. m. 79B, 43CD, f. 252C; 3 pl. gen. 132B, 127CD, accus. 109B, 112C, 130D; see *'e*, *'u*, Introduction, pp. xxxiii–iv, and *GMW* §§ 56, 58.
iach (*iach*) adj. healthy, well 43A.
jaith (*iaith*) f. language 11B, 9CD.
j dan (*i dan*) (len.) prep. under 109B; see *GMW* § 237.
jevangk (*ieuanc*) adj. young 208B, **jevank** 199C, **ifanc** 199J; pl. *jeueingk* 35A, *jeueigk* 38A, *ieueingk* 43A.
i gennyf, i genthi, see *y gan*.
j gyd (*i gyd*) adv. altogether, entirely, completely 77B.
ill (*ill*) gen. pron. 3 pl. before numerals *ill dev* both 45B, *yll dav* 48C, *yll day* 48D; see *GMW* § 107(c).
i mae, j mae, i maent, i mav, see *bod*.
i maes, see *maes*.
imenydd, see *emennydd*.
imgydnabodath (*ymgydnabodaeth*) f. acquaintance 96D.
imgyrhayddyd, see *ymgyrheuddud*.
imweled, see *ymwelet*.
in, see *yn* 2.
inikorn, see *vnigkorn*.
innav (*innau*) aux. conjunct. pron. 1 sg. 58B, **jnnav** 60B, 61C, **jnne[v]** 219B, **inneu** 13A, 183J, **inav** 61D, **ine** 162D; see *GMW* § 62(b).
iro vn. smear, anoint; indic. pres. 3 sg. *ir* 247B, *ira* 237C, *îrâ* 237J.

lladd (*lladd*) vn. kill 89B, 92CD; indic. pres. 3 sg. *lladd* 245B, 149CD; pret. 2 sg. *lleddaisst* 250B, *lleddaist* 186CJ.

lladratta, see *lletrata.*

llafasu vn. dare, venture; indic. pres. 1 sg. *llavassaf* 188B, *llevasaf* 184C; 3 sg. *llevys* 207B; pret. 1 sg. *llevessais* 100B, *llevesais* 101C, *llyfesais* 101D.

llais (*llais*) m. voice, sound 31CD.

llall (*llall*) pronom. (the) other (of two) 176B, 172CJ; pl. *llaill* 176B, 173C, *lleill* 214D; see *naill* and *GMW* §§ 95–6.

llau, see *lleuen.*

llavvr (*llafur*) m. labour, toil, work 65B, **llauur** 15A, **llavur** 66C.

llaw (*llaw*) f. hand in *heb i law* past him 146B, 144C; *rag* (*rrac D*) *llaw* adv. after this, later 18CD; pl. *dwylo* 109D; see *GMW* §§ 218, 235.

llawen (*llawen*) adj. cheerful, glad 124B, 122CD; comp. *llawenach* 125B.

llawenhav (*llawenhau*) vn. amuse, rejoice, gladden 246C.

llawenydd (*llawenydd*) m. joy, gladness 134C, 191J, **llywenydd** 134D.

llawer (*llawer*) pronom. many, much 68B, 18A, 213C, 68D.

llawn (*llawn*) adj. full 129C.

llawr m. floor, ground in *i'r llawr* adv. to the ground, down 111CD.

lle (*lle*) m. place 6B, 37A, 72CD; conj. where 6CD; with neg. *lle ni* 171B, *lle ny* 36A; in ModW, it is followed by *na*(*d*), see *EGC* §§ 62, 234 (ii); see *pa* 1, *yn lle.*

lleddaisst, lleddaist, see *lladd.*

lledradaidd (*lledradaidd*) adj. stealthy 82CD.

llef (*llef*) f. cry, voice 23B, 2A, 30CD.

lles (*lles*) m. benefit, advantage, good in *ar lês* to one's advantage, for one's benefit 243J.

lletrata (*lladrata*) vn. rob, steal 195B, **lledrata** 189C, **lladratta** 189J.

llety (*llety*) m. lodging, abode 79B, 80C, **lletty** 80J.

lleuen f. louse; pl. *llau* 204J.

llevesais, llevessais, llevys, see *llafasu.*

llew (*llew*) m. lion 145B, 142CD.

llid (*llid*) m. wrath 198B; *o lid* from wrath, in anger 75B.

llidioc (*llidiog*) adj. angry 195B, 95D, **llidiog** 95C, 189J.

lliw (*lliw*) m. colour 6BCD.

lloches (*lloches*) f. lair, shelter 71BCD.

llvn (*llun*) m. form, image 191C, **llun** 191J.

llyfesais, see *llafasu.*

llyfr (*llyfr*) m. book 43B, heading C, 46D.

llygad (*llygad*) m. eye 141B, 139CD; pl. *llygaid* 166B, 153C, 108D, *llygait* 165B.

llyma (*llyma*) adv. here is, heading CD.

llythr (*llythyr*) m. letter, letter of the alphabet 5BC, 10D, **llythyr** 2A, 10C, heading D.

'm inf. gen. pron. 1 sg. 65B, 13A, 4CD; accus. 7B, 162CD; see *GMW* §§ 56, 58.

mab m. son; pl. *meibion* 240B, *meibyon* 31A.

mae, see *bod*; (*mai*) conj. introducing a preposed pos. non-verbal constituent, that it is 37B, 8A, 40C, **mai** 40D, **ma'i** 192J; see *GMW* § 148(b)(3).

maen (*maen*) m. stone 224B, 216CD.

maes (*maes*) m. field 140B; *i maes* adv. out 139C; see *GMW* § 247(f).

magu vn. nurture; indic. pres. 3 pl. *magant* 133B, 41A, 130CD.

magyat (*magiad*) m. nurture 50A.

maint (*maint*) m. size in *rrac maint* because of the magnitude 234B; see *GMW* § 102.

mairw, see *marw*.

mal (*mal*) prep. as, like 170C; *mal y* conj. according as, as, in order that 61B, 11A, *mal i* 85C; *mal na* 81C; see *val* and *GMW* §§ 227, 270.

mam (*mam*) f. mother 128B, 20A, 126CD.

man (*man*) m. in *yn y man* adv. soon 111D.

marw (*marw*) adj. dead 56B, 60CD, **mar6** 6A; pl. *meirw* 232B, 223D, *mairw* 223C.

marwol (*marwol*) adj. fatal 237B.

mawr (*mawr*) adj. big, large 80B, 33CD; equat. *kymaint* 56B, 59C, *kymeint* 6A, *kimint* 59D; comp. *mwy* 36CD; superl. *mwyaf* 142B, 87C, *mwya* 140D, *mwia* 87D; see *GMW* § 42.

meddiginiaeth (*meddyginiaeth*) f. medicine 230B, **meddeginiaeth** 254B, **meddigynaeth** 260B, **meddiginaeth** 221C, **meddyginiaeth** 243J; see **meneginiaeth**.

meddwl (*meddwl*) m. mind, thought 50B, 53CD, **med6l** 24A.

medru vn. be able; indic. pres. 3 sg. *meidr* 83B, 85D, *medr* 85C; pret. 1 sg. *medrais* 85B, 86CD; plup. impers. *medressid* 38B.

megys (*megis*) prep. like, as 20B, 47A, **megis** 27B, 20CD; *megys y* conj. according as, as 159B, [*me*]*gys i* 104B, *megis y* 198J, *megis i* 38CD; *megis ir* 50D; *megys na* 117B, *megis na* 69D; *megis nad* 82D; see *GMW* §§ 228, 271.

meib-ion, -yon, see *mab*.

meidr, see *medru*.

meirw, see *marw*.

meithrin (*meithrin*) vn. nourish, cherish, foster 137B, 27A.

melys adj. sweet; equat. *melysed* 175C, *melused* 175J.

menegi (*mynegi*) vn. express, tell 4B, **manegi** 4CD.

meneginiaeth (*meneginiaeth*) f. medicine 221D; see *meddiginiaeth*.

merch (*merch*) f. girl 68D.

meu (*mau*) stressed poss. pron. 1 sg. mine 52A; see *GMW* § 57.

mewn (*mewn*) prep. in 26B, 72CD; *o vewn* prep. within 72B; see *GMW* § 225.

mi (*mi*) indep. pron. 1 sg. 4BCD, 1A; *GMW* § 54(a).

minnav (*minnau*) indep. conjunct. pron. 1 sg. 93B, 54C, **minnau** 258J, **minav** 131D, **mine** 36D, **minneu** 184J; *delyswn minnav* (a misuse of the indep. instead of the aux. pron. *innav*) 218C; see *GMW* § 54(c).

mo, mono, see *dim*.

modd (*modd*) m. way, manner, means 92B, 208C, **môdd** 258J.

mor (*mor*) adv. so 3BCD; with pos. form of the adj. to form equat. 52A, 200C, 225D, **mo'r** 200J; see *GMW* §§ 41(a)(2), 45 N 1.

morvorwyn (*môr-forwyn*) f. mermaid, siren 175B, 171CD, **môrforwyn** 179J; pl. *morforynion* 171D.

morwyn (*morwyn, morŵyn*) f. maiden, girl, virgin 204B, 179C, 199J.

mwnwgl (*mwnwgl*) m. neck 69C, **mwnwc** 69D.

mwy, mwyaf, see *mawr*.

mwyn (*mwyn*) adj. gentle, dear 96CD.

myned (*myned*) vn. go 82B, 84CD, **mynd** 195J; indic. pres. 3 sg. *a* (coalesced with rel. pron.) 110BC, *af* (scribal error for *a*) 110D; 3 pl. *ant* 41A; pret. 1 sg. *euthvm* 158B, *evthvm* 215B; 3 sg. *aeth* (coalesced with rel. pron.) 198B; plup. 3 sg. *aethoedd* 85B; subjunct. pres. 3 sg. *el* 211B, 205C, 72D; see *GMW* § 142.

mynnv (*mynnu*) vn. wish, desire 159B, **mynny** 157C, **myny** 157D; indic. pres. 1 sg. *mynnaf* 4B; 3 sg. *mynn* 33B, 45A, 32C, *myn* 32D; plup. 2 sg. *mynassut* 164B; subjunct. imperf. 1 sg. *mynn6n* 22A; 2 sg. *mynyd* 227C, *mynyti* (agglutinated) 227D; 3 sg. *mynnai* 235B, *mynnei* 28A; 3 pl. *mynnynt* 26A.

mynwes (*mynwes*) f. bosom, breast 109B.

mynych (*mynych*) adj. frequent 22BCD; comp. *mynychach* 28B.

myvi (*myfi*) indep. redup. pron. 1 sg. 51B, 95C, **myfi** 228D; see *GMW* § 54(b).

na 1. (*na*) (len., asp.) dep. neg. 6BCD, 1A; **nad** 14B, 11C, 13D; **nat** 229B, 21A; see *GMW* § 194.
2. (*na*) (asp.) conj. nor 129B, 15CD; **nac** 16B, 126D, **nag** 126C; *na*(*c*) . . . *na*(*c*) neither . . . nor 57B, 21A, 59CD, *na* . . . *nag* 201C; see *GMW* §§ 253–4.
3. (*na*) (len., asp.) neg. imper. 16A; see *GMW* § 195.
4. see *no*.

nakav (*nacáu*) vn. refuse 47B, 49CD, **nackav** 104B; pret. 2 sg. *nakeisst* 51B, *nakaist* 54C, *nakesti* (agglutinated) 54D.

naill (*naill*) pronom. (the) one, in contrast with *y llall* the other 177B, 172C, 173J; see *GMW* §§ 95–6.

namyn (*namyn*) conj. except, besides, but, only 7BD; prep. except, but 3A, 129D; see *GMW* § 255.

natur (*natur*) f. (m. in CD) nature 20BC, 1A, **nattur** 40B, **natyr** 20D; pl. *naturiav* 75B, *naturyeu* 18A, *natturiav* 68B, *natyriav* 68D, *natyrie* 68D.

naturiaeth (*naturiaeth*) f. nature 20C; pl. *naturiaethav* 68C.
ne, see *nev*.
neb (*neb*) pronom. anyone, no one 74B, 22A, 74CD; see *GMW* § 116.
neges (*neges*) f. message, errand 16A.
nerth (*nerth*) m. strength, power 45C, 55D.
nes, nesed, see *agos*.
nev (*neu*) (len.) conj. or 109B, **neu** 34A, **ne** 72CD; see *GMW* § 253(a).
newyd (*newydd*) adj. new 42A.
newyn (*newyn*) m. hunger 33BCD.
ni 1. (*ni*) aux. pron. 1 pl. 99C, 183J; see *GMW* § 62(a).
2. see *ny*.
ninnav (*ninnau*) aux. conjunct. pron. 1 pl. 186B; see *GMW* § 62(b).
ni wyr Dduw expletive, God knows not 128B; see *Duw*, *gwybod*, *ny*.
no (*na*) (asp.) conj. used after comp. of adj. 125B, 27A, 147D, **na** 136CD; **noc** 19B, 80D, **nag** 18C, **nac** 18D; see *GMW* § 46.
noeth (*noeth*) adj. naked, bare 91B, 93C, 100D, **hoeth** 123C; see J. E. Caerwyn Williams, *SC* x/xi (1975/6) 299.
nos (*nos*) f. night 21BCD.
nwyf (*nwyf*) m. energy, vigour 201B.
ny (*ni*) (len., asp.) neg. 22A, 86C, **ni** 13B, 86D; **nid** 16B, 37CD; with inf. accus. pron. 3 sg. *nis* 114BD, *nys* 48A; neg. form of copula indic. pres. 3 sg. *nyt* 49A; *nid amgen* namely 6BCD, *nyt amgen* 19A.

o 1. (*o*) (asp.) conj. if, with indic. pres. or pret. 40B, 17A, 49CD; **od** 161B, 159CD; with copula *os* 41B, 44A, 43CD; see *GMW* § 272.
2. (*o*) (len.) prep. from, of, by means of, on the part of 8B, 4A, 36C, heading D; 1 sg. *ohonaf* 51A; 2 sg. *ohonod* 121B, 120D, *ohonot* 230B, *ohonad* 120C; 3 sg. m. *ohonno* 55B, *ohona6* 5A, *ohano* 58C, *ohono* 58D; 3 sg. f. *ohoni* 112B; 3 pl. *ohonvnt* 176B, *ohonynt* 213D, *onaddvnt* 222B, *onaddynt* 172C, *onaddyn* 213C; see *kwbl*, *kyfflyprwydd*, *llid*, and *GMW* § 63(a).
o achos (*o achos*) conj. because 144D; *o achos na* 6D; prep. on account of, because of, by reason of 40B, 43C, 249J; see *GMW* §§ 232(a), 259.
oblegyd (*oblegid*) conj. because 103B, **oblegyt** 147B, **oblegid** 247J; see *GMW* § 232(c).
ochneidio vn. sigh; indic. pres. 3 sg. *ychneidia* 225D.
oddiaithr (*oddieithr*) prep. outside 78B; see *GMW* § 215.
oddi wrth (*oddi wrth*) (len.) prep. from 80CD; 1 sg. *o jwrthyf* 8B; 3 sg. m. *oddi wrtho* 163B, 94C; 3 pl. *o iwrthvnt* 181B, *oddy wrthynt* 177C, *oddi wrthynt* 177J; see *GMW* § 223(g).
oddwn, see *bod*.
oddyno (*oddi yno*) adv. from there 111CD; see *GMW* § 247(a).
odwyf, oed, oedd, oedd-wn, -yd, oes, see *bod*.

o flaen (*o flaen*) prep. before 132D; *o'r blaen* adv. formerly, before 84B, 19C, 114D.
ofn (*ofn*) m. fear 149B, 147CD; *rrac* (*rag C*) *ofn* conj. for fear, lest 224B, 216CD.
ohano, ohon-ad, -af, -a6, -i, -no, -o, -od, -ot, -vnt, -ynt, see *o* 2.
oherwydd, see *herwyd.*
o jwrthyf, o iwrthvnt, see *oddi wrth.*
oll (*oll*) adv. all, wholly 189B, 10A, 186CJ; see *GMW* § 107.
onadd-vnt, -yn, -ynt, see *o* 2.
ond (*ond*) conj. but 33B, 7C, 12D, **onid** 13B, **onyt** 22A.
oni 1. (*oni*) (asp.) conj. unless 70BD, **ony** 70C; **onyt** 23A, **onid** 245J; with inf. accus. pron. 3 sg. *onys* 76B, 78C, *onis* 78D; see *GMW* § 272.
2. (*oni*) (len.) conj. until 33D; see *yni* and *GMW* § 278.
over (*ofer*) adj. vain 65BC, **ouer** 15A, **ofer** 65D.
o vewn, see *mewn.*
Ouidinus m. the Latin poet Publius Ovidius Naso (Ovid) 55A, **Ovid** 258J, **Ovydd** heading C, **Ouydd** heading D.

pa 1. (*pa*) (len.) interr. adj. what 228B; see *GMW* § 81; *pa le* conj. where 33CD, *ple* 34B; *pa ny* conj. if . . . not 53A; see *GMW* § 274, *PKM*, 247 note, D. Simon Evans, *LlC* vi (1960–1) 117.
2. (*po*) (len. in C) part. used before superl. of adj. *pa mwyaf* (*vwyaf* C) the more 142B, 140C; see *pwy* and *EGC* §§ 52, 238.
paham (*paham*) interr. adv. why 40B, 42CD; see *GMW* § 84.
paid-af, -o, see *peidio.*
pan 1. (*pan*) (len.) conj. when 20B, 9A, 10C, 22D, **pann** 33B; see *GMW* § 273.
2. *pan yw* conj. introducing a preposed pos. non-verbal constituent, that it is 9B; see *GMW* § 87.
parabl (*parabl*) m. speech, utterance, word 6BCD; pl. *parablev* 82B, *parablav* 84C, *parable* 84D.
pawb (*pawb*) pronom. everybody 62BCD, **pa6b** 11A; see *GMW* § 106(a).
pe (*pe*) conj. (with subjunct.) if 225B, 27CD, **pei** 26A, 227C, **bai** 227D; with inf. accus. pron. 3 sg. *pes* 38B, 65C, *bes* 65D; with syllabic form of inf. accus. pron. 3 sg. *pei as* 15A; see *GMW* §§ 59, 274.
pechod (*pechod*) m. sin 173B, 169CD, **pechot** 187B.
pedwar (*pedwar*) num. m. four 157B, 155CD.
peidio (a) (*peidio*) vn. cease, stop, refrain 39B, 211D, **paido** 211C; indic. pres. 1 sg. *paidaf* 42C, *peidaf* 42D; pret. 1 sg. *peidiais* 60B, *peideis* 10A.
pelikan (*pelican*) m. pelican 239B, 229CD.
pell adj. far; equat. *pelled* 82B, 84CD.
pellach (*pellach*) adv. henceforth, hereafter 25CD; see *GMW* § 247(h).

pen (*pen*) m. head 162B, 204D, **penn** 209B, 204C; *vwch ev penn* above them 246B; pl. *pennav* in *ywch i pennav* 225C, *ywch i penav* 224D, *ywch i pene* 225D, *uwch eu pennau* 236J; see *GMW* § 242(a).
perffeith (*perffaith*) adj. perfect 12A.
peri (*peri*) vn. cause 37B, 39CD.
perigl (*perygl*) m. danger, peril 220B.
perthyn vn. belong; indic. pres. 3 sg. *perthyn* 251B, 241CJ.
peth (*peth*) m. thing 5BCD.
pib (*pib*) f. pipe 175CJ; pl. **pibav** 179B.
pigo (*pigo*) vn. prick, peck 244B; indic. pres. 3 pl. *piganhwythav* (agglutinated) 243B, *pigant* 234CJ; pret. 1 sg. *pigais* 249B.
pluen f. feather; pl. *plu* 127B, *pluf* 35A, *plyf* 125CD.
plufio, pluo vn. feather; indic. pres. 3 pl. *plufyant* 38A.
plygain (*plygain*) m. dawn, cock-crow 23BD; **pylgain** 23C.
pob (*pob*) pronom. each, every, all 10B, 8CD; see *GMW* § 106(b).
poen (*poen*) m. and f. pain 36CD.
popeth (*popeth*) pronom. everything 105B, **pob peth** 106CD.
praw, see *provi*.
prenn (*pren*) m. tree, wood 107B, 108C, **pren** 108D.
priod (*priod*) adj. proper, rightful 178B.
provi (*profi*) vn. test, prove, try 105C; indic. pres. 3 sg. *praw* 105D.
pryf (*pryf*) m. insect, vermin, animal 193B, 188CJ.
pryt na (*pryd na*) conj. when . . . not 32A; see *GMW* § 275.
pvm (*pum, pump*) num. five 201B, **pym** 196J, **pvmp** 196C, **pymp** 155D.
pwy (*pwy*) interr. pron. who 173B, 169CD; *a ffwy vwya* and the more 140D; see *GMW* §§ 79–80.
pylgain, see *plygain*.
pysgodyn m. fish; pl. *pyssgod* 177B, *pysgod* 173C.

'r, see *y* 4.
rac (*rhag*) prep. lest, because, against 3B, 8A, **rrac** 18D, **rag** 3C; 2 sg. *rragod* 86B, *ragod* 86C, *rragoti* (agglutinated) 86D; 3 sg. m. *ragddaw* 207B; see *llaw*, *maint*, *ofn*, and *GMW* §§ 63(b), 102, 235.
ragorawl (*rhagorol*) adj. excellent, splendid 122C, **rragorawl** 122D.
ran (*rhan*) f. part, share 181C, **rann** 239C, **rhan** 181J.
rei (*rhai*) pronom. ones, some 25A, **rai** 244C, **rhai** 244J; see *GMW* § 101.
rhedeg vn. run; indic. pres. 3 sg. *rred* 111B, 151D, *red* 151C.
rhydd, see *rroi*.
rinwedd (*rhinwedd*) m. and f. virtue 248C.
roddi, see *rroi*.
rodio (*rhodio*) vn. walk, stroll 72C, **rrodio** 72D.
rof, rrof, rrom, see *rrwng*.
rraid (*rhaid*) m. necessity 18B, 17D, **raid** 17C.
rroi (*rhoi*) vn. give 76B, 85D, **roi** 51A, 85C, **roddi** 77C; indic. pres.

3 sg. *dyrydd* 77B, *dyry* 206C, *rydd* 34C, *rrydd* 34D, *rhydd* 204J, *ry* 204C, 206D; imper. *dyro* 257B, 246CJ; see *GMW* § 175.

rrvthr (*rhuthr*) m. rush, attack 150B, **rythyr** 148C, **rrythr** 148D.

rrwng (*rhwng*) prep. between 44B, 216D, **rwng** 47C; 1 sg. *rrof* 97B, 100D, *rof* 100C; 1 pl. *rrom* 100B, *ryngom* 99C, *rryngomi* (agglutinated) 99D; 3 pl. *rryddynt* 45B, *ryddynt* 48C, rryngyn 48D; see *GMW* § 63(b).

rry 1. (*rhy*) adv. too 241B, 60D, **ry** 60C.
2. **rrydd,** see *rroi*.

rrychwant (*rhychwant*) m. span 216D.

rryng-omi, -yn, see *rrwng*.

rryvedd (*rhyfedd*) adj. strange 239B, **ryued** 16A, **ryvedd** 67C, **rryfedd** 67D.

rryw (*rhyw*) pronom. kind of, sort of 8B, 34D, **ryw** 8C; see *GMW* § 99.

rrywur (*rhywyr*) adv. high time 57B.

ruth[r]o (*rhuthro*) vn. rush, attack 123B.

rwystro (*rhwystro*) vn. hinder, prevent 219C, **rrwstro** 219D.

r(y) 1. (*ry*) perfective part. in *wedyr* (< *wedy*+*r*(*y*)) 122B; see *GMW* § 186.
2. **rydd,** see *rroi*.

ryddynt, ryngom, see *rrwng*.

sampl, see *exampl*.

santaiddrwydd (*santeiddrwydd*) m. holiness, saintliness 145CD.

sathyr (*sathr*) m. footprint, trampling 37A.

sef (*sef*) < *ys*+*ef* that is 46A, 78C.

serch (*serch*) m. love 100CD.

serchawgrwydd (*serchogrwydd*) m. amiability 203C, **serchogrwydd** 203J.

sercha6l (*serchol*) adj. loving 48A.

solaus m. solace 23A; borrowed from French *solas*, *soulas* pleasure, joy, solace.

ssain (*sain*) f. sound 182B, **sain** 177C.

ssantoliaeth (*santoliaeth*) f. holiness, saintliness 147B.

ssarff (*sarff*) m. serpent 90B, **sarff** 92C.

ssarrvc (*sarrug*) adj. surly 123B.

ssomi (*siomi*) vn. deceive (disappoint in ModW) 199B, **siomi** 194C.

ssylvv (*sylfu*, *syflu*) vn. move, stir 207B; see J. Lloyd-Jones, *BBCS* xi (1941–4) 123.

ssynnwyr (*synnwyr*) m. sense 156B, **synwyr** 154CD.

stat (*stad*) f. state 54A.

sy, sydd, see *bod*.

sych adj. dry; equat. *ssyched* 70B, *syched* 69CD.

synwyrys (*synhwyrus*) adj. sensitive, having senses 220C.

syrthio vn. fall; indic. pres. 3 sg. *syrthia* 217C, *syrth* 217D; subjunct. imperf. 3 sg. *ssyrthiai* 225B.

tad (*tad*) m. father 128B, 126CD, **tat** 42A.
tair, see *tri*.
tal (*tâl*) m. forehead 206B.
talken (*talcen*) m. forehead 201C, **talcen** 201J.
talu vn. pay, avail; indic. pres. 3 sg. *tal* 59B, 8A.
tav (*tau*) stressed poss. pron. 2 sg. thine 50B; see *GMW* § 57.
tavod (*tafod*) m. tongue, 84B, 85C, **tafod** 85D.
tebic (*tebyg*) adj. like 127B, 126D, **tebig** 126C, **tybig** 151C.
tebyko, tebyga finneu, tebyg-ir, -wn, see *tybygv*.
tec (*teg*) adj. fair 265B, 21D, **teg** 21C, **têg** 257J; comp. *tekach* 24D.
teiger (*teigr*) f. tigress 188J; see *digerfa, dygerdav*.
telyn (*telyn*) f. harp 179B, 175CJ.
terfynu vn. end, finish; indic. pres. 3 sg. *tervyna* 267B, *terfyna* 259C.
ti (*ti*) indep. pron. 2 sg. 94B, 7CD; aux. 86B, 17A, 3C, 7D; agglutinated in *arnati* 39D, *byosti* 91D, *kyrchaisti* 91D, *delaisti* 119D, *dylyti* 121D, (*dy*) *gariati* 87D, *mynyti* 227D, *nakesti* 54D, *rragoti* 86D, *wrthyti* 14D, *wyti* 104D; see *di* and *GMW* § 54(a).
tirioni (*tirioni*) vn. become loving or affectionate 164B, 163CD.
tithav (*tithau*) indep. conjunct. pron. 2 sg. 235B, **tithau** 195J; aux. **tithav** 16B, 131CD, **titheu** 44A, **tithe** 169D; agglutinated in *dylavtithav* 133B; see *dithav*.
'th (len.) inf. gen. pron. 2 sg. 25B, 20A, 26CD; accus. 192B; see *GMW* §§ 56, 58.
torri (*torri*) 36B, 38C, **tori** 38D; indic. pres. 3 sg. *tyrr* 251CJ.
tost (*tost*) adj. sore, ill, harsh 225D.
tosturio (*tosturio*) vn. pity, have mercy 15C, **tostirio** 15D.
tra 1. (*tra*) (len.) conj. while 3BCD, **try** 117C; see *GMW* § 276.
2. (*tra*) (asp.) adv. very, excessive 56B, 32A, 59CD.
trachefn (*trachefn*) adv. again 231B; see *GMW* § 238.
traed, see *troed*.
traethu vn. speak, relate; indic. pres. 1 sg. *traethaf* 61BC, *travtha* 61D; pret. 1 sg. *treytheis* 11A.
trahaus (*trahaus*) adj. haughty, arrogant 52A; equat. *trahaussed* 89B.
traws (*traws*) adj. cross, perverse 91C; comp. *trawsach* 51C, 98D.
treytheis, see *traethu*.
tri (*tri*) num. m. three 216B, 209C, 224D; f. *tair* 175B, 171CD; see *GMW* § 48.
trigio, trigo vn. dwell, remain; subjunct. imperf. 1 sg. *triky6n* 26A.
tringad, see *dringo*.
tristwch (*tristwch*) m. sadness 36CD.
troed (*troed*) m. (f. in C) foot 73B, 74CD, **troet** 260B; pl. *traed* 109B, 109CD.

troednoeth (*troednoeth*) adj. bare-footed 118BCD.

troi (*troi*) vn. turn 70BCD; indic. pres. 3 sg. *try* 70BCD.

truanaidd (*truanaidd*) adj. wretched 23B.

trugaredd (*trugaredd*) f. mercy 26B, **trugared** 27A, **trigaredd** 26C, 38D.

trugaroc (*trugarog*) adj. merciful 3B, **trigarog** 3C, **trigaroc** 3D.

trwy (*trwy*) (len.) prep. through 9BC, 8D; see *drwy*.

trwydded (*trwydded*) f. sustenance, food 126C; see J. E. Caerwyn Williams, *BBCS* xxvii (1976–8) 224–34; *SC* x/xi (1975/6) 293.

try 1. see *tra* 1.
 2. see *troi*.

trydydd (*trydydd*) ord. m. 71C; f. **trydedd** 72B, 71D; see *GMW* § 52.

tu (*tu*) m. side in *o'r tu arall* on the other side 12B, *o'r ty arall* 11CD.

tuag at prep. towards; 3 sg. m. *tuac ato* 46B, *tiag ato* 49C; see *GMW* § 241.

t6f (*twf*) m. growth 19A.

twyll (*twyll*) m. deceit, treachery 187B, 183CJ.

twyllo (*twyllo*) vn. deceive 194CJ; indic. pres. impers. *twyllir* 193B, 188CJ; pret. 2 sg. *twyllaisst* 266B, *twyllaist* 258CJ, *twyllaissti* (agglutinated) 193B.

twyllodrys (*twyllodrus*) adj. deceitful 181C, **twyllodrus** 181J.

ty, see *tu*.

tybiaid (*tybied*) vn. suppose, think, imagine 197B, 14CD, **tybied** 192J; subjunct. pres. 3 sg. *typio* 73B, *tybio* 74D.

tybig, see *tebic*.

tybygv (*tebygu*) vn. surmise, think 134B; indic. pres. 1 sg. *tybygaf* 186B, 182J; impers. *tybygir* 184B, *tebygir* 180CJ; pret. 1 sg. *tybygais* 135B; subjunct. pres. 3 sg. *tebyko* 74C; impers. *tybyger* 34C, *tybyker* 34D; imperf. 1 sg. *tybygwnn* 238B, *tebygwn* 230C, *tybygwn* 230D; see Henry Lewis, *BBCS* x (1939–41) 301–4.

tydi (*tydi*) indep. redup. pron. 2 sg. 97B, 20A; see *GMW* § 54(b).

tyfy (*tyfu*) vn. grow 47D; pret. 3 sg. *tyvoedd* 100C, *tyvodd* 100D.

tynnu vn. pull, draw; indic. pres. 3 sg. *tynn* 108B, 139C, *tyn* 139D; impers. *tynnir* 155B, 153C, *tynir* 153D.

tyrr, see *torri*.

'u inf. gen. pron. 3 sg. m. 70C, f. 194C; see *'e*, *'i*.

val (*fel*) prep. as, like 142B, 39CD; *val y* conj. according as, as, in order that 36B, *val i* 50C, 23D, *fal y* 188J, *fel i* 253J; *val na*(*d*) 80B, 82C; see *mal*.

uchel adj. high; comp. *vwch* 149B, *ywch* 147CD; see *GMW* § 42.

vchenait (*uchenaid*) f. sigh 234B.

vddunt, udunt, see *i* 1.

velly (*felly*) adv. therefore 85B, 34A, 22C, 24D, **uelly** 41A, **felly** 174J.

vn 1. (*un*) num. one 14B, 18A, 13CD; **un** 175J: see *GMW* § 48.
2. see *yn* 2.
vnbennes (*unbennes*) f. lady 67C, **vnbenes** 67D.
vnigkorn (*unicorn*) m. unicorn 204B, **vnikorn** 199C, **inikorn** 210D, **unicorn** 199J.
vnion (*union*) adj. straight, direct 162B.
vnwedig, see *enwedic*.
vry (*fry*) adv. above 44A; see *GMW* § 247(g).
vwch, see *uchel*.
vy (*fy*) (nas.) gen. pron. 1 sg. my 4B, 2A, 1CD, **fy** 183J, **vyn** 1B, **vyng** 46A; *ymod* (*vy+bod*) 97D; *ynghyflwr* (*vy+kyflwr*) 14D; see *GMW* § 56.

'w inf. gen. pron. 3 sg. m. (len.) 71BC, 49D, f. (asp.) 79B, 204J; 3 pl. 127B, 126CD.
wedi, wedyr, see *gwedy*.
wf, see *bod*.
wllys, see *ewyllys*.
wrth (*wrth*) (len.) prep. to, because of, at, with 13B, 119C; 1 sg. *wrthyf* 3BCD, *6rthyf* 25A; 2 sg. *wrthyt* 250B, *6rthyt* 29A, *wrthyd* 102BD, 164C, *wrthyti* (agglutinated) 14D; 3 sg. m. *wrtho* 76CD; see *GMW* § 63(c).
wy (*wy*) aux. pron. 3 pl. 131B, **6y** 27A; see *GMW* § 62(a).
wybrol (*wybrol*) adj. ethereal 129CD.
wybyr (wybr) f. *sky* 35D.
wyd, wyf, 6yf, see *bod*.
wyllys, see *ewyllys*.
wyneb (*wyneb*) m. face 147B, 145CD.
wynt (*wynt*) indep. pron. 3 pl. 241B, **6ynt** 25A; see *GMW* § 54(a).
6ynt6y (*wyntwy*) indep. redup. pron. 3 pl. 26A; see *GMW* § 54(c).

y 1. (*i*) (len.) prep. to, for 17A; 1 sg. *ym* 15B, 10A, 135CD, *ymi* 21A, 25D; 2 sg. *yt* 4B, 44A, 16D, *ytt* 47A, 42D, *ytti* 52A; 3 sg. m. *yddo* 150C; 3 sg. f. *yddi* 83C; 2 pl. *y6ch* 14A, *y ch6itheu* 13A; 3 pl. *yddynt* 127CD; see *i* 1.
2. (*y*) affirm. part. and oblique rel. part. 11B, 2A, 182J; **ydd** 1B, **yd** 8A, **yr** 26B, 237J; see *i* 2.
3. (*y*) (len.) predicative part. 251B; see *i* 3, *yn* 3.
4. (*y*) def. art. 6B, 1A, 20C, 10D; **yr** 28B, 4A, 31CD, **vr** 90B; **'r** 8B, 9A, 11CD; see *GMW* §§ 27–9.
5. (*ei*) (len.) gen. pron. 3 sg. m. his 5A; see *ei* 1, *i* 5.
6. see *yn* 1.
7. see *yn* 4.
y ar (*y ar*) (len.) prep. from on 39A; see *GMW* § 223(b).
ychneidia, see *ochneidio*.

ychwaith, see *chweith*.
ychydic (*ychydig*) pronom. little, few 59B; see *bychydic*.
ydenydd, see *adain*.
yderyn, see *ederyn*.
ydiw, see *bod*.
ydnabydder, ydnapo, see *adnabod*.
yd-wyd, -wyf, -ynt, -yw, see *bod*.
ygadvydd (*agatfydd*) adv. perchance, perhaps 173B, **ag atuyd** 25A; see *GMW* § 150.
y gan (*i gan*) (len.) prep. from 24A; 1 sg. *i gennyf* 130B; 3 sg. f. *i genthi* 199B; see *gan* and *GMW* § 223(c).
y gyt ac (*i gyd ag*) prep. together with 40A; see *GMW* § 210.
ymadrodd (*ymadrodd*) m. prose, story-form 53B, 56CD, **ymadra6d** 3A.
y mae, see *bod*.
ymaith (*ymaith*) adv. away 110B, 195CJ, **ymeth** 111D.
ymborth (*ymborth*) m. food 131B, 41A, 128CD.
ymchwel, -yd vn. return; indic. pres. 3 sg. *ymchwel* 12B, 10D, *ymchoel* 10C.
ymddangos vn. appear; indic. pres. 3 sg. *ymddengys* 11CD.
ymddiddan (*ymddiddan*) vn. converse, talk 15B, 7CD.
ymddigryfhav (*ymddigrifhau*) vn. delight or amuse oneself 196B.
ymenydd, see *emennydd*.
ymeth, see *ymaith*.
ymgelu (*ymgelu*) vn. conceal, hide 80B, **ymgelv** 83B, **ymgely** 81CD; indic. pres. 3 sg. *ymgel* 81B.
ymgydnabod (*ymgydnabod*) vn. acquaint oneself 93B, 96C; see *kydnabod*.
ymgyrheuddud (*ymgyrhaeddyd*) vn. reach, attain 25B, **ymgerheuddud** 35B, **ymgyrhaeddyd** 25C, **imgyrhayddyd** 25D, **ymgyrhayddyd** 38D.
ymgyvydnabod (*ymgyfydnabod*) m. acquaintance 96B; see *kyvydnabod*.
ymhell (*ymhell*) adv. far 78B, 36CD, **ympell** 26A.
ymhellach (*ymhellach*) adv. further 255CJ.
ymhenn (*ymhen*) prep. at the end of, after 233B, 224C, **ymhen** 224D; see *GMW* § 245(c).
ymhennydd, see *emennydd*.
ymlid vn. pursue, chase; indic. pres. impers. *ymlidiyr* 254C, *ymlid* (error for *ymlidir*) 254J.
ymod, see *vy* and *bod*.
ymoglyd (*ymoglyd*) vn. avoid 86B, **ymoglut** 227B, **ymweglyd** 86C, **ymochelyd** 86D, **ymochlyd** 212D.
ympell, see *ymhell*.
ymronn (*ymron*) prep. on the point of 250C.
ymryddhav (*ymryddhau*) vn. free oneself 199B.

ymwelet (ac) (*ymweled*) vn. visit 241B, **ymweled** 231C, **imweled** 231D.

ymwisgo (*ymwisgo*) vn. dress oneself 103C, 120D, **ymwisgaw** 103D.

yn 1. (*yn*) vn. part. 1BC, heading D, 6A; with inf. gen. pron. 1 sg. *y'm* 104C, *i'm* 104D; 2 sg. *i'th* 88B, 90D, *y'th* 90C; see T. Arwyn Watkins, *BBCS* xviii (1958–60) 362–72.

2. (*yn*) (len.) adv. part. 5BCD, 1A, **in** 71C, **vn** 7B; see *GMW* § 250.

3. (*yn*) (len.) predicative part. 10B, 43A, 9CD; see *i* 3, *y* 3, and *GMW* § 244 N.

4. (*yn*) (nas.) prep. in 6B, 31CD; with inf. gen. pron. 1 sg. *y'm* 166B, 187C; 1 sg. *ynof* 27B; 3 sg. m. *ynddaw* 147B, *ynda6* 40A, *ynddo* 5B, *yndo* 5C, *ynto* 5D; 3 pl. *ynddvnt* 234B, *yndynt* 226C, *ynddynt* 226D; see *GMW* § 63(b).

5. (*ein*) gen. pron. 1 pl.; *yn dav* both of us 174B, 170CD; see *ein*.

yna (*yna*) adv. then 21BC, 37A, 207D.

ynghenol (*ynghanol*) prep. in the middle of 201C, **ynghanol** 201J.

ynghwaneg (*ychwaneg*) pronom. more 249J.

ynghyd (*ynghyd*) adv. together 35CD.

ynghyflwr, see *vy* and *kyflwr*.

yni (*oni*) (len.) conj. until 50B, 34D, **yny** 131B, 42A, 33C; see *oni* 2.

ynifail, see *anivail*.

yn lle (*yn lle*) conj. where 107B; prep. in *yn lle gwir* in truth, verily 130B, 21A; see *GMW* § 245(h).

yno (*yno*) adv. there 108BC, 34D.

ynt, see *bod*.

yntav (*yntau*) indep. conjunct. pron. 3 sg. m. 162B, 161C, **ynt** (scribal error) 161D; aux. **yntav** 22B, 250C, **yntau** 250J, **ynte** 206D.

yny, see *yni*.

yn y (*yn y*) conj. where 7B.

yr, yrot, see *er*.

yr awr conj., see *awr*.

yr hyd i, see *hyd*.

yrwnn, see *y* 4 and *hwnn*.

ysgavael (*ysgafael*) m. prey, spoil 71C, **ysgafel** 71D.

ysgidiav, ysgidie, see *essgid*.

ysmala (*ysmala*) adj. importunate, persistent 245CJ; equat. *yssmalhaet* 256B; see Melville Richards, *BBCS* x (1939–41) 240–1; *PKM*, 287.

ysmalhau (*ysmalhau*) vn. importune, persist 246J.

yssgavaeth (*ysgafaeth*) f. prey, spoil 71B.

yssgrivenedic (*ysgrifenedig*) adj. written 5B, **ysgryvenedig** 5C, **ysgrifenedic** 5D.

yssgr[iv]enn (*ysgrifen*) f. writing 10B, **ysgryven** 8C, **ysgrifen** 8D.

yssmalhawch (*ysmalwch*) m. importunity, persistence 258B.

ysstlys (*ystlys*) m. and f. side 252B.

ysstryw (*ystryw*) f. trick 226B.
ysstyriaw (*ystyrio*) vn. consider 16B, **ystyrya6** 12A, **ystyriaid** 61CD.
yssyd, yssydd, ysydd, see *bod*.
ystriwiaeth (*ystrywiaeth*) f. trick, cunning 107D.
ystyriaeth (*ystyriaeth*) f. consideration 107C.
ywch, see *uchel*.